Petals & Promises

Elizabeth Knight

Creative Wonder Publishing

Knight, Elizabeth
Petals & Promises
Editing: Swish Editing
Cover artist: Chaotic Creatives (Brittany Franks)
Formatting: Creative Wonder Publishing
ISBN: 979-8-88958-067-6 (Paperback) / 979-8-88958-019-5 (ebook)

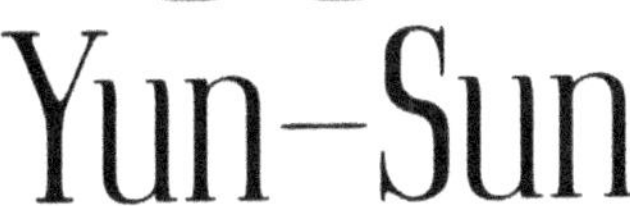

Yun–Sun

Leaving Bailey-Rose at her studio was harder than I ever thought it would be. Gareth got behind the wheel and dropped his head to it, unable to even start the SUV. Eventually, he managed to pull himself together and get us to the Scent Matchers' headquarters for the city of Windermere. The organization was located on the top three floors of a skyscraper in the central downtown area, like you'd expect from a company that molded people's lives every day.

When we walked into the lobby, the security was intense, requiring us to walk through metal detectors before reaching the building services desk. Once we showed our summons, two armed men escorted our group to their offices, ensuring that we were supposed to be there. Satisfied that we weren't a threat, the security left, and we were ushered into what looked more like a living room than any meeting space.

"Can I get any of you something to eat or drink?" the receptionist asked.

"No, thank you," Gareth stated. "How long until someone is available to meet with us? I'm not trying to be a dick, but we really need to get back to our Omega."

The woman smiled at us as if she found the situation adorable. "I understand... the first few weeks with your Omega is something quite special. One of the Matchers should be with you shortly. I promise this is a matter they take quite seriously."

Gareth grunted as he leaned back into the sofa. "If that were the case, they never would have pulled us away during our leave."

Her response was another smile before leaving the room and shutting the door behind her.

"You know that was the dumbest thing you could have done," Warrick grumbled. "If you pulled that shit at my restaurant, I'd make you wait longer just for being an ass."

Gareth leveled Warrick with a look that warned me a fight was about to break loose. Before I could step in, Vili was way ahead of me, shooting to his feet.

"No," he barked out. "We all upset, on edge. This is no time for fighting." Narrowing his eyes at the others, Vili lowered his voice. "I bet they have cameras, listening, watching, studying us. Do not give them a reason to take our kitten."

Having put everyone in their place, Vili took his seat, and the room fell silent. Why none of us had considered the fact they were probably watching us shows how unprepared we were for this meeting. Thankfully, it only took another five minutes for a woman to knock on the door before entering.

I instantly knew she was an Alpha, not because we Alphas recognize each other, but the way she presented herself was a dead giveaway. The woman looked like she'd just stepped out of a designer magazine with her matching skirt suit and gaudy jewelry. I wasn't one to focus on women's hair or makeup, yet I had to wonder how much hairspray she used to keep the style from moving even an inch. The other thing that made it impossible not to stare was the color of lipstick she chose—it was so pale it practically made her lips vanish off her face.

"Hello, gentlemen, I'm Mira Chambers, Head Matcher for this location," Mira introduced herself.

We all stood to shake her hand and introduced ourselves like the proper Alphas we were raised to be.

"Thank you all for coming to meet with me. I know it was short notice and during your leave of all times," Mira offered as we took our seats. "I hope you understand this is a rather unusual situation with Bailey-Rose. Since it's our duty to ensure the health and happiness of future generations, you can understand why we removed Miss Thatcher from the database."

The stormy look on Ulysses' face told me he absolutely didn't see their reasoning. So before he could rip this woman apart, I took the lead.

"Mrs. Chambers, as a lawyer, I can see why the Scent Matchers have the rules they do. If we can eliminate a problem for many, a few might need to suffer. However, you will have to understand we are Bailey-Rose's matches, and it's hard for us to listen to someone speaking ill of her." I held up my hand to stop her from speaking, already knowing what she's about to say. "Forgive me for cutting you off, but even if you tell me that wasn't your intention, as an Alpha yourself, you understand that's not how it works. Your Omega becomes your everything, and we are a pack who hasn't had the chance to bond, making our tolerance lower than most."

My brusque manner seemed to throw her slightly off-kilter, almost as if she was a little surprised to have gotten such a strong reaction. "You make a valid point, Mr. Lee. I will choose my words more carefully from now on."

I inclined my head, not feeling a verbal affirmation of human decency needed to be offered.

"Mrs. Chambers, your summons said further information was needed. What questions can we answer for you?" Warrick asked, falling into the role of a prominent mogul's son.

It was the perfect move, though, as she responded well to his tone and slight smile, which she returned. "Oh, well, thank you for bringing it up, Mr. Shaw. That makes my job easier. There's never a great transition into digging into people's personal lives."

I can't see why you'd have an issue with that when it's your entire purpose.

"Miss Thatcher is from a high-profile family, as are each of you," Mira pointed out as she opened a leather padfolio, looking over something before pulling her pen free. "Could you tell me how you and Miss Thatcher were introduced? I'll also need to know if her genetic condition was shared upfront or if you discovered this information another way."

Catching Ulysses' eye, I gave him a look to see if he was up for answering her questions. With a subtle nod, he cleared his throat and shifted forward. "Crew Thatcher, one of Bailey-Rose's older brothers, is my best friend. I've known the entire family for many years and was well aware of Rosie's condition. In fact, I've spent many days in the hospital keeping her company. After I graduated college, I took a job that had me traveling until now. When I went to visit and let everyone know I was back for good, I discovered Rosie was my Scent Match. So, to answer your second question, her situation has never been a secret to us."

The slight widening of Mira's eyes told me that was the last thing she expected to hear. "Well..." she said, then let the words drift off, unsure where to take this next.

A nagging feeling had my skin itching as I sensed this woman expected us to want to dump Bailey-Rose and not fight to keep her. My suspicions that none of this was making sense grew the longer we sat here.

"Are there any further questions, or was the concern we were kept in the dark the true purpose of this meeting?" Gareth challenged, his tone snide as he crossed his arms.

Mira looked down at her papers, shuffling through them as if searching for anything else she could use. "No, there are no further questions," she admitted, turning her gaze back to us. "However, I would like to warn you that if you plan on having children with her, they won't be brought into the program. As you so eloquently said, we try to prevent what we can from being passed on. Which means not aiding in the procreation of children who could only add to the problem."

That's when Gareth lost it. He'd been holding on by a thread, but hearing her say something so callous caused it to snap.

"You bitch," Gareth snapped, shoving to his feet. "How dare you. No child brought into this world should be considered a *problem*. I don't know if we plan on having kids or if Bailey-Rose even can, but I sure as fuck wouldn't want you ever to be involved in my child's life. Those who are meant to be together will find each other... we are proof of that. So put up all the rules and regulations you like, but stay the hell away from my family."

In the next second, all our phones went off at the same time, an alarm blaring so loud since five devices were amplifying it. The sound had my gut clenching since this alarm was tied to Bailey-Rose's monitor. Notifications were flying across the screen as an ambulance was dispatched to her location, and the hospital was alerted to an incoming patient. Dr. Arbour would also be getting these, so he was onsite at the hospital when she arrived. Each of us surged to our feet and headed for the door.

"Gentlemen, silence your phones this instant and sit back down. We aren't done here," Mira ordered.

Vili was the only one who paused to address the woman. "Yes, we done," he stated and slapped a card on the coffee table. "You have more questions, speak to our lawyer."

Since Bailey-Rose showed up and joined our family, it's brought out Vili's Alpha side. The man might choose to be the happy-go-lucky goof we know and love, but underneath was a lion waiting to take on anyone who dared to threaten our girl.

We rushed right past the receptionist, who was hurriedly speaking to someone before dropping the phone and trying to stop us. "Wait, you can't leave. Stop right there, or I'll call security."

Pressing the button on the elevator to close the door, we ignored the women's protests. I doubted they would call security. There was no reason for them to detain us, and if they tried, I would bury them in every lawsuit I could think of. I might resent the type of lawyer my father was, but I'd spent my whole life watching him decimate those who slighted him, so it was hard not to pick up a few things.

"Doc, do you know what's going on?" Ulysses asked, having called the hospital. "No, we aren't with her. The Scent Matchers called us in for a pointless meeting." He paused, listening to whatever Dr. Arbour was saying as he paced the small space, rubbing his forehead. "She was fine, Doc. I promise we never would have left her if there was any indication of a problem. Thank fuck we gave her the new monitor before we left. Do you know if the paramedics got to her yet?"

Ulysses looked at this watch and nodded, mumbling to himself. The elevator doors opened to reveal three security guards waiting for us.

"They're going to beat us to the hospital since it seems we've run into a small problem," Ulysses said. "Doc, I don't fucking care what you have to do or what it costs, but don't you fucking dare let her die."

"You're gonna have to come with us," one of the security guards announced.

Gareth rolled his shoulders and cracked his knuckles before stepping forward and decking the man right in the mouth. "The fuck we are."

I panicked when Gareth pulled the gun out of the guard's holster, causing me to lunge forward to grab his wrist. "Let me try. If they still don't budge, then you can shoot them. Right now, they have no reason to hold us, but that will give them one," I hissed out.

Gareth clenched his jaw but nodded, but I still didn't let go of his arm as I turned my attention to the guards. "You have no right to detain us. We have an emergency to attend to. Our Omega has a heart condition and is being rushed to the hospital. Let us go, or I promise the five of us will make your lives a living hell. If that still doesn't change your mind, then I have zero issues allowing my pack brother to shoot you if you leave us no other choice."

The guards looked at each other for a moment, then backed off, allowing us to pass.

"Gareth, give the man back his gun," I instructed. "We don't need it, and Bailey-Rose wouldn't be happy with you for pulling this kind of stunt."

Ejecting the magazine and clearing the chamber, Gareth tossed the gun back to the guard, dumping the bullets in the trash can as we ran out of the building. Ulysses dove into the driver's seat, starting the car and waiting long enough for everyone to get in before peeling out of the parking lot. Traffic laws didn't mean anything to us as Ulysses blew through lights and forgot a brake pedal even existed. Screeching into the hospital's complex, he followed the signs to the emergency room and parked in front of the entrance.

Tumbling out of the SUV, I shoved past a couple exiting the building, mumbling my apology.

Warrick slid to a stop, crashing into the nurse's desk, talking a million miles a minute. "Where is Bailey-Rose, Bailey-Rose Thatcher? Dr. Arbour's patient with a heart defect, rainbow hair, utterly adorable in every way. An ambulance should have brought her here. Please tell me the doc has her."

"Ah..." the nurse behind the desk said, trying to process everything the man just spouted at her.

"Boys, over here," a voice called.

Our heads snapped in that direction, and we spotted Nurse Harlow, Dr. Arbour's assistant, waving at us.

"Follow me, and I'll fill you in," she said, swiping her card to open the emergency room doors to let us in. "At this moment, she's in the operating room. Dr. Arbour just got her stable enough to start the surgery. He wanted me to tell you that he's doing the experimental procedure, there's no other option, and to wait would only risk her that much more."

I stumbled over my feet hearing this and had to catch myself against the wall. Ulysses caught my arm, keeping me steady as I took a few shaky breaths. "Tell me this will work," I begged. "Please, we-we can't lose her."

Nurse Harlow hid it well, but I knew she was as worried as we were. "What I can tell you is Bailey-Rose is one of the strongest people I've ever known, and Dr. Arbour loves that girl like his own. She will fight hard to get back to you, and Dr. Arbour will give it everything he's got, and that is a combination I choose to believe will win out."

Ulysses wrapped his arm over my shoulder and gave me a tight side hug. "She's right. Rosie isn't going to give up, so neither are we. I've seen her do it before. Rosie had a close call once with pneumonia, but our girl kicked ass then, and she'll do it again. I know it."

"Come on, let me show you to a private waiting room," Nurse Harlow urged. "This is going to be a long surgery, but I will keep you updated on the progress no matter how long it takes."

Heading up to the fourth floor, we passed the door to the surgical rooms, and I knew our girl was back there fighting to come back to us. They were right. Bailey-Rose was stronger than any superhero, and when she came out of this, if the procedure were successful, she'd have a new lease on life. While this isn't how any of us wanted it to happen, it just proves if we can make it through this, we can make it through anything.

The room Nurse Harlow showed us to was simple but private and comfortable. It even had a coffee and tea station for us to use along with a phone to call down to the cafeteria if we needed food. There was also a television, but none of us felt the urge to turn it on. Roughly, a half hour later, Eli and Crew joined us with some news that had my blood boiling.

"What do you mean Randall was there?" Ulysses demanded. "How do you even know that?"

Eli, Bailey-Rose's oldest brother and a man I did not want to end up on his bad side, glared at Ulysses. "Did you really think I wouldn't put up cameras and have a security system if I was ever going to feel comfortable with her being there alone? Thank God I did, so now we know the full story."

"Don't—" Ulysses started, but Crew rested a hand on his best friend's shoulder, stopping him from saying something he'd regret.

"I get it, man. I really do, but you're not the only one who's pissed off about this," Crew reminded. "LouLou has been ours to look after for a long time, and frankly, that mentality isn't going to change. Let's all just take a deep breath, and I'll show you the footage we caught. Eli already sent a copy to the police, and they're looking for him now. It won't be long until he's caught. LouLou got him good before he ran off."

Eli handed over a tablet with the video footage already pulled up for us to watch. It took everything in me not to throw the tablet and watch it shatter so I didn't have to witness my precious *omae* being attacked by this animal. There was a burst of pride as we watched her stab him, getting him to drop whatever he was about to inject into her.

"How did he know she'd be there?" Vili questioned. "We didn't know she'd be there till the letter showed up."

"Letter?" Crew repeated.

"Yeah, some bullshit from the Scent Matchers about Bailey-Rose not being in the system and making sure we were aware of her *circumstances*," Gareth spat. "We were instructed to come without her, so she decided going to the studio would be a good idea. There's no way Randall could have known unless he's been stalking her."

"Not her," Eli corrected, reading whatever had just been texted to him. "Her phone. The police found it at the studio, and when they looked it over, there was a tracking app hidden in the background. It doesn't work if the phone is off, though, but he'd know she never has it off. It's one of my rules, and Randall knew that. I gave him a list."

With a groan, Ulysses dropped onto the couch, cradling his head. "This is our fault."

"How could that possibly be?" Eli challenged.

"We all knew he'd been harassing her with texts since they ran into each other at Warrick's restaurant. Since we were all together, I had her turn her phone off," Ulysses explained, looking up at Eli. "That is until this morning, knowing she was going to be on her own."

"Mom said he showed up a few days ago demanding that we give her back to him. Now that nonsense makes a little more sense," Crew commented, rubbing the back of his neck. "Hold on, didn't he cheat on her? Why the hell would Randall think they were still together after doing something like that?"

"Because he did it for her benefit," Warrick muttered. "The idiot told her to her face that because he couldn't have sex with her the way he wanted to that Randall hired whores to sleep with. He claimed it helped to keep the edge off so he could be what she needed. Talk about a load of bullshit."

"Excuse me?" Eli growled out. "Are you telling me he admitted to sleeping with other women the whole time he was with *my sister*?"

I waited for the phone Eli still had in his grasp to shatter with the way he was squeezing it to the point his knuckles were turning white. Believe me, I was right there with him. If I didn't need to be right here, waiting for news about the woman I loved more than anything in this world, I would be hunting Randall down.

"Chief, it's Eli Thatcher. I need to know everything there is to know about Randall Steele, the bastard who attacked my sister," Eli ordered. "Yes, I'm standing here with her pack right now. No, we don't plan on being anywhere else. Fine, but we *all* expect answers when you show up in an hour."

With that hardly-veiled threat, Eli hung up and dialed another number. "Hello, my name is Eli Thatcher, and I would like to hire a team of men to guard my sister and her pack. She was attacked by an ex-boyfriend who wasn't happy she found her scent matches. Yes, the police are aware and investigating, but he tried to drug and kidnap her. Thank you. I look forward to speaking with him when he's available."

"Eli, you need to stop," Crew warned. "It's not our place to make these calls anymore. It's theirs," he said, gesturing to us.

"He's right. A few of us can make those same phone calls too," Warrick pointed out. "Not that we aren't grateful for the help, but she's our Omega."

"Our father appointed me to be her guardian, to look after her no matter what," Eli shared. "I don't mean to over-step, but pack or not, in a situation like this, there's no way you're keeping me from protecting my sister."

"That's not what we want either," I interjected, standing. "Instead of instantly making a phone call, take a second and let us know what you're thinking. We are family, and we're all here together because we all love Bailey-Rose. It's going to take time for us all to adjust. I, for one, appreciate you being here. I'll admit I didn't even consider this more than her heart acting up." Eli's intensity calmed a little at my words, trusting we weren't looking to keep him from being part of this.

"I'm assuming the second call was to a security company, yes?" I asked, and he nodded. "Well, I happen to have a connection with a man who runs an operation here in town.

He helps protect women, children, and Omegas who have been abused while they are still at risk of their abuser finding them again. Gideon knows how these men think and the laws to use against them. So my suggestion would be to loop him in on the situation as well as your added security because I'll be damned if he slips away based on some technicality."

Eli nodded and took a seat, resting his arms on his legs. "That's a smart call. I've seen and heard one too many news articles about people who should have been locked up getting away. Randall Steele won't be that lucky."

Vili

A mere two hours have passed since my sweet kitten was taken into surgery. I've been sitting here trying to sketch out a few new pieces that I'd come up with that would look stunning on our Omega, but nothing seemed good enough for her. Finally, I gave up and pulled out my phone, knowing there had been a few work emails that I'd been avoiding. Mostly the ones coming from my fathers.

Feeling like punishing myself, I pulled up the email from my father, Wilhelm, the creator of Silveda.

> *Vili,*
>
> *I would like an explanation as to why I learned that you are on courting leave from an out-of-office note on your calendar. We had agreed you'd be taking a break from your search for an Omega during our peak season. This is a blatant show of disrespect, and I don't appreciate you ignoring all phone calls to discuss this. I expect a prompt response from you, Vili, or you'll force me to do something drastic.*

That was sent three days ago, and I had zero intention of responding. However, the controlling bastard would now see that I read it since he likes to attach notifications of his emails being opened for situations like this. I contemplated what his drastic measure could be when I was far too valu-able to the business for him to let me go. In the past four years, my designs have been the top sellers, making up most of our profit. If there was one thing my family liked more than their status and reputation, it was money. Which honestly made no sense since every person in their pack has been rich since birth.

Even if Wilhelm dared to cut me off from family money, I was their only child, not to mention I owned the rights to those designs, and they paid me a royalty for using them. If there was one thing my family taught me well, it was to learn how to do business like someone was going to screw you over. I'd even had Yun look over my contracts just to be sure, but he agreed they were pretty ironclad.

Pulling off my glasses, I rubbed my eyes, knowing the dull ache behind them was from how stressed I was. Glancing at my watch, I groaned, seeing only another fifteen minutes had passed. There was a knock at the door before Nurse Harlow stepped in, pulling a cart with food trays stacked, ready to hand out to patients.

"I figured you guys wouldn't leave this room or think to use the phone, so I brought up some sandwiches," she shared. "Boys, I know you're worried, but trust me when I say this is going to be the longest day of your life. If you don't eat or rest, then none of you will be of any use to Bailey-Rose. You know that girl, she'll be so worried about everyone but herself, so I suggest you don't give her something to fret about."

Everything Nurse Harlow said was true. I'd seen that side of my kitten when I was left to deal with an angry knot after she'd passed out from not eating. The silly woman was far more worried about me than the fact she passed out. Tucking my phone back in my pocket, I stood and hugged the woman.

"Thank you," I said, taking one of the trays. "Alphas are

stubborn, forget the big picture, and need others to remind them."

"Oh, you're most welcome," Nurse Harlow tutted. "It's my job to look after Dr. Arbour's patients, and in this case, it means all of you. That darling girl would never be able to rest if you lot weren't all right."

"That's the damn truth," Crew said, grabbing a tray. "That LouLou is a tyrant when she thinks something is wrong."

We all chuckled at how true that was.

"I ended up in rut a few days ago and tried to keep my distance, but she wouldn't hear of it," Yun-Sun shared. "Instead, she decided we needed to take a trip to see Dr. Arbour so we would stop worrying about hurting her."

"Sounds about right," Crew agreed between stuffing his face. "Eli had to pretend to leave for business trips when he had to deal with his bouts of rut."

That raised some eyebrows from us.

"Dammit, Crew," Eli muttered. "You made that sound incredibly inappropriate. What he's trying to say is that I couldn't be in the house with Bailey-Rose while in rut because she doesn't understand how overprotective Alphas get during that time. If I told her I needed some space for a couple of days to let my rut pass, she'd take it as a personal challenge to 'fix' whatever upset me."

"Let me guess, she kept telling you that you'd never hurt her," Yun-Sun added dryly.

Eli gave an answering grin. "Something like that, but it wasn't her I was worried about. There was a reason no male tutors were ever allowed to work with her. One time, I caught her math tutor staring at her butt instead of the whiteboard, and I didn't know my rut was due. The man left rather suddenly with two black eyes so he couldn't look at anyone for a while."

That had Gareth laughing and shaking his head. "Sounds like he deserved that punishment."

I was distracted as my phone started to vibrate, and I looked down to see my father, Jonas, had texted me.

JONAS:

I'll be arriving in Windermere in two days. I expect you to be there to pick me up.

The ping on my phone was a flight schedule so I knew when to collect him from the airport.

VILI:

I can't stop you from coming here but I won't be the one to pick you up.

JONAS:

So you do have the ability to respond, that's good to know. Son, we will be having a conversation while I'm there.

I rolled my eyes at Jonas daring to call me his son. His sperm might have been the one to assist in my creation, but the only time he ever involved himself in my life was when I found myself in trouble. It would seem I've truly pissed off my fathers, and Jonas coming here was the drastic move Wilhelm alluded to. Let him try and talk to me while I had something monumentally more important to focus on. Lucky for me, the security company Eli called had agreed to take the job, so all I had to do is tell them Jonas would be a threat to my precious kitten, and he'd never step foot near us.

It was truly sad that things had to come to this, but I refused to even resemble the type of people they were. I chose to be a person I could look in the mirror and respect. Someone worthy of having the love of a woman like Bailey-Rose. If I had it my way, she'd never find out the cruel nature of the people who brought me into existence, claiming to be my parents.

VILI:

Take this as my final response, Jonas. Come near me or my true family, and I'll take everything you value in this world from you. Stay in Numoland and forget you ever had a son.

GARETH

Four hours into the surgery, and so far, all the updates had been positive. The riskiest part of this whole thing was repairing the valve and creating one from her own tissue. Nurse Harlow had just left after sharing the good news—it worked. Now, all that was left was to put everything back where it belonged and get her heart beating on its own again.

The police chief hadn't arrived yet, letting us know they'd caught a lead and were running it down. Honestly, I didn't want the chief to show up here because that meant he wasn't out there looking. Something in my gut told me they wouldn't find him, at least not today. There was so little time from him leaving, the ambulance showing up, and cops being called with zero trace of where he'd disappeared to.

None of that mattered, though, not right now, at least. What I was praying for over and over again like a fucking mantra, willing it into existence, was the chance to look my baby girl in the eyes and know she was still here with me.

I thought losing Callie was going to break me, but that was nothing compared to this ache I felt in my chest. The power of determination was keeping me from shattering into a thousand pieces, but if Nurse Harlow steps foot in here with that look on her face, that would be it for me— everything would be over, and there would be no point in existing in this world without Bailey-Rose in it.

Before, when people talked about the bond between an

Alpha and their scent-matched Omega, it sounded absurd. How could one moment, one whiff of a scent change your life forever? It didn't make sense.

Until it happens to you.

Then you wonder how you ever questioned the bond that filled the emptiness inside you. Bailey-Rose changed everything for me, our pack, and the trajectory of our lives. Now, all of that was at risk of being taken from us before there was ever a chance to enjoy this new adventure. I had so many things I wanted to share with Bailey-Rose, and that was the hope I chose to cling to. There would be a day I get to take her to Watson Ranch, introduce her to my mother, roast s'mores over a fire, and stare up at the stars you could see so clearly away from the city. That was the life she could have now with this surgery.

I have no doubt the recovery from this surgery will take time, and she will need time to adjust. However, once the doctor cleared her, there was no more holding back. We would show Bailey-Rose the world that had been kept from her, making millions of new memories to wash away the bad. Hell, I didn't care if I had to quit my job to make that dream a reality. I had more than enough money in my trust and what I'd saved preparing for the day our pack had an Omega to spoil.

All I knew was I never wanted to live with an ounce of regret or missed moments with my Bailey-Rose. And if anyone dared to fuck with my Omega ever again, there would be no hesitation in the hell I would rain down on them. I lost one person I loved with all my heart because I wasn't there for her, and that wasn't going to happen again.

Ulysses

Everything took six long, agonizing hours, but my Rosie pulled through. I was now looking at her as she rested in the ICU where the nurse could keep a close eye on her. While the surgery went well, there was still a chance something could go wrong. As Dr. Arbour reminded us, this surgery was still experimental, and they didn't have a whole lot of data to go on, especially when it came to someone like Rosie.

I let my fingers brush over her cotton candy-colored hair, needing to touch her to prove to myself this wasn't a dream.

Over the years of knowing Rosie, I'd spent a good deal of time in the hospital with her, but the majority of that time, she'd been awake, smiling and laughing while receiving treatment. Looking at her lying in this bed with numerous wires, tubes, and sensors going in every direction, it scared me to touch her. Gareth was braver than I was, holding her hand, pressing kisses to it to comfort himself.

Lifting my gaze, I found Crew standing across from me, trying to hide how scared he was. If Crew was worried, I have no idea how the rest of us were even standing right now. No matter how tough things got, Crew was always the one to offer the silver lining. He'd told me once that he'd been put on this earth to be Rosie's cheerleader so she'd never have the chance to doubt if it was worth fighting to go on.

Seeing him like this had me a little worried about what

he would do now that we were taking over his role in Rosie's life. I shook that thought from my mind. There was only so much one person could worry about. Right now, the woman fighting to come back to us was my sole focus.

"Gentlemen," Dr. Arbour greeted as he entered the ICU suite. "I just wanted to come by and fill you in on what we're looking for in the next twenty-four hours. After any surgery, there is a concern with bleeding. If you notice anything that causes alarm, please ring the nurse. We'd rather it be nothing than risk it to be something. I'm keeping her sedated for the time being... the less stress we can put on her body, the better. My hope is by the time she is ready to go home, I will be able to prescribe an accelerant."

"An accelerant?" I asked, having never heard the term.

"Yes, it is a recent break in medical technology," Dr. Arbour explained. "Think of it like a dialysis machine, but instead of filtering the blood, we are temporarily super-charging the body's ability to heal. If she can handle the treatment, it would cut Bailey's healing time in half. Meaning instead of eight to ten weeks, possibly even longer, we're looking closer to four or five weeks."

"Oh yeah, that's something LouLou would be all for," Crew commented. "The older she gets, the harder it is to convince her to stick to bed rest."

"Yes, I'm well aware of her feelings on that particular treatment." Dr. Arbour chuckled. "If you'll excuse me, I'm going home to eat and get some sleep. I suggest you all do the same since she won't be waking up anytime soon. If you need anything, my physician assistant, Timmon, is taking over her care for now. He is someone I trust completely to make the right call for Bailey-Rose in my absence."

Eli reached out and shook the doctor's hand. "Thank you seems like such a small thing to say for saving my sister's life, but I'll say it anyway. Thank you from the bottom of my heart, Dr. Arbour."

We felt the same way but didn't know how to express it, so we followed Eli's example, except for Gareth, who hugged the older man. "You didn't just save her life today, Doc, so thank you for saving us all."

Dr. Arbour returned Gareth's hug and patted him on the back. "I appreciate your words, young man, but I should be thanking all of you. If she didn't have you to fight to come back to, this could have gone very differently. I suppose this is why they say it takes a village, and everyone has their roles to play."

With a final wave and a goodnight, Dr. Arbour left us to watch over our girl. Standing there at the foot of her hospital bed, looking at her so small and vulnerable, had me almost in tears. The soft beep and whir of the medical equipment kept the room from being too silent, but it didn't have the same feel I was used to being here with her. In the back of my mind, I feared that this experience would cause me to keep her in the cage of the life she'd been living just to keep her safe. Yet that's the last thing Rosie deserved from us.

For too long, she was told it wasn't safe for her to experience the world like everyone else. Once she was healed and back on her feet, this surgery would change everything for her. Nurse Harlow walked through what to expect as we waited for Rosie to be placed into a room.

"Before I tell you all the amazing things that will change for Bailey-Rose, you need to keep in mind there will still be things to watch out for. The most important part of this surgery is allowing her heart to beat correctly. With the valve replaced and

the spot where the hole had been as a child reinforced, it gives her the chance to experience a fairly normal life. She'll be on blood thinners for life, but in exchange for that, she won't need to worry about a heart monitor," Nurse Harlow shared, all of us cheering and smiling.

Pausing, she glanced at the brothers and cleared her throat before shifting to face us more directly. "Once she has passed all her tests and we confirm everything is healed, Bailey-Rose will no longer need to take suppressants. However, I would strongly urge you to have an honest conversation about children and if she's willing to wait a few years for her body to adjust to a properly beating heart. I'm not saying she can't have children, but Dr. Arbour and I both feel it would be in her best interest to take some time. A body healed to function and live life isn't the same as what's needed to carry another life."

Knowing Rosie couldn't go into heat or rather shouldn't, none of us had really talked about children. Personally, all that mattered to me was that Rosie was healthy and happy— anything else was a bonus. I glanced at the others out of the corner of my eye, and none of them were giving anything away with their expressions, but I knew we all would agree on is whatever was best for Rosie.

"We will keep that in mind to talk about once we are out of the woods," Yun-Sun said with a kind smile. "There had been some concern on her end about bonding since that would throw her into a heat. Does that worry no longer apply, or should we also wait on that as well?"

Nurse Harlow grinned at the question and how Yun was phrasing it since Eli and Crew were sitting in the room. "My answer to that would be, as long as she is cleared for normal physical activity, and there are no apparent complications Dr. Arbour mentions, then she would be cleared to resume normal life. Just to be clear, when I say normal, I mean normal for the average Omega who never had a heart problem."

Eli cleared his throat loudly and shifted uncomfortably in his seat but didn't say a word. That man had more self-restraint than a monk, but as we saw today, when he reaches the limit of his restraint, you better watch out.

"You mentioned there would be things we need to be careful of," Warrick reminded.

"Yes, yes I did," Nurse Harlow mumbled as she pulled a few pages off her clipboard and handed them to Warrick. "While many things won't be a concern in day-to-day life, there are a few areas of her health we won't be able to fix. Her diet will need to remain much like it was, but the one thing that isn't a negotiation is no caffeine. By that, I mean no coffee, energy drinks, stimulants, or drugs. We fixed the plumbing issue of her heart, but the genetic aspect of this messes with the electrical signals, and getting mixed messages from things like caffeine isn't going to be helpful."

Warrick offered me the sheets he'd been handed, and I looked over the list of post-surgery concerns which seemed fairly typical. Flipping to the next page, I found bullet points and explanations for lifestyle changes, many of which Rosie had already been adhering to.

"What does this mean, sudden drops in blood pressure?" I asked. "I thought you said she didn't need her monitor anymore?"

"I suppose that was a bit hasty for me to say," Nurse Harlow admitted. "She won't need it to track her heart rate as precisely as she once did or if her blood pressure rises due to activity. Now, you'll be looking for the opposite. It's a side effect of some of the drugs she'll have to be taking for the rest of her life to prevent any rejection of the foreign material used. Normally, it wouldn't be a problem, but..."

"Bailey-Rose isn't a normal case," Crew said, finishing her

thought. "Yeah, I was waiting for that to come up... it always does."

Nurse Harlow shifted so she could see him, her expression heartbroken for ever having to bring it up. "You know we do everything in our power to give her the best life possible. However, there simply isn't any other choice. On a bright note, it does put her in the category of patients who can request a service dog. I know she's always been hoping that would be an option for her."

Feeling Rosie's foot twitch under my hand pulled me out of past conversations and back to the present. There was an odd blip on the heart monitor, followed by another. Vili, who was sitting next to her, started to sing softly. A gentle croon in his native language had her relaxing, and the small frown between her brows relaxed hearing Vili's voice.

Could it be that she'd gotten worried when we stopped talking?

"Guys, I think she needs to know we're here," I pointed out. "Remember how they always say people in a coma can still hear what's happening around them? I would bet anything hearing us close by is comforting her."

"Makes perfect sense to me," Yun-Sun agreed. "Just like right after we met, she had an instant attachment to us, and it was hard for her to be away from us."

"Pretty sure that goes both ways now," Gareth added. "I can't even process the thought of ever going back to work. It's not like they really need me. It's just assumed if you're a Watson, then you work at the family business."

Feeling a wave of fatigue wash over me, I sank heavily into the open armchair. "God, I can't even think that far ahead right now, but I understand where you're coming from. What could possibly be more important than being with her?"

"Guys, think about it... our Omega owns four percent of The Snuggery. None of us would have to work if we didn't want to," Warrick reasoned.

His idea received a rather disgruntled sound from Eli, pretending to sleep on the other couch.

"I didn't say that's what we were *going* to do, just that it was possible," Warrick muttered, crossing his arms like a pouting kid. "Besides, I don't need to run The Fat Mule. I choose to. If I brought in a manager I trusted to run the place, I could be hands-off dealing with things from home pretty easily."

Yun sipped on his coffee from where he stood near the window of Rosie's room. "Might I suggest we see how things go with her recovery before we make any major life changes? Today has been traumatic not only with what happened with Bailey-Rose but with our meeting with the Scent Matcher. We all need time to process as does the one person who can't share her vote on this matter."

"Yeah, we know how much she loves it when we make choices for her without telling her," Gareth said with a huff of laughter then leaned forward. "Hey, what was Nurse Harlow talking about when she mentioned the service dog? Somehow, I think that should be something we do a little research on."

"Let's tackle that tomorrow. Right now, I think we should take turns getting some sleep," I suggested. "If Rosie needs to have one of us talking to her, that means someone should be awake. Vili, you good to stick with her for like an hour or so?"

Vili shot me a thumbs-up, letting me off the hook as my body seemed to melt into the armchair. I don't know what it is about hospitals, but they seem to put you in a time freeze. Right now, I had no concept of what time it was or if we were still in the same day. The only reason I knew it was nighttime was because of the window in the room. Flipping the legs up on the armchair, I attempted to get some rest. Now, if only my brain were as tired as my body, it would slow the hell down enough to let me sleep.

Warrick

A pair of mismatched eyes stared up at me as I grinned down at the most beautiful woman in the world. She was born to be an artist with one eye the color of the clearest blue water you've ever seen and the other a soft light green that I would dare to call seafoam. While my Care Bear's eyes were open, they weren't quite focused. Dr. Arbour decided she was doing well enough to test bringing her out of sedation.

"Bailey-Rose, it's Doc Arbour. If you can hear me, squeeze my hand," he instructed as he flicked a small flashlight into her eyes. "Good, very good, Bailey-Rose. Now let's try to wiggle your toes... both feet, please."

We all watched her dainty, uncovered feet for her to wiggle them and let us know there was no damage to her mind during surgery. A grin pulled at my lips as an irrational amount of joy flooded through me at the sight of her pretty purple polished toes as they did a little jig.

"Wonderful, simply wonderful," Dr. Arbour praised, squeezing her hand. "Now, I have no doubt your throat is pretty sore from the ventilator. Would you like an ice chip or two?"

She nodded, so I plucked a smaller-size chip from the cup I was holding and held it against her lips. Most of it melted before she got it in her mouth, but the sigh of relief was music to my ears. I went back for another, and she turned her head to look at me, a smile growing on her face.

"Hi," she croaked out as my Care Bear tried to lift her arm, reaching for me.

Fuck the ice chips, I decided and dropped the cup on the side table so I could grasp her hand in both of mine. "Hi back," I whispered.

Some of the guys were still sleeping, having just laid down. Dr. Arbour didn't want me to wake them in case things didn't go well, and we put her right back to sleep. So far, things seemed to be going amazingly well.

"You're..." She paused then coughed only to then let out a shrill, painful whimper.

Instantly, every Alpha in the room was awake and rushing to the bed, hearing her distress. A nurse rushed in and offered a syringe to the doctor who immediately administered it through a port on her IV tube. When the nurse started to place a heart-shaped pillow near Bailey-Rose, Gareth took a step only to have Eli yank him back. This caught the doctor's eye, and he was none too pleased.

"Boys, remember where you are and what Bailey-Rose has been through. I don't want to hear one growl or see you so much as glare at my staff. It's going to take us a moment to figure out the right balance of medication to manage Bailey-Rose's pain," Dr. Arbour snapped. "Fighting your instincts is hard, especially when it comes to your Omega, but if my staff can't do their job, then the only person it will hurt is Bailey-Rose. Do we have an understanding?"

We all agreed and understood why he felt the need to nip the attitude in the bud. I'm sure they've run into issues before.

The doctor turned his attention back to Bailey-Rose, who looked miserable. "I'm sorry you needed to hear that, kiddo. No one is mad at you, and you did nothing wrong. I just needed to set the ground rules. I did the same thing to your brothers many years ago... you just weren't in the room. Let's leave trying to talk for a little later when your throat isn't so angry. You can have all the ice chips you like, so take full advantage of that."

Snatching up the cup once more, I grabbed a chip at random to offer her. She took it greedily and gave me a look of appreciation, squeezing my hand. Gingerly, I lifted it and kissed the inside of her palm since she had an IV taped to the back of it.

"Now, kiddo, do you remember being taken to the hospital?" Dr. Arbour asked. She shook her head and seemed a little alarmed at that. "That's fine, it's okay. I didn't expect you would. I'm not going into all the details right now, but what you need to know is we did the surgery."

Care Bear's eyes went wide and slowly used her other hand to tentatively touch her chest. Of course, she was bandaged up so she couldn't feel the incision, but I'd seen it when they changed the dressing, and it was from her neck to her navel. My sweet, tender-hearted Care Bear already had an underlying fear of the scars she'd had from other surgeries, worried that we would see her as imperfect. Nothing in the world could happen to her that would make me think she was anything less than perfect. I knew she wouldn't believe me or the others right away, but that simply meant I got to convince her every day for the rest of our lives how beautiful I thought she was.

"You gave us one hell of a scare, Care Bear, but you did it. You pulled through and beat the odds," I told her, staring deeply into her eyes, trying to look super serious. "Bailey-Rose, you are a total badass."

Tears rolled down her cheeks as she smiled, trying not to laugh or burst into hysterics, I'm not quite sure. However, the look in her eyes told me she truly didn't believe she'd survive if forced to go through the surgery, yet here she was.

"Those better be happy tears because there is no use for sad tears right now," I reminded her as I wiped them away with the sheet. "Things are only going to go up from here, I know it. We sat the entire six hours in the waiting room, dreaming up things we wanted to do together. Even your brothers gave us a few ideas. Let me tell you, boy have we gotten in some bonding time with them. Crew is lucky to be alive after how loud he snores, but we'll forgive him because we're family now, right?"

"My family," she managed to whisper then looked at the others gathered at her feet. "My pack. People I love."

I ducked my head as tears welled up in my damn eyes at hearing her say that. *Fuck,* this woman had a chokehold on my heart and didn't deserve her love, but I was going to damn well strive to be a man who did.

"All right, I think it's time we give you something to help you rest and take away the pain for a little while. It's going to be a rough recovery, I'm afraid. But if there's one thing I know about you, kiddo, it's that you're not afraid of facing a challenge," Dr. Arbour said, giving her a wink before turning one of the medications back on.

Within seconds, her eyes fluttered closed and was once more fast asleep. I cradled her hand for a little longer before I stood, letting Crew take my spot for a while. Wandering over to where Gareth was once more hunched over his laptop, I plopped down beside him. Glancing at the screen, I saw a series of tabs open about service dogs.

"Wow, you're really latching on to this idea, aren't you," I commented.

He paused in his reading to hand the laptop over to me.

"Read this article and tell me it doesn't seem like the perfect thing for our girl."

"Ah… this is about a guard dog, not a medical alert dog," I pointed out.

"Just read the damn article," Gareth grumbled before shoving up to get another cup of coffee.

Out of all of us, he'd been the one to sleep the least. I suppose it made sense with everything that happened with his sister. I'd be an irritable asshole, too, if I were being haunted by a loss from the past. Focusing on the article, it didn't take me long to see why this idea had turned into his obsession. It appears certain breeds of dog could be taught to be both a medical alert dog and a guard dog, especially with a situation like Bailey-Rose where she didn't need mobility help and wasn't at risk of stumbling over them if the dog were trying to herd them away from a situation.

"Okay, I'm in," I stated once Gareth sat back down. "So what kind of dog did you pick, and when is it showing up?"

Gareth blinked at me for a second then laughed. "What—"

"Nope, don't even pull that shit. I know you, Gareth," I said, cutting him off. "Spill."

Instead of answering, he pulled up a page showing a massive dog that Bailey-Rose could ride if she needed to. It had a light golden coat, making it look like a fucking lion, having me question if it was a dog. Scrolling down, I saw his name was Waffles, and according to the message that popped up, Waffles would be arriving at our home in two weeks. Bailey-Rose was going to lose her mind, and I couldn't wait to see it.

BAILEY-ROSE

"Put me down, Gareth."

It's been two weeks since my surgery and one week that I've been back home. While I was recovering in the hospital, working with various physical therapists, the guys had decided to make a second nest on the main floor of the house, meaning I didn't need anyone to carry me around. In fact, I needed to get in at least fifteen to thirty minutes of purposeful activity each day.

"Baby girl, we are about to sit down with two detectives, who will ask you to talk about what happened. You're just gonna have to suck it up because having you safe in my arms is the only thing that's going to keep me from chewing their asses out. It's been two fucking weeks, and they still haven't found the bastard," Gareth grumbled as he carried me down the hall to the living room.

Since coming home, the guys had been amazing and doing their best not to smother me. Before I stepped one foot back into our home, I sat them down, and we had an honest conversation about how we were all feeling. While I was the one who had been attacked, fought back, and landed herself in the hospital, this had been hard on them too. We agreed that if I had a night nurse who left in the morning after making sure everything I needed was pulled together, the guys wouldn't try to smother me. For the most part, it was working.

"Maybe that's why I don't want you holding me," I countered. "I'm not thrilled with the fact my crazy ex-boyfriend is out there waiting for the next chance to drug and kidnap me."

Ulysses, who'd been walking ahead of us, stopped and whirled around so fast Gareth had to lurch to a stop, making me hiss in pain.

"Fuck, I'm sorry, Rosie, I didn't realize you guys were that close behind me," Lysse apologized, reaching out to take my hand, searching my face to make sure I wasn't in too much pain.

We had to hold off on my next dose of pain meds because it made my memory foggy, and I wanted to make sure I could tell the cops everything.

"I'm okay," I said after a second of taking slow, deep breaths. "Just didn't have time to prepare myself for abrupt movement. You know, if I were walking, this wouldn't have been a problem."

Gareth just gave me an unamused look. "No, it would have been worse."

"He's right. Sorry to break it to you, but on your own, I'm a hundred percent certain you would have crashed right into me instead of stopping in time," Ulysses agreed, kissing the back of my hand. "Anyway, the reason I felt the need to pull a U-turn is because I want to make it perfectly clear that *Randall* isn't ever going to get that close to you ever again. One close call is all any of us, including your brothers, are willing to risk."

I let out a sigh and squeezed Lysse's hand. "Add me to that list as well. That's one experience I would like never to repeat again."

"Talking to the detectives will be a good step in the right

direction. We've told them what pieces you've shared with us, but I know they have a lot of questions to ask as well," Gareth shared. "If it gets to be too much, then you say the word, and we'll tell them to come back another time. What you have to share is important, but, baby girl, your mental health is more important to me, no matter the guilt trip they try to lay on you." He nuzzled a kiss to my hair, which had me preening under my Alpha's attention.

"Okay, let's get this over with," I urged. "Besides, you said a surprise was showing up later today as well. With this much excitement, I'm gonna need a nap between these major events."

The two men chuckled, smiling at me as they walked side by side the rest of the way to the living room. Probably a smart choice after our close call.

My other three Alphas were there with two people I didn't know—a man and a woman dressed in suits. Gareth carried me over to the chaise lounge so I had the most room to get comfortable. Everyone waited as I tucked pillows where I needed them before Gareth curled around me. Warrick chose to sit at the end of the chaise so he could rub my feet for me. Something we discovered helped keep my mind off how uncomfortable I was.

"Here, kitten, it's your favorite," Vili said, offering me a mug that looked like an adorable blue llama.

Taking a sniff of the beverage, I sighed in happiness. "Thank you, Vili."

"Miss Thatcher, I'm Detective Vogal, and this is my partner, Detective Kelsen," the man introduced. "While I'm sorry we have to meet under these circumstances, I'm glad to see you are recovering well. If you don't mind, I'd like to cut right to the chase since we have yet to apprehend Mr. Steele."

"Of course I understand," I assured him. "Thank you for giving me time to recover before having to relive this nightmare."

Vogal glanced at Yun with irritation before focusing back on me. "You have some rather persuasive Alphas," he muttered before flipping open his notepad. "We've seen the footage of your studio space, but it didn't have any audio. Could you tell us what exactly Mr. Steele intended to do when he showed up at your studio?"

I took a sip of the tea Vili handed me, knowing it would help to keep me calm. Once I remembered everything that happened, I'd been having nightmares, but my therapist felt they would dissipate once I was off some of these heavy pain meds and sleep aids. She'd also suggested that helping the police might offer some relief since it allowed me to participate in Randall's capture.

"I get lost in my world when I sketch. Add in the music playing, and I had no idea Randall was there until he tapped my shoulder. To say I was surprised and confused to find him there is an understatement. I'd told him my dreams for that building and how much I loved it, but not in a way he'd go there to look for me. When I talked with my family, none of them had mentioned to Randall their plan to turn that place into my studio," I shared, looking down at the burnt orange color of the tea.

Gareth kissed my shoulder, reminding me he was here with me while Warrick firmly squeezed my foot.

"Randall told me I was his and that my pack had no right to take me from him," I looked up at the two detectives. "I don't understand why he would think that. Everyone knows when you meet your scent matches, everything changes. Anyone you were with before no longer matters. It's a harsh and cruel reality when you're the person who's rejected, but it's not uncommon enough for Randall not to know."

"Are you saying Mr. Steele planned to kidnap you?" Detective Kelsen pressed.

I nodded, taking a gulp of tea now that it had cooled. "Yes, he planned to drug me then head for Trastle, where we would start a new life. The bastard picked there because there was another top hospital for people who have my medical issues. He'd even found a doctor willing to take me on as a patient. What Randall didn't get is if he used that tranquilizer on me, it would have killed me."

Kelsen jotted down various notes as I talked. "Do you know what hospital or the name of the doctor?"

"I don't know the name of the doctor, but I'm positive the hospital he was talking about is Fairview Heart Medical Center," I offered. "Dr. Arbour had mentioned the other group of doctors performing the experimental surgery I just had were located there. If you ask around who would be able to conduct the surgery, it will narrow down your list of doctors to talk to."

"Thank you, Miss Thatcher, that is helpful," Vogal said, then flipped back a few pages in his notes. "The last thing I want to touch on is the number of harassing phone calls and text messages you received prior to the attack. It seems they appeared after a week of total noncommunication. Would you have any insight into what caused this escalation?"

Before I could answer, Warrick jumped in. "I've already addressed that. He came into my bar, grabbed Bailey-Rose, and tried to drag her out of the place. You already know he believed they were still together but was giving her space. There is no need to rehash something when I was a witness."

Vogal's jaw muscle twitched at Warrick's intervention. "It

is helpful to hear about situations from other perspectives. There might be some information Miss Thatcher remembers that you didn't hear. Eyewitness accounts are deeply unreliable."

Hearing the dismissive tone in Detective Vogal's words had my blood boiling. "Detective, if you would like my continued cooperation, then I suggest you watch how you speak to my pack. We are the victims here, or have you forgotten that?"

Vogal seemed taken aback by my outburst, but Detective Kelsen just smirked and gave me a wink of approval. It would seem not many people called Detective Vogal out on his shitty attitude.

"My apologies, Miss Thatcher, I didn't mean to come across too callous," Vogal said, backpedaling like the best of them. "I'll be honest, it doesn't make sense why we can't find him. Nothing in what we've learned or discovered in his home or place of work suggests he would be capable of hiding from the cops this effectively. Do you know anything else that might help us get this guy?"

I chewed on my lip, replaying that moment over in my head, then I remembered something. "This isn't the first time he's done this," I blurted. "The first time I met Randall was at the hospital while I was recovering from a chest cold. He told me back then he was there visiting his brother who'd been hurt, but that was a lie."

My hands began to shake as I thought back to that day and how lucky I felt to have found someone who understood. Little did I know I played right into the hands of a madman.

"He'd had a pack, one he was scent matched to, but got rejected when his Omega wouldn't let him mark her. I guess the reasoning she gave the Scent Matchers was he scared her. This made him angry enough that he beat her to the point she ended up in the hospital. Claimed she was telling lies and needed to be honest and speak the truth," I explained. "The brother he claimed to be visiting was actually the Omega he beat up. When one of the other Alphas in his previous pack got pissed at Randall for being there, Randall beat him up too."

Ulysses stood with a snarl as he began to pace behind the couch. "Tell me, how is an animal like that not put in jail? The laws about abusing Omegas are clear and enforced no matter what, or so I thought."

"There is no mention of this altercation or the fact Mr. Steele ever had a pack on file. We are going to need to dig a little deeper into this new information. It's possible he might be using a different name to keep that off his record. Either that or he has family and friends in some high places to keep this sort of thing quiet," Vogal admitted, tucking away his notepad. "Thank you for your time, Miss Thatcher. Is it okay with you if I reach out with any further questions?"

"Absolutely, if there is anything I can do to help put Randall behind bars, I will," I said, shaking both the detectives' hands. "Although, since I need to get a new phone and number, it might be best to call Yun if you need to get in touch."

Yun-Sun had made it known he was the point person with this matter. Anything to do with Randall or the Scent Matchers was to be directed to him. I was more than happy to hand that responsibility over to the most qualified member of our pack. Plus, it seemed to give Yun purpose and something to focus on besides me.

"Not a problem," Detective Vogal assured me before following Yun, who showed them out of the house.

The guys were quiet as Vili handed me my pain medication, which I took, gulping down the rest of my tea. Vili let his fingers glide through my hair, brushing it back and out of my face. "Are you okay, kitten?"

With a half-hearted smile, I nodded, then sank against Gareth's warm, comforting body, allowing myself to be enveloped by his sweet tea and lemon scent. "I just can't believe I didn't see it before now. We dated for six months, so shouldn't that have been long enough to know if someone is batshit crazy?"

Warrick shifted to sit on the ottoman so he could see my face. "Have you heard about the three-month rule?" I scrunched up my face in confusion. "All right, I'll take that as a no. Well, there is a theory that it takes a person three months before they start showing their true colors to someone they are dating. At that point in your relationship, you left for three months to finish school. So It's possible you didn't know because he could still hide the crazy."

I rolled that thought over in my mind, trying to see if that made me feel any better. While I was at school, we mostly talked in short bursts on the phone, over video chat, or through text messages. Anyone can fake their personality for such a short time, even after three months have passed. This knowledge didn't make me feel better, but it did keep me from beating myself up.

"What do you say we watch a movie until your meds kick in?" Gareth suggested. "I believe next on our list of Disney movies is *Peter Pan*. Personally, I think it's one that if you fall asleep during the middle, you won't miss much."

During my time in the hospital, Crew told the guys about my hobby of picking some tangent to turn into a movie marathon. I've done it by director, theme, word in the title, anything to give me a goal to accomplish while I was stuck in bed. This time, I let the guys pick since they would be subjected to the choice as well. In a surprising turn of events, they chose Disney movies in order by release date, and they weren't talking about just the animated files. They truly meant anything created by Disney.

"You also said that about *Treasure Island*, but you were glued to the screen the entire time," I reminded him.

He nipped at the shell of my ear, making me gasp as a pleasant tingle ran through my body. They'd taken me off my suppressants and put me on birth control since I agreed I was in no shape to risk the chance of getting pregnant. Not that I was getting any action with how sore I still was, even with the special treatments Dr. Arbour had me on to speed up healing the past few days.

"It's dangerous to tease me, Gareth," I warned. "You heard the doc. The accelerator will help me heal but also removes medications lingering in my system. There are no suppressants left to keep my heat at bay, and that has left me *incredibly* sensitive."

Gareth nuzzled my neck, pressing a soft kiss there. "So you're telling me I could get you off with a flick of my tongue?"

Instantly, my mouth went dry, and my pussy was soaked from hearing the offer. "Gareth," I whimpered.

Sitting up, he looked down at me, realizing I was not kidding about how horny I was. For the first time since I was thirteen, I haven't been on suppressants. Dr. Arbour warned me I might feel like a randy teenager since my body hasn't had to regulate my hormones until now. All of us were under strict instructions that sex wasn't allowed to happen until Dr. Arbour gave the all clear.

"Holy shit," Gareth swore. "I'm so sorry, baby girl. You were being serious, and I clearly wasn't listening."

"Fuck, do you smell that? Is she perfuming?" Ulysses

asked. "This absolutely can't happen right now. Gareth, why don't you give her a little space, and I'll message Doc."

"Good idea. I'll grab the neutralizing salts," Warrick announced.

Neutralizing salts were used mainly by Alphas who needed to get a scent out of their head. It was meant to be used during rut if they had to interact with others outside their pack. Warrick returned with a small glass jar and held it under my nose so I could take in a few deep breaths. To my surprise, it cleared my body's fixation on Gareth's scent and the promise of what he offered.

"Wow, that stuff is impressive. His scent is totally gone, wiped from my memory," I said as I let my head flop back onto the couch. "That was close, a little too close. Don't get me wrong, there is nothing I would like more than to get lost in the lust-filled fog of a heat and let you guys ravage me. Yet somehow, I don't think it's a wise choice now."

"Sweetheart, if you're trying not to create that situation, I highly suggest you don't paint such a vivid picture like that for us," Yun warned, a low, rumbling sound mixing with his words.

Twisting my head to look at my Alpha, I saw his brown spice-colored eyes zeroed in on me. In their depths was equal part hunger and dominance. As much as I wanted to stare into them forever, I knew it would only spark the flame I'd just put out, and none of us could afford that.

"Someone said something about *Peter Pan*?" I squeaked out, slapping a pillow over my face. "I think now would be a great time to watch something so wholesome and absolutely not at all suggestive."

"I don't know, those mermaids, though..." Warrick commented in a teasing tone. Peeking over the pillow, I glared at him. "Teasing, Care Bear. I'm just teasing."

Soon, we were all lost in the world of lost boys and fairy dust before I fell asleep in my nest of couch pillows. Who knew I would actually need an entire bin full of pillows to get comfortable after this surgery? Lucky for me, I had some amazing Alphas who didn't bat an eye at taking the entire thing to go.

BAILEY-ROSE

My surprise Gareth promised was delayed a few days because of crazy weather. It was being flown in, and with all the canceled flights, it took a bit for the airlines to sort themselves out. Despite all that, today was finally the day, and Gareth got confirmation my surprise had landed and was now en route to our home.

I was so excited I couldn't keep still, so I did my walking for the day out in the backyard. After three days of rain, it was nice to be outside feeling the fresh air and sunlight on my face. Before the incident, I hadn't spent much time exploring the property, but now it was a good excuse. From the back patio, you could see the pool, but what was hidden was a small garden the groundskeepers looked after. There was also a walking path along the border of the property paved with compacted gravel.

"What's Numoland like?" I asked Vili, who'd joined me on my stroll. "You've been in Preidon for three years now, right?"

"Yes, my kitten, it three years last month," Vili answered. "Numoland is vast, green, and many mountains. They say we hardy people because we live off the land. I say when you good to the land, it good back to you."

"Do you miss it?"

Vili slowed to a stop, and since we were holding hands, so did I. He looked up at the sky and closed his eyes as if he was drinking in the peace our quiet surroundings offered. "I miss places and things sometimes, not people. The people there should stay there, let me live free here."

Stepping closer, I rested a hand on his chest. "You mean your family should stay there and leave you alone?"

In the sunlight, you could see more of the copper tones in Vili's strawberry-blond hair which always seemed to be mussed. It had me curious to see if it might be curly if he let it grow longer. Lowering his gaze to meet mine, I couldn't help but smile at the joy in his caramel-colored eyes. His golden-rimmed glasses only helped to set off his features while making him look smart and sophisticated—which he was.

"Would it upset you to know it is family?" he asked, using his other hand to stroke along my jawline. "You lucky, my pretty lady, to have family who truly loves you. Not all have this in their lives. A short time, I had true love from one person, then she died. I pray and pray she my real mother, but she wasn't. It took time to accept my family is who they are, but I not like them, which made them angry. Now that I think about it, I should be happy... by sending me away, they gave me you and the others."

Bending down, he softly kissed my lips, but I wanted more. Grabbing the hair at the back of his neck, I kept him from pulling away as I popped up on my tiptoes to deepen the kiss. Seeing what I was after, I felt his smile against my own as he scooped me up so I could wrap my legs around his waist.

"You must be good," Vili warned. "Only kisses, my kitten."

"I'll take kisses all day long if they are from you," I whispered.

Vili wasn't willing to go all in on this make-out session I was trying to instigate at first. When he realized I wasn't going to shatter, he became bolder until he finally gave in. The feel of his hands gripping my ass, holding me tight to him, had me moaning. I rolled my hips, trying to find the friction I needed, but that came to a halt as the movement pulled at my healing incision. Tomorrow, Dr. Arbour was coming to take out my stitches and give me a progress report, but I knew he wasn't going to give me the all clear.

"What did I say, kitten... only kisses," Vili scolded, feeling my body tense up. He gave me one more life-altering kiss before setting me back on my feet. "Come, let's finish the walk... surprise should be here by then."

Just when I didn't think I could be walking higher than cloud nine after a good make-out session, we rounded the corner of the house. The guys were in the driveway talking with a man who had a golden wooly mammoth sitting next to him. There was no leash keeping the dog at his side, but it was clear to me that the fluffy monster wasn't going to budge an inch.

Vili led me over to the group, and out popped a little black and white dust bunny from between the bigger dog's legs. The little guy wagged his tail and was all wiggles as he slowly crept toward me. Using Vili as support, I dropped to my knees and offered the back of my hand to the happy floof. Instantly, he snuffled my hand and quickly licked it before bounding back to the much bigger dog.

It took everything in me not to squeal with delight and shatter everyone's eardrums, but I managed to pull it together. "Your dogs are beautiful. What are their names?" I asked as Vili hoisted me up by my armpits.

"Well, little lady, this here is Waffles, and the tiny fella is Nugget," the man answered and extended his hand. "My name is Hank, Hank Sharp, and these two aren't mine."

"Oh?" I questioned as Hank gave Waffles a hand signal, which had the dog standing and approaching me.

If Hank said anything after Waffles bumped his large head against my hand asking for pets, I didn't hear it. The fur under my hand felt like silk on the surface, but it was incredibly dense, allowing my fingers to sink a few inches into his fur. Sweet brown eyes looked up at me, and he gave an approving chuff before pulling an about-face, then plopping his wooly butt next to me. I felt him lean against me as if offering his support so I felt more stable standing here.

Looking up, I found everyone watching the interaction with smiles and a pouting Nugget in Hank's arms. "What?" I asked.

"Well, Miss Thatcher, the thing about this breed of dog is they have to choose the person," Hank explained. "It's one reason they aren't used for this type of work all that often. That's why I make it a rule there is no exchange of paperwork until a meet and greet is done. You, little lady, now have yourself a medical alert guard dog and lifelong loyal companion in Waffles."

My jaw literally fell open at his words. I glanced down at Waffles then back at the guys, finding it hard to believe this was truly happening. "This is for real... right?"

"Yeah, baby girl, it's for real," Gareth assured me. "Nurse Harlow told us you qualified for a medical alert dog, and I just took it one step further. No matter where you go or who you're with, I want you to feel safe, and I think Waffles will help achieve that."

Tears welled in my eyes as I gazed down at Waffles and sniffled when those sweet brown eyes looked back. "What do you think, Waffles? Do you want to be part of this family?"

His answer was to boop his nose against my hip, causing

me to smile at him. Waffles got to his feet and nudged me again with his nose, harder this time.

"Little lady, I think it's best if you sit down right now," Hank ordered. "Better yet, laying down would be best."

Waffles nudged me again with a slightly worried whine to accompany what I now realized was an alert. I'd been so overwhelmed with emotions I didn't notice how lightheaded I was feeling. Thankfully, the driveway was paved so I wasn't lying in gravel, but it didn't mean it was much more comfortable. Once Gareth and Vili helped me lay down, Waffles wriggled his large body under my legs to send more blood to my heart by keeping my feet elevated.

"Rosie, talk to us. How are you feeling?" Ulysses asked, placing a cool cloth on my head.

"I'm a little lightheaded, but that's about it," I shared, trying to keep my guys from worrying too much. "Maybe I overdid it with the longer walk after having my accelerator treatment done."

Yun-Sun kneeled next to me with a cup and straw, offering it to me. "Sweetheart, why is this cup practically full?"

One of the things I had to monitor and adjust to was how much water I needed to drink. Not only would it help keep my blood pressure stable, it was also needed for the accelerator treatments. As my blood was being super-charged to assist with the rapid healing, I needed to flush out all the bad shit, or it could wind me up on the pavement with a dog under my legs.

"So ah, how long do I stay like this?" I asked.

"Don't worry... Waffles will let you know when it's safe," Hank assured me. "When he does, would you indulge me by letting him help you to your feet? This is part of the service he is trained to offer, and I just want you to feel comfortable taking the offered help."

"Yeah, no problem, but you'll have to check with these worrywarts to see if they'll actually let me do that," I teased, sipping on my special electrolyte water.

Most of my guys gave me scolding looks, but Warrick and Vili just snickered, knowing how accurate what I said was.

"Rosie, this is why we got Waffles. If we don't let him do his job, then what was the point?" Ulysses reasoned.

Tilting my head, I looked up at him, where he was sitting behind me. "Oh, I'm well aware of that. I just wanted to make sure you guys were on the same page."

Waffles cut off any further argument as he crawled out from under my legs and shoved Warrick out of the way. Warrick clearly hadn't been expecting that and toppled over, but thankfully, he'd been crouched beside me so he didn't have far to fall.

"Sorry about that," Hank muttered, helping Warrick to his feet. "This particular breed is a one-person-only type. They won't be a danger or threat to anyone else unless there's a reason, but I definitely wouldn't call them a friendly breed."

"Good to know," Warrick said, brushing himself off. "Although, I have to say I like that trait for this particular situation. It means that nothing and no one will be a distraction or even tempt him to leave Bailey-Rose's side."

"That's the heart of it," Hank agreed, dropping to one knee by me. "All right, little lady, I'm going to put Waffles' harness on him and show you a few key things. Don't worry if you can't remember it all. Part of buying a dog from me is that I spend a few days working with you. The most important thing about a working dog is learning to speak the right language."

Hearing that I would have something purposeful to do made me giddy. The past two and a half weeks had been rough as Dr. Arbour warned me. Although it wasn't in the way you'd think. I was used to going through various therapies after a long hospital stay, and the pain was the worst I can remember, but the inability to do anything was the real torture—restrictions on how much I could lift, not going up and down stairs, and feeling utterly exhausted after a ten-minute walk. Learning to work with Waffles was going to be the mental game I needed to keep from losing my shit.

"Are you able to sit up on your own, or will you need his help with that?" Hank asked once Waffles was suited up.

"I *can* do it, but it's rather painful right now," I admitted.

Hank nodded and proceeded to show me how to call Waffles over, where to grab the leather harness, and tips to get back on my feet once I was sitting up. It was like I'd climbed Mount Everest with how accomplished I felt to have managed that on my own.

"This is a soft-handled harness, but you can easily switch it out for one with a semi-rigid top handle if need be. Personally, I don't see you needing it once you're fully recovered," Hank reasoned. "I hope I'm not overstepping when I say I think we should call it here for the day. Sounds like you've had a lot going on, and it would be good for you and Waffles to just spend time together. I'll have you take the harness off when you're ready so you know how. Nothing you do will break or damage it, so don't be shy."

"Thank you, Hank. You really have no idea what this means to us," Gareth said, shaking Hank's hand. "If you follow me, I'll show you to the guest house where you can settle in."

"Oh, there's one more thing..." Hank admitted, setting Nugget on the ground, who instantly bolted to sit between Waffles' legs. "I hope you don't think me dishonest, but Nugget and Waffles are a package deal. Nugget was trained to be a psychiatric service dog, but the poor fella got attacked by a stray, and since then, Nugget has been a nervous Nellie about most things. However, when he's with Waffles, Nugget is fearless and able to live a happy life. We aren't charging you for him since you're doing us and Nugget a favor by taking him on too."

"Will there be any issues with Waffles doing his job with Nugget around? Or companies, for that matter, having two dogs in tow?" Yun-Sun inquired.

"Not at all. You put service gear on Nugget, and he'll mind, knowing he's on the job. The problem is Nugget doesn't think he can do his job without Waffles. Guess you could say Waffles is Nugget's support animal," Hank explained. "One of these days, Nugget might find his footing again, but who knows how long that will take. Either way, he is a fully certified and trained service dog, so you're not lying or breaking any laws by putting him in his vest. Plus, he's the snuggler out of the pair, so it's a nice balance."

Grinning, I kneeled to pet Nugget, beyond excited to have him added to our family as well. "Welcome to the pack, you two."

BAILEY-ROSE

As I sat on the table in the exam room waiting for Dr. Arbour to come in, I absently swung my legs, trying not to get too excited. Today marked five weeks since my surgery, and while I still wasn't at a hundred percent, I would safely say I was at a solid ninety percent back to normal. All the goals Dr. Arbour wanted to see me accomplish before clearing me I'd met, and then some. There was nothing I wanted more than to be released from medical restrictions and free to get started living my life again.

Waffles lay on the floor with Nugget sitting alert beside him, his little black nose taking in all the scents of the room. Hank and I worked together for about a week as he taught me all the commands needed to work with Waffles. He'd been trained in a different language, and if I didn't say the word just right, Waffles didn't react fast enough. Hank gave me an audio recording to listen to so I could hear the inflections in the correct areas.

When it came to the medical alert tasks, Waffles did that on autopilot as did Nugget. Up until a week and a half ago, I'd been sleeping alone. Dr. Arbour and the guys feared rolling on top of me or rogue limbs smacking into me before I was healed enough. Thankfully, I had Nugget. He'd curled up right next to my head and would be there with a comforting lick when I woke up from nightmares. Now that I was off all the heavy medication, they were much better and less frequent, but there were still some nights I woke up in a cold sweat seeing Randall's face looming over me.

Since the beginning, two of the guys would sleep in the room with me on mattresses they set up. They would comfort me until I fell back asleep, but it was nothing like the feeling of being safe and wrapped in their arms. Just this week, I returned to my nest, and one of them snuggled up with me for the night. My hope was once Dr. Arbour gave me the all clear, I could convince them to get their asses back in my bed. Then maybe something else they'd been reluctant to test the limit on would happen. This Omega was getting needy, and there was only one solution to sort out that issue.

"Hey, kiddo, sorry to make you wait," Dr. Arbour said in greeting as he went straight to wash his hands. "I was waiting for the lab to send your stress test results back so I could look them over. Seems they are training some new people, and it got lost."

"Here I was thinking you just wanted to torture me," I shot back with a grin. "After you clear me today, I won't need to see you for the next three months, and this is payback."

Dr. Arbour chuckled and began his physical examination, which caused Waffles to sit up, watching the doctor carefully. I held up a hand, telling him to stay just to be sure he didn't decide Dr. Arbour was doing something to hurt me.

"You'd think after our third meeting, he'd know I wasn't going to harm you," Dr. Arbour muttered. "Deep breath, as deep as you can and hold it. Now let it out all the way until there is nothing left. Good and good. Lungs sound excellent, no fluid buildup or restricted movements."

Next, he swiped the torture device off the desk and handed it to me. Glaring at it, I placed the tube between my lips, took a deep breath, and blew as hard as I could to get that damn little red ball to the black line. Out of everything, this was the one task I struggled with the most. My lungs were slightly underdeveloped due to the genetic issue I faced, as well as not being able to push the limits of my body to strengthen them.

"Okay, okay, that's enough… you're turning purple, kiddo," Dr. Arbour said, grabbing the device and pulling it away. "You know I don't expect you to hit the line yet, but you sure came damn close that time. I bet at your next appointment in three months, it will be easy-peasy for you to do."

My eyes grew wide. "Wait, does that mean you're clearing me?"

"It sure does, Miss Thatcher," Dr. Arbour announced, scribbling something on my chart. "As of this moment, all medical restrictions are removed. Hold on, there," he said, cutting off my escape. "There is a reason I asked to have this appointment in private. I know those men love you and want the best for you, but some matters are yours to decide for yourself."

That made me curious. "Like what?"

"Birth control," he stated. "I know you're already on it, but what I want to ask is how long do you want to be on it? There are many options besides pills if you choose to be on it for the near future. I can inject an implant that offers two, three, or five years of protection. Then you don't have to worry about missing a dose. However, if you want to try for kids in the next year or sooner, then I'd suggest sticking with what you're doing now."

"Why would you need to ask me this alone?" I pressed.

Dr. Arbour let out a sigh. "You have not had to experi-ence the pressure many Omegas face since until now, you couldn't have children. In many packs, not all, there is an understanding that children will be part of an Omega's duties. I realize that sounds very old-world, but I've found the answer I get with the Alphas in the room and without are entirely different. So now, as a rule, I have this talk in private so we can have an honest conversation."

"Huh," I mused aloud. "I can see why that makes sense."

"Do you have questions, concerns, or anything else you want to know about?" Dr. Arbour offered.

In some ways, talking to him about this was weird, having been his patient since I was a baby, but he was a professional and simply looking out for me. "I know for sure I'm not looking to build a family in the next year. There is so much I want to see and do now that I have that freedom. Let's go with the three-year implant. That way, I have time to think about it after living a little. Plus, not having to worry about taking another pill would be magical."

"That sounds like a wise choice to me," Dr. Arbour said with a nod and gathered the supplies he needed.

Moments later, with a little poke, some numbing, and a giant-ass needle, my arm was being wrapped up.

"Give it one day before testing out how effective this is," Dr. Arbour cautioned. "You've lasted five weeks, so I'm sure one more day won't be that bad. One last thing, then you can go live a beautiful life."

Dr. Arbour settled his hands on my shoulders and gave me a sweet yet watery smile. I could feel panic starting to rise, causing Nugget to let out a sharp bark when he couldn't reach me. Dr. Arbour scooped up Nugget and placed him in my arms, patting my knee affectionately.

"No need to fret, kiddo... this is good news," he assured me. "I am retiring at the end of the week. My practice will be handed over to Timmon and another surgeon I trust to care for my patients. You were the reason I continued to work this long because I couldn't trust anyone else with your care. Bailey-Rose, you are like a granddaughter to me, and I can't tell you how happy I am to see you grow up, find love, and be given a second chance to see the world."

This had been the last thing I'd expected him to say. "You're not that old... you can't retire."

"Oh, you sweet girl, but I am that old. Hell, I was old when I helped bring you into this world." He laughed. "This is a good thing, Bailey-Rose. I had one more surgery left in me, and I saved it for you. Now it's time to let the younger generation make their mark in the world. For years, I lived in this hospital more than my own home with my pack. It's time for us both to travel and have wild adventures. Who knows, we might run into each other on the beach or hiking a mountain. That would be a memory worth making, don't you think?"

A tear rolled down my cheek, but it was a happy one, even though I was going to miss these moments with the man who saved my life more times than I can count. "It would be the best memory."

"That's the spirit," Dr. Arbour cheered, clapping his hands together. "Come on, kiddo, let me walk you and your pack out one last time so I can make this memory too."

"Maybe we should take a picture, just in case you get really old and forgetful," I suggested.

"What a brilliant idea. I'm sure Nurse Harlow is lurking somewhere nearby," Dr. Arbour whispered conspiratorially, making me laugh and reminding me this was a happy moment.

We were so excited that I was finally free from all restrictions. Now it was up to me to learn what my body could handle with my newly repaired heart. In a few ways, it was a little intimidating. I wanted to try everything, yet the fear I've lived with for twenty-five years kept whispering in my ear, making me doubt if this was really real. How could a heart that had once been a ticking time bomb in my chest suddenly become the thing that will give me a full and happy life?

The guys were too excited to return to the house after the appointment, so we decided to go for an early dinner. I was more than happy to do anything that got me out of the house. So Warrick was nominated to pick the place, and we ended up at Just Like Mom's. It was a diner meant to replicate the old-fashioned feel when diners were in their glory. However, when I sat in the booth, I immediately knew why Warrick picked this place—the milkshakes.

These were not your average milkshakes. No, these masterpieces came topped with whole doughnuts, slices of cake, cinnamon rolls, and brownies. You name it, they could make it happen and put you into a sugar coma you'd never regret. The rest of the food looked amazing too, but I knew Warrick was playing to my sweet tooth.

"Guys, if I eat one of these, you're going to have to roll me out of here," I said, staring at the two-page spread of pictures.

"Care Bear, today is a day to celebrate. Don't get bogged down in the details. Get what speaks to you, and we'll deal with whatever comes after," Warrick reasoned.

Gareth reached over and turned the page back to the normal food. "Pick your meal first then decide if you want a shake. I'm sure they can make them to-go as well if you think it will be too much now."

"Oh, I like that plan." I grinned. "I feel like my stomach has shrunk over the past weeks since I was never hungry. Knowing I can come back to eat the milkshake when I'm ready changes everything."

The waitress came over to greet us and take our food and drink orders. "Coming right up," she announced. "I'll be back with your drink and shakes."

"So, Care Bear, what's first on the bucket list?" Warrick asked, resting his chin on the palm of his hand. When I looked at him confused, he seemed a little surprised. "Are you telling me you don't have a list of things you've wanted to do but couldn't?"

"Not really," I admitted. "It was easier to accept things when I didn't fixate on what I couldn't do but created lists of all that I *could* do."

Yun-Sun got up from his seat, walked over to the main counter where you could sit, and asked the lady serving there a question. Moments later, Yun returned with a white paper placemat and a small box of crayons.

"What's all that for?" I asked, watching him take out the blue crayon.

He glanced up at me, his stunning eyes filled with mischief. "We are going to create an adventure list."

"An adventure list..." I repeated.

"This has nothing to do with death or dying, so I don't feel like a bucket list is the right term," Yun-Sun explained. "You will get to put down whatever you like, but each one of us gets to add an adventure we'd like to experience with you. I'm going to put down taking you to a theme park. Not many people know this, but I'm a roller coaster junky."

While something like that shouldn't surprise me, it did. Out of all the guys, he was the most calm and collected.

Perhaps that's why he enjoys roller coasters—it's all about controlled chaos.

"I've only been to fairs but never ridden on anything more exciting than a Ferris wheel or merry-go-round," I shared, bouncing in my seat, jostling Nugget, sitting in the corner next to me. "This sounds amazing and something I'm not sure I would have thought of on my own."

Yun-Sun passed the paper over to Ulysses, who took the crayon and tapped his chin with it. Then his face lit up as an idea struck him. "Rosie, do you remember that day, years ago, I picked you up, and we drove two hours to that place where you could swim with dolphins?"

Instantly, I knew what he was talking about. It was a memory I treasured. Not only had I gotten to spend the day with just Lysse, but then being able to see dolphins up close and personal was amazing. That had been one of the lowest days of my life after Papa Addy died, and I don't really know if Lysse knew how much it meant to me he did that.

"Of course, I remember. It was the day I fell in love with you," I admitted confidently, since I knew he loved me too.

My frankness seemed to catch Lysse off guard as he choked on the soda he'd just taken a sip of. "Really?"

Grinning, I nodded. "What can I say? You were my prince charming who came to rescue me from the depths of my despair."

"Is that why you never told anyone what we did?" Lysse questioned.

"Some things a girl just needs to keep for herself," I explained. "So, what idea did you have that connects back to that moment?"

"Ah..." he mumbled, trying to gather his thoughts. "Right, so I was thinking that we should go snorkeling. Take a trip somewhere where the reefs are full of fish and other things to see. You don't need to be certified like scuba diving, and we can even rent the gear if we want."

Our conversation was put on pause as our food arrived, and we dug in. I was grateful for the chance to take a moment and process the fact these men were not holding back when it came to these ideas. Here I was thinking that going for a bike ride on a path that wasn't flat would be a thrill ride. Clearly, my ability to see life like everyone else was skewed. This was going to be the bigger battle—relearning what I was capable of. I needed to stop marking things as impossible and truly consider what would hold me back from doing things like snorkeling or riding a roller coaster.

The answer to that was nothing but me.

Vili licked his fingers clean from the chili dog he was eating and grabbed a crayon. "This idea not so thrilling but still an adventure."

Gareth looked over his shoulder, frowning at what was written. "Vili... what exactly do you mean by go see whipped cream? Is there some kind of whipped cream factory or something you want to go see?"

Vili chuckled. "That be fun too, but *Whipped Cream* is ballet performed in Numoland. I saw it as a boy and feel that kitten would enjoy seeing it too. The show once traveled but now only found in Numoland."

Warrick pulled out his phone, leaning close to me as he searched the name of the ballet. When he clicked on a video, it brought up a series of clips revealing the story was all about a baker and various sweets dancing across the stage. Everything looked so bright and colorful, something to truly make you smile while watching.

"I don't think it's possible there could be a ballet more suited to you than this, Care Bear," Warrick commented, then looked up at the others. "Um... so are we required to do all these adventures as well?"

"I say no," Vili voiced. "My hope was it would be me and kitten, alone. Well, Waffles and Nugget too."

Gareth snatched the list and a different crayon from the table. "I agree with Vili, but I have something to add to that. Instead of just one, we write down two adventures, so we each get a one-on-one outing plus the group activity."

Warrick snapped his fingers before pointing at Gareth. "That is one brilliant idea because I thought of something, but I wasn't sure I wanted to share it with all of you. It seemed more of a Care Bear and me thing."

Seeing how excited the guys all got about this change to the rules had me laughing. "This is ridiculous. We have the rest of our lives to go on hundreds of adventures."

"Yeah, but these are going to be the most memorable since it will be the first adventures you get to experience," Lysse reasoned. "Which means we need to make them count."

"Right, because I will never remember all the ones after these. Come on, Lysse, you know better than that," I scolded playfully. "Mind of an elephant right here," I added, tapping my temple.

The paper made its way around the table twice so the guys could put down all their ideas. I was laughing so hard my sides started to ache, and my cheeks felt like they were about to cramp up. Just as my majestic unicorn milkshake to-go was set before me, Yun-Sun got a call. Instantly, I knew it wasn't good as his serious face fell into place, and he got up from the table. The joy I'd been feeling, allowing me to forget the darkness that lingered on the edge of my mind, now became a rock in my stomach.

Nugget butted his head against my arm, pulling my

attention away from Yun to look at him. Watching me carefully, Nugget cocked his head this way and that, trying to get a read on my emotions before crawling onto my lap. He licked my chin and leaned into me, offering all the support his little body could offer. Waffles' head appeared from under the table where he'd been lying at my feet. Without any preamble, Waffles flopped his head across my knees and let out a heavy sigh.

To my surprise, my body took a cue from him, and I, too, sighed, releasing some of the tension built up in my body. Warrick took my hand, stroking the back of it with his thumb. "No matter what it is, Care Bear, we'll figure it out together."

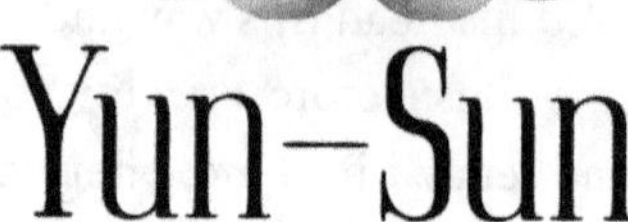

Yun–Sun

"What do you mean he broke in again?"

I realized I shouldn't be yelling at this officer who was only doing his job. It wasn't his fault that Randall showed up once more to the studio. How the security system and cameras didn't go off or alert us to someone being there made no sense. Everything had been upgraded and codes changed to one that no one could figure out with a well-educated guess.

"Sir, I'm aware of the situation, and I understand why you're frustrated, but the fact of the matter is that Randall Steele broke into the same building he tried to abduct Miss Thatcher from a month ago. Only this time, when he couldn't find anything to tell him where she was, it appears he took it out on the building. I hate to ask you this, but it would be a great help if Miss Thatcher could come down here and tell us if he might have taken anything or if there is some meaning to what damage he did do," the officer explained.

Rubbing my forehead, I growled out my frustration. The last thing I wanted to do of all days was to drag Bailey-Rose back into that moment. Her nightmares had finally started to lessen, and I feared if we brought her back, it would start all over again.

"How bad is the damage?" I asked.

"Most of it is in the downstairs level. Seemed like she might have been working on something, and whatever it was sure pissed him the hell off. He even left her a note," he admitted.

Rage hummed in my veins that the bastard dared to speak to her after almost killing her. He'd left her no choice but to push her body to the limit in order for her monitor to go off. If *anything* else had gone wrong or the ambulance was delayed, I wouldn't have an Omega to curl up in my arms and whisper in her ear how much I loved her.

"Tell me," I demanded. It came out as an Alpha bark, putting the power of my rank into those words.

There was a sharp intake of breath, telling me this man was a Beta. While they didn't react to a barked command like an Omega would, it still had influence over them.

"Give her back to me," the officer answered. "He used some kind of yellow paint he found in the studio and drew something that resembles a bumblebee below the words. Does that mean anything to you?"

"It was the nickname that sick bastard gave her," I spat. "Guess he wanted to make sure to leave a clue, just in case we didn't know who he was talking about. Take all the pictures you need of that message, then cover it up, or I'm not bringing her there. She's suffered enough trauma from this man, and I won't let him steal one more ounce of happiness from her. Do we have a deal?"

"Yeah, I can work with that. Give me about twenty minutes, then it will be documented and destroyed," he assured me.

"Good, we'll see you in twenty minutes." Hanging up, I took a moment to take a few deep, calming breaths like I'd heard Bailey-Rose's therapist instruct her to do when things got too overwhelming.

Once my emotions were in check and I wouldn't risk snapping at my girl, who was the last person who deserved

it, I returned to the table. The guys looked at me expec-
tantly, but my attention was focused on the pastel beauty
who was being smothered by two dogs. If Waffles felt the
need to add his help, she was not okay.

I turned to Warrick and with a gesture, asked him to
move so I could sit next to her. He obliged and took my seat
as I slid in, wrapping an arm around the most important
person in my life.

"*Omae*," I whispered, pressing a kiss to her hair. "I know
nothing I say right now will change the way you feel, so I
will state facts that cannot be argued. You are safe in this
diner and at this table with your pack. Waffles is not on alert
or guarding the table, which means there is no immediate
threat to you or us."

Another thing we'd learned from her therapist was how
to help her when she woke up from her nightmares. The
hardest part for the person experiencing them was knowing
what was real and what was imagined. So it was best to offer
them facts they could see and acknowledge, helping their
brain to realize they'd been dreaming.

"But that phone call was about *him,* wasn't it," Bailey-
Rose stated.

"Yes, it was," I admitted. While I wouldn't let Randall's
actions harm my Omega if they could be avoided, I wasn't
going to outright lie to her face. If she found out about the
message, then I'd own up to that too, but I was going to
protect her for as long as I could.

Bailey-Rose looked up at me, her normally bright, joyful
gaze had shadows behind them that weren't there before.
Those shadows weren't always there, but moments like this,
where she had to face that memory head-on, it dulled the
sparkle. "What did he do?"

"He broke into the studio again," I divulged. "I don't know how he did it without us knowing, but he did."

"Why? Why would he need to go back there?" she asked, her tone pleading for me to give her an answer that would have all this make sense.

Reaching up, I brushed my fingers along her jaw, wishing I had that answer. "I wish I knew, sweetheart. The cops asked for your help. They need you to tell them if he took anything, left something, or any possible thoughts you might have as to why he came back."

"Do I have to?" she whispered.

Leaning down until our foreheads met and our noses brushed, I shook my head. "No, *omae,* you do not."

"But I should," she added as if she knew I'd held back from saying it. "The more they have to work with, the sooner they can catch him, right?"

"That is true, but you matter more," I remind her. "If this will only hurt you, then fuck it... they can manage with what they've got on their own."

Bailey-Rose fell silent for a moment, soaking in my touch and scent as she decided. "Okay, I'll go."

"Okay," I murmured, kissing her as I cradled her face with my hand, trying to infuse all the love I had into the kiss.

Once more, this tiny, gentle soul who held my heart showed me what true strength and courage looked like.

BAILEY-ROSE

The studio was trashed, and not just the back section where the working space was. In his anger, Randall had punched holes in walls, broken windows, and smeared paint everywhere. The office upstairs was the only untouched area, probably because the door to that area wasn't obvious.

Waffles was glued to my side on high alert as I carried Nugget, not wanting to get his mostly white fur covered in paint. There was so much anger displayed in this space that I didn't know what to make of it. Everything I was seeing seemed so different from the man I'd dated. Part of me wondered if there was another factor as to why he'd become so volatile.

"Miss Thatcher, I'm Officer Fawlk," the officer greeted, keeping his distance with a wary eye on Waffles.

I reached down and placed a hand between my wooly companion's shoulders. "He is impeccably trained, Officer Fawlk. Waffles won't act without my order, or you make the first move of aggression."

Officer Fawlk nodded but didn't seem convinced. "We know for certain Mr. Steele was the person who broke in and destroyed the place. His fingerprints are everywhere... he didn't even bother to hide them. What would be the biggest help to us is understanding why he'd come back here. In addition, if you could share with me if he stole anything or left something behind."

"I don't know how much help I can be, but give me a chance to look around, and I'll let you know if I spot something," I offered.

With the guys flanking me, I entered the workspace where most of the damage had been done. Every surface was covered in paint, drawers of supplies were dumped, and the canvas I'd been working on was absolutely destroyed. Squatting, I picked up what was left of the frame and noticed what looked like part of Ulysses' head was scribbled out with a marker. It was like Randall was trying to erase them from the picture, and if he couldn't do it in real life, then he'd make do with the picture.

Thankfully, I hadn't gotten much further than sketching it out, but it still made me sad to see it ruined. Something caught my eye, and I stood, walking over to a pile of paint tubes that looked like someone stomped on. Sticking out was the corner of what might be a card of some kind. I found a spot where the paint was dry and set Nugget down.

"Stay right there, mister," I ordered.

Nugget instantly dropped his butt to the floor and wagged his tail, making me smile. "Good boy."

Moving aside the paint, I realized they covered a bouquet of flowers, pink peonies to be exact. Randall and I had been on our third or fourth date when he gave me a bouquet of them. He said they reminded him of me with how happy and soft they were. The downside had been they attracted bees to our picnic lunch which is when he started calling me Bumblebee. I was the sweet-smelling flower that had attracted him. It had never made sense to me, but Randall was adamant it was the perfect pet name.

"Officer Fawlk," I called. "I found something."

He wandered over, slipping on a pair of gloves before picking up the letter. The paint covering it made it a little hard to open, but he managed to pull out a get-well-soon card. Flipping it open, he scanned the inside, frowning before flipping it around for me to read.

A hand settled on my shoulder before another blocked my view. I was surrounded by the comforting scent of sweet tea with a tang of lemon, letting me know it was Gareth. "You don't have to read it, baby girl."

"Yes, I do," I countered. "I don't want to be afraid of him, Gareth. Randall haunts my dreams and sends me into a panic when the police call. He has no right to take up this much space in my life when he means nothing to me. If I can help the police figure out what's going through his head so they can catch him faster, then that's what I'll do."

Gareth dropped his head to rest on mine for a moment before pressing a kiss to it and dropping his hand. "All right, baby girl. It's your call."

Leaning into him, I looked up, offering him a smile. "Thank you, Gareth."

He returned my smile and kissed my forehead. "You're welcome, baby girl."

Taking a deep breath, I focused on the card.

BUMBLEBEE,

I'M SORRY I RAN, LEAVING YOU ALL ALONE. THEY SAID YOU WERE TAKEN TO THE HOSPITAL AND RUSHED INTO SURGERY. I TRIED TO VISIT AND GIVE YOU THESE FLOWERS THEN, BUT THEY REFUSED TO LET ANYONE VISIT. MY FACE IS ON THE NEWS, AND THEY ARE SPREADING LIES AGAIN. DON'T LISTEN TO THEM. I WOULD NEVER HURT YOU, BUMBLEBEE. I LOVE YOU. I PICKED YOU OUT OF EVERYONE TO BE

MINE.

I HOPE THESE FLOWERS MAKE YOU SMILE AND REMEMBER HOW PERFECT WE ARE TOGETHER.

XX R

"He said that to me before," I murmured. "Something about how I was rejected, but he picked me and was told he could have me. I don't understand it, but obviously, it means something to him."

Officer Fawlk tucked the card back in the envelope, handing it off to someone else who placed it in an evidence bag. "In my experience, that type of entitlement comes from people who have been born into privilege. They don't know what the word 'no' means. Did Mr. Steele talk about his family much?"

"Come to think of it... no," I answered as I thought back over our conversation. "The only thing he ever said specifically is that they came from money so I shouldn't be worried he was after me for that. When I asked what his parents did, he brushed it off, saying he didn't want to talk about it. I just figured he didn't have a great relationship with them, so I didn't want to press the matter."

"Well, any detail helps us narrow down what his last name might really be," Officer Fawlk commented as he made notes.

"I'm sorry, his real last name?" I pressed.

The officer's gaze flicked to me then Gareth for a second, as if judging if he'd spoken out of turn. "Yes, I just spoke with the two detectives on your case, and they mentioned the last name he's using now only started showing up in the system about a year ago. This leads us to believe he used a different one previously. If someone wanted to keep the incident related to his previous pack quiet, changing his last name would be the easiest place to start."

An idea popped into my head. "Did you look at who owns his apartment? He told me it was owned by his family so he could live there as long as he liked."

Officer Fawlk grinned at me. "I see we have a detective in the making. I'm not on the official manhunt for Mr. Steele, but everyone in the department knows about it. So let me know what the address is, and I'll make sure to run it past Detective Vogal. They might already have the information, but it never hurts to ask."

I rattled off the address by heart, having it memorized since I had to give it to every taxi driver since I couldn't drive myself.

"Thank you, Miss Thatcher, you have been a huge help," Officer Fawlk said, shaking my hand. "I hope you believe me when I say we are doing everything we can to get this guy off the streets. No one deserves to feel like the boogie man is lurking behind every corner." Shifting his gaze to Gareth, he continued. "If I have any further questions or information to share, we'll reach out. You guys have a better rest of your day, and we'll make sure this place is secured the best we can."

Gareth shook the officer's hand then bent down to scoop Nugget up before twining our fingers together and leading me out of the workspace. I was surprised to see the others talking with Eli, who looked like he came right from the office.

"Thank you for the offer, but Infinery owns the building even though it's Bailey-Rose's to do with as she pleases. I've already called the insurance company, and they'll be sending someone by to look at the damage," Eli explained, then he spotted me.

Things at the office had been crazy for him as a merger

with another offshore oil company was taking place, meaning we hadn't seen each other since I got out of the hospital. It didn't help that his righthand man and personal assistant, Joss, had to quit, leaving him to find a replacement. I wouldn't say Eli was a bad boss, but the man was a perfectionist. He had zero problems pointing out people's mistakes, but in his mind, he believed he was helping them improve. Forty interviews and three tries later, Eli managed to find Joss. I can't wait to see how things will work out this time.

"Hey, big bro," I greeted, flinging my arms around him. "I feel like it's been ages since we've seen each other."

Eli returned my hug with a gentle squeeze. "Well, B, I suppose that's the downside of not living under the same roof."

When I didn't let go right away, Eli wasn't bothered and continued to hold me close.

"B, I know it's been a little while, but when did you acquire a lion pretending to be a dog?" Eli whispered.

Laughing, I released my hold and took a step back. "Eli, meet Waffles, my personal medical alert guard dog. Oh, and Nugget, he is a trained psychiatric service dog who is struggling with his self-confidence."

"Is a service dog allowed to work if they have an issue like that?" Eli questioned.

Gareth snorted, trying to cover up his laugh. "I should have known the deal for Waffles was too good to be true. Turns out it's because Waffles and Nugget are a package deal. This little tyrant does his job perfectly as long as Waffles is around to give him the support he needs."

Eli blinked a few times, processing that information. "So a service dog has his own emotional support animal?"

"Pretty much," I agreed. "But Hank says there is still

hope Nugget might work through his issues, and if that happens, he might pick his own person to help one day.”

“Hank is the trainer,” Yun-Sun offered. “He spent a week working with Bailey-Rose on how to use the personal protection commands Waffles is trained to respond to.”

Eli’s eyes went wide. “Wow, you guys don’t know how to do anything halfway, do you? I certainly would think twice if I had to face off with Waffles.”

“That was exactly what I hoped for,” Gareth said with a proud smile. “Plus, it was a way for all of us, Bailey-Rose included, to feel confident enough to do things on her own, especially now that she’s fully cleared to resume all activities.”

“Little B, that’s amazing,” Eli cheered, pulling me into another hug, spinning us in a circle. “Oh God, there couldn’t be any better news to hear.”

Setting me on my feet, he pulled out his phone, and the next thing I knew, my parents and Crew were on the screen.

“Are you all right? What’s wrong?” Daddy Rawr demanded, looking slightly panicked.

“Eli, why did you send the emergency SOS message?” Mother asked, rubbing sleepy eyes. “Where are you? Oh my God, what happened to the studio?” she blurted, seeing the damage behind me.

“Guys, maybe we should stop asking questions if we want answers,” Crew reasoned as he slid his headphones to wrap around his neck, telling me he’d been working in the recording studio.

“Ah... hi, guys,” I offered with a wave then glared at Eli. “Did you seriously use the panic button for this?”

“Little B, this is absolutely a situation that warrants an instant response,” Eli argued. “Now tell them so I don’t look like the boy who cried wolf.”

Rolling my eyes, I faced my family with a shit-eating grin and gave the good news. "Who's got two thumbs and is free to live her life to the fullest? This girl!"

"What?" Crew blurted, nearly falling out of his chair. "LouLou, that's incredible."

"Oh, sweety, that's so wonderful," Daddy Rawr said, elation lighting up his face.

Mom cheered and clapped her hands before snatching the phone away from Dad. "Darling, I knew this day would come. I prayed for it constantly. Oh, your papa must be doing that awful dance he does when he's excited about something up in heaven. Eli was right, this is absolutely the right time to use that alert. Tell me, what are you going to do first? Skydiving? Climb a mountain?" She lowered her voice. "Have lots and lots of sex?"

"*Mom*," all three of us kids yelled.

"What? The poor thing has had to be so careful, and none of you know what it's like to be an Omega. We have needs, you know," Mother grumbled.

Ulysses' face appeared over my shoulder. "I can answer that, Mrs. Thatcher."

"Jolene, please. We are family now, Ulysses," Mother corrected.

Ignoring the request for the millionth time, Lysse continued, "Two days from now we are flying out to Prio Gria where we will be spending some time in the sun and ocean."

Shocked at this announcement, I looked at the guys who looked far too pleased with themselves.

"Oh, I love Prio Gria. It's a wonderful tropical country with amazing food and the most welcoming people. You have to take the time to see Valfail Reef. It's one of the most beautiful reefs I've ever been to," Mother chattered on, completely oblivious to the fact I was no longer paying attention.

Eli took pity on me and reclaimed his phone, taking the conversation outside the studio to give us a little privacy.

"Was this already planned, or did you just decide this second?" I asked.

Placing a hand on my back, Lysse urged me toward the door. "Do you mind if we have this conversation back home? I don't feel like happy conversations should be happening here of all places."

That was hard to argue with since I felt the same way. "As long as you know you're not getting out of this conversation."

"Believe me, Rosie, we want to have this conversation more than anything in the world," Lysse assured me.

Back home, I sat at the kitchen island and scrolled through pictures of Prio Gria's private island resort. This place was stunning, something you dreamed up but didn't think was real. The main building offered all kinds of restaurants, bars, activities, a spa, and anything else you could imagine. Instead of rooms like a normal hotel, the bungalows were built over the water. Each one had a wooden walkway from the shore to the private bungalow, and when I say private, I mean private.

The next bungalow was far enough away you weren't concerned about being overheard or seen by anyone but who you brought with you. You could pick various sizes of bungalows with different features, but the one Warrick pulled up to show me was called the Packmoon Suite. It was listed as the perfect place to bask in the glow that came from being a newly bonded pack.

"Wait..." I started then paused, looking at the five men standing across from me. "Are you... is this... *for real*?" I squeaked out.

They all nodded, smiling from ear to ear as they gave me a moment to process this.

"But the Scent Matchers—"

"Can go to hell," Gareth stated, cutting me off. "They have no grounds to keep us from being a fully acknowledged bonded pack, baby girl. Whatever that shit was we got pulled in for meant nothing. Yun had our lawyer check into it, and we're already in the system as a legitimate scent-matched pack, which means that once we are bonded to you, we can submit that paperwork, and no one can ever dispute our family."

"So what say you, kitten? Will you be ours forever?" Vili asked, reaching out for my hand.

There was no doubt in my mind what the answer would be because there is no place I would rather be than with these men. "Yes. Yes, I will be yours as long as you will be mine?"

"Fuck it, let's go to Prio Gria right now," Warrick suggested. "We have our own plane, and what do we need to pack when we're all going to be naked for most of the trip?"

"No, we can't go now," I blurted, yanking my hands back to gesture for them to stop.

Ulysses frowned. "Is there something we should know, Rosie? I thought Dr. Arbour cleared you?"

"He did. It's not that, though," I assured him and pointed to the bandage that wrapped around my bicep. "I got a birth control implant, and we have to wait twenty-four hours before having sex."

Warrick stretched out over the counter as if he wanted to tell me a secret, so I leaned in. "There are so many other things we can do without having sex, Care Bear. If you'd like, I'd be happy to show you what they are."

My cheeks burned as I blushed, my pulse rising at his words and slick gathered between my legs. It was clear my brain was the only one worried about waiting the day like I'd been instructed to. *Was it really that big of a concern?* I had been on oral birth control since my surgery. In fact, I'd taken one this morning with my pill regimen. *So what was the reason for holding off?*

Gareth grabbed Warrick's shirt and dragged him back. "Don't go there, man. If we get started down this road here at the house, we're never going to make it to Prio Gria."

"Yes, I agree with Gareth," Vili added. "Plus, now we get to shop for bikinis."

Suddenly, everyone was on board with the idea of leaving in two days, and tomorrow we were going shopping.

BAILEY-ROSE

Our flight was early in the morning. I mean, the sun wasn't up early. Thankfully, none of the guys expected me to be alert or responsive, taking care of everything. Soon, Warrick wrapped me up in my blanket like a burrito and carried me out to the waiting limo. Nugget was already inside, curled up in a plush dog bed we'd gotten for him to sleep on in the plane. Waffles, my faithful shadow, hopped in after us and settled on the floor. He also had a bed, but it was probably in the trunk with the rest of the luggage.

"Why are we going so early? Don't we tell the plane when to leave?" I asked, snuggled between Warrick and Vili.

Vili stroked his fingers through my hair, making it incredibly difficult to focus on his answer. "Time change, my kitten. We want all the time we can get."

"You all filed for bonding leave, so no one is expecting any of us to communicate with the outside world for at least two weeks," I mumbled. "Do you really think we'll need a full month to get past the bonding bliss?"

Hearing the guys chuckle at my question, I cracked open an eye to look at them. The excitement and primal energy filling the limo had me perking up a bit. My Omega instincts told me that something was shifting in our dynamic, and my skin tingled with delight. I knew I was perfuming, but I wasn't sure if they could smell it since I was wrapped up as snug as a bug in a rug.

Seconds later, Warrick and Vili started to purr, nuzzling their faces against my hair. I was in heaven engulfed in the spiciness of Warrick's scent and the marshmallow sweetness of Vili.

"Kitten, they give month for a reason," Vili whispered, nipping the tip of my ear. "It has nothing to do with Alphas, yet everything to do with Omegas' needs."

A shiver ran through my body, and I was already panting, desperate to be touched.

"Once a pack decides they are going to bond, the shift in intentions of the Alphas triggers a response from the Omega. That is what you're feeling now," Warrick explained, his voice low and raspy. "Each bite bonding you to us will change everything in your body chemistry as well as ours. It's how you know when someone is bonded to another even if you don't see their marks."

I was no longer listening as Warrick traced his finger along my jaw, neck, and collarbone. A whine slipped out of me as I rubbed my legs together, needing to *feel* them touching every inch of me. The small taste I'd gotten of what it was like to be in heat was nothing compared to the way my body *demanded* my Alphas to mark me. Wiggling in the blanket, I tried to get free, but Warrick had expertly trapped me.

"You did this on purpose," I accused. Irritation at being thwarted made me snap at him.

Warrick nodded, tipping my chin up to meet his citrine-colored eyes. "This is why we are given a month off and most packs go into seclusion because, my sweet, perfect Omega, this is just the tip of the iceberg of what you're going to experience."

Before I could yell at him for teasing me if he wasn't going to do anything about it, Warrick fused his lips to mine, cutting off all responses. Moaning, I sank into Warrick's hold as he shifted me to sit on his lap. The sensation of his tongue stroking mine seemed to zing right to my throbbing clit. My panties were soaked as slick poured out of me in preparation for what was to come. Only I would have to wait five more hours for that need to be fulfilled.

Breaking the kiss, Warrick pulled back to gaze down at me. "Fuck, Care Bear, you smell so goddamn addictive. Like the perfect lazy summer day, lying naked in the sunshine, as the sweat from fucking you senseless dries off my body."

My whole body spasmed like I was having an aftershock, making me groan in discomfort at the lack of actually experiencing the orgasm. "Please," I begged, my fingers slipping between my legs to relieve my aching clit. "I can't wait. Either one of you helps, or I'll take care of it myself."

Hands gripped my legs, turning me so my back was to Warrick's chest, allowing Gareth to unwrap my legs. He only freed the lower part of my body, keeping my arms trapped to my sides as Warrick held me tight. Seconds later, my sleep shorts and panties were stripped off me before shoving my legs wide. I cried out in pleasure at the feel of Gareth's tongue stroking over my pussy.

"Yes, oh God, please don't stop," I whimpered.

Stopping was the last thing on Gareth's mind as his mouth latched onto my clit, and he started to purr. The vibrations were all it took to send me rocketing over the edge into orgasmic bliss. Next, he slipped two fingers into my pussy, teasing my G-spot, causing another climax to slam into me. A scream ripped out of my throat as my body trembled, but Gareth didn't bother to slow down, aiming to pull a third orgasm out of me in a matter of seconds. With the magical addition of his tongue, I was flying high in the clouds of euphoric bliss.

So this is what it feels like to have intimacy with no restraint or worry. Yeah, we're definitely going to need the whole month.

Gareth's triple-decker delight took the edge off my need and knocked me out so when I woke up, we were an hour away from landing. The private plane was Vili's, or I suppose the more accurate statement would be it was Silveda's. However, it was meant for Vili's personal use since he needed to travel back and forth to Numoland for business.

I gazed out the plane's small window, still wrapped in my blanket, with the guys all snuggled up around me. It appears they didn't like being up so early for the flight either, or I was rubbing off on them, having never been a morning person. Out of necessity for school, I adapted, but since my surgery, my sleep schedule has been all over the place. Something tells me this trip wasn't going to offer any help in creating a new normal.

The comforting scent of fresh, warm blueberry muffins had me purring before Yun-Sun's lips touched my neck. "The mark I gave you is almost faded," he murmured.

Arching against his body which was melded to my back, I rubbed my ass against his stomach. "Then it's a good thing the next one you give me won't ever fade."

A deep rumbling purr erupted out of him as Yun let his teeth scrape along my neck. "Trust me, sweetheart, I plan to leave my mark where I can always see it on you. That way, I know everyone else will too."

The possessive tone and the way he let his fingers wrap around my throat in a claiming gesture nearly had me turning into a blob of pudding, wishing he'd lick me off the spoon. "I never thought this would happen," I admitted as I worked one hand free to stroke his arm. "I'd given up hope that there was anyone out there who'd want a rejected and broken Omega like me."

"You were never broken," Lysse growled out, drawing my gaze to where he lay in front of me.

I smiled lovingly at him, stroking his cheek, feeling the stubble under my fingertips. "I know that now, but before you walked back into my life, only my family told me that. Tell me, would you believe your parents over the rest of the world?"

"Probably not," he admitted, caught my hand, and pressed a kiss to my palm. "But I would have believed you."

"That's because I'm always right," I teased.

A warning glint was in his eyes, my only clue before I was under a tickle attack. I tried to get away, but Yun betrayed me and dragged me back, getting in his own attacks on my ribs until I was laughing so hard I was crying and begging for mercy.

"Uncle, I plead uncle. Someone save me," I tried to yell, but I couldn't stop laughing.

A deep bark was our only warning before Waffles charged his way onto the bed and dragged the guys by their shirt or shorts away from me. Once they were all dumped on the floor, Waffles draped himself over my legs, keeping me right where I was and ensuring the guys kept their distance.

"Waffles, it's okay, buddy. We were just playing," I cooed, petting the silky fur on his giant head.

He gave me a look that told me he didn't agree and booped his damp snout against my shoulder.

Surprised at the alert, I checked my monitor, and sure enough, my blood pressure was rapidly dropping. "Okay, it seems a tickle fight might need to be something to work up to," I sighed, flopping back onto the bed.

There was a low warning growl from Waffles as the bed dipped.

"*Nien*," I ordered, telling him to back off.

Instantly, the growl stopped, and Waffles got up to position himself under my legs instead of on top of them. This was the only downfall for a dog who had two jobs. While he alerted me as he was trained to do, Waffles had been in guard-dog mode, not medical. Once I'd released him from the need to actively guard me, he conducted himself in the manner of his medical training.

"Sorry about that, guys," I apologized as the guys stood around the bed with Warrick sitting on the edge, attempting to check on me. "I'm still learning his moods."

"Don't sweat it, Care Bear. We are learning how best to interact with him too," Warrick said, crawling over and placing a hand on my forehead. "You feel pretty warm. Did you overheat trapped in your blanket?"

"Could be part of it," I answered with a shrug. "I didn't even consider that being a problem."

"Planes are not the best at temperature control... it's either freezing or a little too warm," Ulysses added. "I'll be right back with some water and a cold towel."

Warrick turned my wrist so he could look at my monitor. Now, having the chance to really wear and use the other features of the new monitor they got me, I was impressed. It tracked my temperature, heart rate, blood pressure, and steps, and, of course, had a GPS locator in it. The feature I liked the most was that I could ping one of the guys or all of them if I needed. So if I was in the house and only Vili was home, I could just alert him I desperately needed more hot chocolate.

"Temp is two degrees higher than normal," Warrick shared. "I'm gonna shoot Dr. Arbour a quick message just asking if that's normal for Omegas during heats and bonding."

"Don't bother him. He's retired, remember?" I pointed out. "Did you get the direct number for PA Timmon?"

Warrick pressed a quick kiss to my cheek before rolling off the bed. "Yeah, we have his number, but Dr. Arbour said he is happy to answer questions for us over the next few months since we're still not sure what aftereffects the surgery will have, good or bad."

If Dr. Arbour volunteered to have them reach out, who was I to tell them differently? Just as Lysse returned, Waffles crawled out from under my legs and jumped off the bed but didn't go far. Stacking up a few pillows, I sat up, took the offered water, and used the cool cloth to wipe down my face and neck. It felt gloriously refreshing.

"Please take your seats as we prepare for our final descent into Pago," a voice called over the speakers.

"Well, that couldn't have been better timing," Gareth said, trying to fight back a grin.

I cocked an eyebrow at him. "What's with you?"

"Oh, nothing," he answered with a shrug. "I'm just excited to land since it means I'm that much closer to making you scream my name again. Only this time, it will be while I'm buried balls deep in that pretty pussy, as I leave my mark forever etched on your sexy body."

Well, fuck. I certainly wasn't worried about low blood pressure now.

Warrick

S ome moments will live in your brain forever, and the expression I saw on Bailey-Rose's face as we pulled up to the overwater bungalow was one of them. I thought her eyes were going to pop out of her head with how wide they got. Thankfully, Ulysses had an arm wrapped around her waist, keeping her close until the small boat we were in docked. A second boat filled with our luggage pulled up to the slip next to us.

This was one occasion I didn't mind using my family connections to my advantage. While the Shaw family didn't own this resort, they invested quite a bit of money in the renovations two years ago. So when I called the owner out of the blue asking for his most exclusive and sought-after bungalow, he didn't hesitate to make it happen.

What made this resort so exclusive wasn't the fact it only had twenty bungalows but that it was on its own private island. They'd turned the middle of this island into a self-contained ecosystem growing all their own fruits and vegetables. Fresh seafood was caught daily and prepared for the guests, while select amounts of other meats were imported from the mainland. There is just something whimsical about needing to take a boat to get to your destination. It adds that extra bit of magic to an already stunning landscape.

Sunset Dreams Resort was truly a place you believed could only exist in your imagination. The pure white sands, palm trees, crystal clear water, and a soft breeze made the humidity bearable. I couldn't think of a more perfect place to start the beginning of forever with Bailey-Rose.

Part of me hated that Randall showing himself again was the driving factor in getting us here, but I wasn't going to dwell on that. Eli promised to deal with things back home and would keep us updated on any progress in hunting the bastard down. We Alphas agreed Randall wouldn't have a chance in hell of touching our girl ever again if we were on the move, living life to the fullest. None of us would give him the satisfaction of knowing Bailey-Rose was living in fear of him, so we created a plan to do just the opposite.

"How is something like this possible?" Bailey-Rose gasped as she entered the bungalow. "The floor is all glass."

Nugget proceeded to pounce on a fish that was swimming past and was deeply offended when his efforts were thwarted.

"Sorry, little guy, but you're gonna need to get in the water if you want to nab one for real," I explained as I picked him up, ruffling the fur between his big ears.

Waffles, the dutiful companion that he was to my Care Bear, moseyed behind her as she explored the place. There wasn't much you couldn't see from the entrance since it was an open floor plan. One of the coolest things I'd been excited about was a sunken couch that gave you an even better view of the ocean beneath us.

"Guys, why does it say, press button for one-hundred-eighty-degree viewing?" Bailey-Rose asked.

Gareth walked up right behind her and, without a second thought, hit a button. The sound of gears running caused Gareth to drag her back a few steps as the wooden walls opened like curtains being pulled back. When it stopped, half the bungalow was open to the view of the ocean.

"I'll admit I'm impressed," Yun-Sun mumbled under his breath.

Coming from a family like mine, I understood his hesitation to give into the lavish life after seeing what it did to our parents. When you didn't have to work for anything, it changed how you viewed the world and everyone in it. We quickly realized that was something we had in common as a pack. Each of us was inherently wealthy, having been born into money, but none of us like to take something we didn't earn, making us the odd man out.

A shrill squeal of delight burst out of our Omega as she took a running start and launched herself onto the bed. Much like her bed at home, it was round, but instead of being hung, it was sunken into the floor like the sofa. A curtain of bug netting would surround the bed when pulled closed, but for now, it was half open. Pillows in all sorts of tropical colors filled the bed, making it like an adult ball pit but with pillows.

I couldn't help but smile as I watched the woman I was hopelessly in love with enjoying the space we would be in for the next two weeks. Rolling onto her back, she stretched out her legs and pressed her arms over her head, causing her shirt to ride up. My gaze locked onto the bare skin that was revealed, and an almost overwhelming urge to place my mark on her skin took hold.

Since we'd asked Bailey-Rose to be ours, and she accepted, the need to complete the bonding was growing more intense every day. It's said that science, biology, and instinct drive us to fulfill this act, but I couldn't disagree more. The single thought I had running through my mind since she said yes was holy shit, I'm one lucky bastard.

Biology might have brought us together, but how I felt about this tiny, badass warrior who brought so much light to my life had nothing to do with science. It had everything to do with who *she* was as a person.

The feel of fingers combing through my hair surprised me, and I froze. Somehow, I'd lost myself to my needs and found I was nuzzling my cheek against Bailey-Rose's stomach. Okay, maybe they weren't totally wrong about the instinct part of bonding. Clearly, that was playing a higher role in this than I expected, but *fuck,* she smelled so damn good, I just wanted a taste. Giving in to the urge, I licked the bare skin along the top of her shorts, causing her to shiver. The only thing that kept me from going further was the angry grumblings from her stomach.

Turning to look up at her, I cocked a brow. She was doing everything possible to keep from laughing, even clamping her hands over her mouth. Despite her efforts, the telltale shake of her body told me she was cracking up. So I did the only thing I could and blew a raspberry over the spot I wanted to mark. Peals of laughter filled the bungalow, and I knew without a doubt this was how I wanted to spend the rest of my life—experiencing moments with her.

"Come on, you... sounds like we need to feed the monster who's living in your belly," I teased, pulling her to her feet.

"So how does food work here?" she asked as Yun lifted her out of the pit of pillows. "I don't see a kitchen, just a fancy table for us to eat at."

Vili held up what I thought was a book until he flipped it open showing it was a tablet. "You pick from here, kitten. This has all yummy things to eat or drink."

The man settled onto an oversized padded lounge chair that would fit three or two people side by side. He then tugged Bailey-Rose onto his lap so they could look over the menu together. Taking out my phone, I took a picture of them and sent it to her family. Yesterday, we'd called to tell her parents our plan to bond our pack together over this trip, and we'd be a little hard to get in touch with. They were so excited for us and had zero issues as long as we kept them up to date on our location. This was the agreement they had with their children, and now we had to follow as well.

It would be Jolene's birthday while we were gone, so Bailey-Rose came up with the idea of sending her mother a picture frame so we could send photos to as a gift. It made our lives easier because then any of us could take a picture and send it to the frame, keeping them included in our travels. Family was incredibly important to our girl, and I saw why. They were pretty amazing people who welcomed us with open arms, and I never wanted Bailey-Rose to feel she needed to pick between us or them. So, if we needed to send pictures and keep her parents updated on our travels, it was the least any of us could do.

"I'm not eating snails," Bailey-Rose blurted. "I don't care what you say, Vili, it's not happening."

"Why is so good," Vili insisted. "Fine, I get some for me then... maybe you might try."

"I doubt it," she muttered. "Now pineapple chicken sounds amazing. Oh, look, they have little steamed dumplings that look like bunnies. We're definitely getting some of those."

Ulysses stood next to me, his arms crossed, wearing a dopey grin as he watched our Omega. "Hey," I whispered.

It took him a second to come back down to earth and turn his attention to me. "What's up?"

"We're doing the right thing getting her out of town,

right? I mean, I know we are, but shouldn't we be more honest as to why?" I asked, feeling a moment of doubt.

Ulysses turned to fully face me with a curious look on his face. "Do you think Rosie doesn't know that there's more to us leaving so soon after what happened at the studio?"

"I..." Pausing the moment I started to speak, I realized he was right. Bailey-Rose Thatcher, while carefree, pure-hearted, and adorably clumsy, was no idiot. "You're right, man. I guess I just hesitate at the thought that we were not being honest."

"Look, we've all seen what it looks like when a pack doesn't trust or respect each other. They must have at some point, but situations happened to break that trust, and now they live the rest of their lives resenting their pack. None of us want to be them, and the way we keep that from happening is by having conversations like this. You had a concern, and instead of ignoring it and letting that fester, you spoke up." Ulysses grabbed my shoulder and gave it a friendly squeeze. "If you want to talk to her about it, then none of us will stop you because we don't want to keep secrets from her either."

Feeling better about the situation now that I'd had a chance to get my fear off my chest, I decided to let the matter drop. None of us wanted Randall to ruin this time for us, and at the heart of it, that's why none of us wanted to bring it up in the first place. It's better to leave the darkness trapped in the shadows than darken the room to let it free.

"Done," Bailey-Rose exclaimed. "It says food should be here in twenty minutes."

"Which is impressive because you ordered half the damn menu," Gareth added.

"Anyway," she cut in, drawing out the word. "I think we

should get in a quick dip in the water since you shouldn't right after eating."

Yun-Sun frowned at that. "Sweetheart, you know that's a myth, right? There is no truth to that other than parents not wanting their kids rushing through lunch just to get back in the pool."

"What?" Bailey-Rose demanded, utterly flabbergasted at this news. "I've been lied to my whole life?"

Yun shrugged. "I'm sorry, but it's the truth."

It took her a good minute to come to terms with that knowledge before popping to her feet. "Either way, I'm going to change and test out the water."

I wish I could say I was a bigger man who could resist watching his girl change, but I'm not. It was clear she wasn't planning on stepping into the bathroom like she once would have. Nope, our Omega was embracing the reality that we were all going to be naked together a lot in upcoming days.

While I could one hundred percent appreciate a woman who had abundant assets, the woman who stole my breath away had curves in all the right places with a solid handful on top and in the back to grip onto. When she bent over buck-ass naked to grab her swimsuit, I nearly tackled her to the bed seeing her pussy glisten with slick in the sunlight.

"Holy fucking shit," Ulysses bit out. "Is she trying to turn us into senseless rutting Alphas?"

"I'm gonna go with yes," I answered, my hands balling into fists. "Otherwise, she has no goddamn idea what she does to us."

Soon, our visual feast was covered with a lavender-colored string bikini with little silver beads on the ends of the strings that glinted in the sunlight. It had been pure torture to watch her shop for them since anything Bailey-

Rose put on was perfect. We walked out of that store with twenty different options, and I doubt she'll put another one on after this. Oh well, there will be other occasions she'll need to have clothes on.

"Any of you joining me?" she asked, batting her lashes at us, proving the woman knew exactly what she was doing.

"Sure," I offered, then stripped off my clothes, tossing them closer to the bed. "Ready?"

Now, it was her turn to get a taste of her own medicine as the scent of her perfume hit my nose. Instantly, I started to purr, pleased to get such a reaction from sight alone. I gave her a wink and headed out to the deck, where we had a plunge pool as well as steps leading into the ocean. The sound of small feet running up behind me had me grinning, that is, until she blew past me and leaped into the water.

The need to protect my Omega reared up as all the worst possible outcomes ran through my head. We didn't know how deep the water was or how far the stairs extended. What if she hurt herself? Sprinting to the edge, I jumped just as she popped out of the water, grinning from ear to ear. Thankfully, I'd aimed to the right of where she was so I didn't land on top of her. It was far deeper than I expected, and there was zero risk of Bailey-Rose getting hurt. Now satisfied that everything was fine, my heart rate began to slow as I resurfaced.

"Isn't this *amazing*?" Bailey-Rose yelled as if she were trying to tell the world her opinion.

Treading water, I waited for the others to join us, diving into the water. Only Yun-Sun wore swim trunks while the others followed my example.

"What are you worried about, Yun," I teased. "You know she's already seen all there is to see."

"Yeah, but the guy delivering our food hasn't," he countered. "I'd prefer to keep a limit on who I expose myself to, and a stranger isn't one of them."

That was a point I couldn't argue with, but it did raise another question. "So what are we supposed to do once we're lost in the haze of the bond?"

"Already taken care of," Yun shared, waving off my worry. "I found a whole menu section for bonding care, which includes leaving food outside the door in coolers for us to bring in. They are dropping the first one off tonight that will have enough snacks and drinks for at least two days. Then each morning, another will arrive, and they'll take the empty one. I just mark down food we don't want, and the rest is up to them."

"Nice, that might be my favorite thing about this place," Gareth said, grinning. "No need to make choices about things that don't matter when we have something, or should I say someone, to focus our attention on."

Bailey-Rose blushed, dipping under the water to hide, then swimming out to the floating platform a few feet away. Watching her climb out of the water, my mouth went dry at the sight of the water cascading off her milky white skin. In the back of my mind, I made a note to ensure I took extra care to slather her in suntan lotion. We couldn't let our girl get sunburned, and it offered me the chance to feel her smooth skin under my hands. My dick pulsed at the idea, and I'm pretty sure I was leaking a little extra salt into the water, telling me I was reaching the end of my rope. The food better get here soon, or our girl wasn't going to be eating anything but my cum.

BAILEY-ROSE

Five pairs of eyes were a heavy weight to bear as my Alphas watched me stretch out on the raft, tossing an arm over my eyes. Another growl from my stomach reminded me I truly was hungry. I knew if I ignored it and didn't get the chance to eat before the tension building between us broke, there was a high chance I'd pass out again. The last time that happened, poor Vili was left in so much pain as he pulled out of me before his knot shrunk. I'd seen how awful that had been for him, and I wasn't looking to repeat that experience.

Climbing up here had been the only option to control the urges coursing through me. One thing I hadn't considered about them being naked and swimming was how clear the water was. There was nothing to keep how turned-on they were from sight. Even Yun-Sun had an obvious tent in his swim shorts, and I knew how good that cock felt.

The raft dipped and shifted as one of my guys climbed up to join me. Water droplets landed on my skin, telling me that whoever it was hovered over me. In the next second, a gust of wind hit just right, and I was lost in the scent of sweet milk chocolate and bright notes of orange, creating the perfect balance. Smiling, I kept silent, curious to see what my first love was going to do now that he'd joined me.

"I see you smirking like the Cheshire Cat, Rosie," Lysse whispered in my ear. "Could it be that you know exactly what you're doing to us? Has my sweet little Rosie turned into a sultry tease?"

Unable to keep from looking into his blue eyes that matched the water around us, I lowered my arm. "I don't know what you mean. I'm just here relaxing and soaking up the sun."

"So tease it is," Lysse determined with a laugh. "Well, two can play that game."

Reaching up, he tugged on the strings tying the top of my bikini until they released. My breath started to pick up as I felt my newly repaired heart thundering in my ears. Since I was lying on the back strings, Lysse decided to just tug what remained down around my waist. Taking a fist full of my wet hair, he pulled, tipping my head back to stare up at the cloudless blue sky. The first touch of his lips over my scar had me sucking in a sharp breath.

"Lysse..." I whispered.

All the guys had made it incredibly clear to me that in no way did they see this mark as ugly or something to be ashamed of. However, it was hard for me to look at it, knowing how long it took for the reddish-purple color of a healing scar to dissipate. With my fair skin, it stood out, drawing people's attention and causing them to quickly look away, feeling guilty for looking. What I hated most about the scar wasn't how it looked but the fact it sometimes felt like a brand. To the average person who saw it, I was marked as imperfect, and that infuriated me to the point of tears some days.

"Shh, Rosie," Lysse whispered, a hand gliding down my side to settle on my hip. "Let me worship this body of yours as it deserves. It's been through hell, fought many battles, and has brought you out the other side stronger than ever."

Tears leaked out of my eyes at his words and the feel of his lips brushing my skin.

"This scar..." he said, pausing to press open-mouthed kisses down my sternum, "... is a badge of honor, a mark of strength, and proof the woman I love will be able to share a long life with me."

I tried to reach up to touch him, but he caught my hands and pinned them to the raft. "No, there is only so much control I have. Right now, I just want to taste every inch of you until the food gets here."

Which was exactly what he did. When he reached the end of the scar, he worked his way back up until he reached my chin. He saw I'd been crying and licked the salty trail before kissing me so deeply it seemed we shared oxygen. Releasing my lips, he moved down, nuzzling the side of my neck and letting his teeth scrape along certain parts, pulling a moan from me.

The real tease, however, was feeling the tip of his cock as it brushed along my stomach. As he worked his way down, so did his dick, making me shiver as it grazed the top of my mound. What I craved was so close yet still too far away, but if I tilted my hips, the tip would catch at the top just above my clit, making me cry out.

"Tell me, Rosie, do you still enjoy being a tease?" Lysse asked as he cupped my pussy. "God, you're fucking drenched down here, ready and waiting for your Alpha to fuck you until his knot swells and locks you to him like the good little Omega you are. Do you want me to fill you with my cum as I place my mark on your body?"

A whine erupted from me as my body all but short-circuited at the lack of orgasm with all this stimulation. "Please..." I gasped, thrashing from side to side, desperate for any kind of friction. "I want it all, Lysse. I want to be fucked hard. To feel like you're going to split me in half as you hold me together. I need you to flood me with your cum, trapping it in me with your knot until I'm marked inside and out as yours forever."

Something between a snarl and a growl rumbled out of Ulysses as his mouth latched onto my nipple. I arched, feeling his teeth bite down but stopped just before they would break the skin. Then the next second, he was gone, leaving me a needy, shivering mess.

"Kitten," Vili cooed, brushing a hand over my hair. "Come back to me just for a moment."

Lifting me so I was sitting, he slid in behind me and lifted something to my lips. The second I got the taste of peanut butter and banana, I started to guzzle down the cool, refreshing smoothie. The shock of cold hitting my stomach helped bring me back to reality. I saw Yun and Gareth escorting an irate Ulysses back into the bungalow.

"This is packed full of protein," Vili murmured as I took over, grasping the glass bottle. "Slow down, kitten. I have another if you need," he shared, pointing to the pink-colored glass bottle.

It tasted so good and was exactly what I needed. I'd been just as thirsty as much as hungry. Finishing off the bottle, I sighed, leaning back against Vili. "Thank you. If you hadn't stopped him, this would have ended much like our time together."

Vili hugged me tightly, kissing my temple. "This why we have pack. It takes us all to look after each other. As for that moment between us, not matter how it end, I treasure the feeling of being with you." Picking up the second smoothie, he opened it and offered it to me. "Now we prepare so we can make many more memories together and have no fear."

Chuckling, I took the drink and sipped it a little more

slowly. This one was a blend of tropical fruit that was an explosion of exotic flavors in my mouth. "Yes, this time everything will be different, and I get to explore all the things I never had a chance to discover."

"Yes, kitten, there are many things we want to teach you," Vili murmured as he started to purr and let his hands cup my breasts. "Many things to try."

Shivering, I arched into his touch as he flicked my nipples, working them into peaks begging to be given attention. "I think I've had enough to eat," I decided, unable to keep my other pressing needs at bay.

"Is that so," Vili commented as he pulled my hips back so I could feel his hard dick pressing against my ass. "Then you won't mind if I pull these."

I wasn't sure what he was talking about at first until what was left of my bikini top fell off, and my bottoms were held on by my legs clenched together.

"This makes things easier... nothing should keep you from us," he reasoned before standing and pulling me to my feet, shedding the last of my swimsuit. "So perfect you are, my kitten. Now be good girl and swim to your waiting Alphas," Vili instructed with a sharp swat on my ass, urging me into action.

Diving into the water, I swam as quickly as I could, knowing what awaited me once I stepped back in the bungalow. No longer would I be the rejected Omega, forced into life alone and unwanted. Within the walls of this tropical nest were the people I was meant to share my life with, to plan for forever, and trust with the pieces of my beautifully broken heart.

Emerging from the water, I climbed the steps, head held high, shoulders back, fully embracing the power of owning my sexuality. Hell, I was an Omega, a being genetically wired to have a high sex drive to match that of their Alphas, who were created to fit with me perfectly. Today was when everything changed, and the six of us became a true family connected in the most intimate act of bonding. With each mark given and received, a window to the soul would be created, allowing the partners to feel what they feel with no words needed. Once a bond is created, there were no more secrets between an Alpha and their Omega.

Entering the bedroom side of the bungalow, I locked eyes with Ulysses first, drawn to the primal scent pouring off him. Much like the effects of an Omega's perfume, the musk an Alpha in rut created was like crack. One moment he was across the room, then the next, he was right in front of me, scooping me up in his arms. I wrapped my arms around his neck, curling my fingers in his hair as he devoured my mouth. Two fingers thrust into my aching pussy from behind, causing me to moan in delight. Finally, I was going to be filled, giving my pussy something to cling to. All too soon, those fingers were removed as my back connected with a wall, making me squeak in surprise.

"I wanted our first time to be sweet and gentle like you deserve, Rosie, but I *need* you," Lysse managed to explain as he used the wall to hold me up while he positioned his cock at my entrance. "Don't worry. I promise to make it up to you over and over again until I'm sure you've forgiven me."

Not waiting for an answer, Ulysses shoved me down on his cock, thrusting the whole thing into me at once. I cried out, digging my nails into his skin as my body erupted with pleasure. "Finally," I gasped. "I finally have you inside me after so many years of dreaming about this moment."

That information only seemed to add fuel to the blaze that was already burning in my Alpha. He growled so deeply it caused his cock to vibrate inside me, causing my eyes to roll back at the euphoric feeling. Then Lysse began to move, thrusting into me as if he wanted to split me in half. I could feel the wood of the wall scraping along my back, but I didn't give a fuck. All that mattered was the feeling of this man pounding my pussy and not giving a damn what my heart rate was.

"Goddammit, Rosie, you feel so good. I knew you would be... this is incredible," Ulysses praised as he pulled me tightly to his chest, holding me as he snapped his hips, thrusting deeply into me.

I nuzzled my face against his neck, getting drunk off his scent to the point I was licking his skin, hoping it would taste like chocolate. Frustrated that what my nose was telling me and his taste didn't match, I decided that further action must be taken. Latching my mouth on his neck, I bit down hard, sending a shockwave from the strongest climax I'd ever experienced through my body as I tasted the faintest tang of blood. Ulysses let out a roar as he dropped to his knees, clutching my head to his neck as I licked the wound I'd created.

"Holy fucking shit," Lysse panted. "I was not expecting the bond to pack such a punch. You just had to make the first move this time, didn't you, Rosie?"

Realization of what I'd just done crashed through me as I released my hold on him. "Lysse, I'm so sorry."

Ulysses relaxed his arms so I could see his face. The expression I found was a mix of adoration, love, and awe as his eyes welled up with tears. "Don't you fucking dare apologize for claiming me as your Alpha, Bailey-Rose. You have given me the most amazing gift I'll ever be able to receive." Cupping my face with his hands, he kissed me tenderly. I could feel every emotion in it as if it were my own. "Now, it's my turn to return the favor, but I think we should move this to the bed just to be safe. I nearly dropped you."

Without pulling out, Ulysses rose and cuddled me close as he stepped to the bed, laying me on my back. "I hope you don't mind, but I want to watch your face as I mark you."

Hearing him say something like that shouldn't make me blush, but it did. Biting my lip, I nodded, pulling him down to kiss me as he started to fuck me again. The frenzy had dissipated slightly, giving Lysse more control over his actions. This Alpha of mine wasn't holding back, but he was more deliberate in his movements as he started to purr. Vibrations deep inside me teased places I never knew existed, setting off fireworks under my skin. Breaking our kiss, I tossed my head back, crying out in nonsensical words and sounds, trying to convey just how good this was feeling.

Then, for a split second, everything stopped, and my world exploded, revealing I'd been living in a muted state of being. Colors were brighter, sounds were clear as a bell, every touch to my skin was mind-blowing, and I knew I'd never be alone in my life ever again. Just as fast as the moment happened, it was over, but a new energy hummed in my chest that tethered me to Ulysses. Now I understood why he cried after I marked him because the sensation of being his was overwhelming in the best way.

"Mine," Ulysses stated as he released my breast where he'd decided to leave his mark, the same place he almost claimed out on the raft. "My perfect Omega," he mumbled, running his tongue over the mark, which had me coming instantly.

As my pussy clenched, I realized Ulysses had knotted me, but I'd been lost in the bond to notice. Even his warm breath over the mark had me twitching and spasming around his knot. Even though he was locked to me, he managed to rock into me, hitting all the perfect places to keep me on edge.

"More," I croaked. "I want to feel more."

Ulysses' eyes dilated at my request. "Whatever my sweet Omega desires, her Alpha will provide."

Seconds later, I was screaming and writhing as Ulysses sucked on my nipple and his mark while sliding two fingers between us to rub my clit at the same time. There was nothing my body could process but pure pleasure that was almost on the cusp of being too much. A brush of emotions through my connection to Lysse swirled around my blissed-out brain.

Adoration.

Disbelief.

Gratitude.

Unconditional love and devotion were what Ulysses was feeling in this moment.

Now I understood why people said a bond was a connection of souls—the deepest connection two people could ever have and why bonding should never be taken lightly. Give this vulnerability to the wrong person, and it could destroy you just as easily as it could restore you. I wasn't sure how the connection worked or how to share with him what I was feeling. I kept my emotions open and put my heart behind them, praying he would understand.

"Rosie," Ulysses whispered, resting his head against mine. "Breathe for me, my love. There's no need to panic. I hear you loud and clear. It's the purest song to my ears that will never be drowned out."

The brush of his thumb along my cheek as he wiped away my tears had me curling tight against him. I loved this intimacy we were sharing, yet I felt I was missing other things that were just as important. Then that feeling vanished as the rest of our pack curled around us, sharing in the moment. Lifting my head, I found Warrick stretched out above me, grinning.

He reached out and tilted my chin so he could kiss me. "One down, four more to go, Care Bear. Who will you claim next?"

Smiling, I let my hand slide down his chest to grab hold of his cock. "Why not you?"

As if Ulysses' body understood that I had places to be, more men to bond with, his knot relaxed enough for Warrick to pull me to him. Sitting cross-legged, Warrick cradled me in his lap, enjoying taking his time kissing me as I rocked slowly against his hard cock. The feel of his hands running down my back and along my thighs before retracing their steps had me purring in delight. Even though I'd just had my world rocked by Ulysses, I was craving each of my Alphas with the same fervor.

Twisting, Warrick laid down, stretching out on the bed while I sat perched on his hips. "I want to watch you ride me, taking your pleasure from your Alpha," he informed me, tracing two fingers down my scar until he reached my clit, slowly circling the sensitive nub. "Let me hear how good I make you feel, Care Bear. No one will hear us, so don't you dare hold back."

I squirmed a little, feeling Ulysses' cum leaking out of me onto Warrick as my slick prepared me to take his cock. "Do you want me to clean up first?"

Not having experienced sex with multiple partners before, I didn't really know how they'd view interacting with what others left behind. Warrick pushed up on one arm as he slid the hand teasing my clit between us, sinking two fingers into my pussy. Slowly, he thrust them as deep as he could, lazily scissoring and stirring up whatever was left inside my pussy.

"There is no need for you to do that because I have a feeling there will be many times one of us will want to leave our mark inside you," Warrick commented. "This is just part of being in a pack. We all get used to seeing each other naked, dicks might touch, and leftover cum just becomes extra lubrication, my sweet, thoughtful Care Bear."

Pulling his fingers out of me, he raised them to my lips, and I opened, sucking them clean, causing Warrick to groan and his cock to twitch with excitement.

"Fuck, why is that so hot?" he asked, gripping the back of my neck and crashing our lips together.

Sliding up his body, I moved off his cock so I could grab hold, guiding it to my pussy, then easing myself onto it. We both moaned as he stretched my walls, being slightly girthier than Ulysses. Once I had him fully seated in me, I pushed up, breaking our kiss so I could ride him as he wanted. With my legs being so short, I tucked my feet over his hips, allowing me to have better leverage. Head tossed back, I closed my eyes, trusting my body to know what it wanted. Warrick grasped my thighs, his fingers digging into my skin, but I reveled in the possessive touch.

"Yes, just like that," Warrick praised. "God, I love watching your tits bounce as you move, begging for my attention."

I gasped as he pinched my right nipple, giving it a slight tug, sending a jolt of pain that quickly turned to pleasure. He was more gentle with the left nipple where Ulysses had marked me, but I noticed there wasn't the same euphoric feeling when Warrick touched the area compared to Lysse. *Could it be because it was Lysse's claim on me?* That was a worry for another time as a third hand brushed down my back, pushing me slightly forward. Knowing only men I trusted with my life were here with me, I gave in to the request, tilting to a more forward angle. This changed where Warrick's cock hit, but for the better as the pressure was more focused on the happy button.

Sucking in a breath, warm liquid started to cascade down my back, followed by strong fingers massaging it into me. I groaned in pleasure at the touch along with the feeling of tension leaving my body. "That's it, *omae*, give your body over to us," Yun-Sun whispered, his lips brushing my ear.

Soon, Yun was controlling my movements, his hands urging me to take Warrick deeper and slightly faster. More warm liquid was added, creating more slip as Yun's hand worked lower and lower. Finally, Yun pressed me flat against Warrick, who took over the work, pumping his cock into me. I tensed slightly as a finger circled my asshole, but when I realized he was simply going to massage the area, I relaxed once more.

"Good girl," Yun praised, kissing the small of my back where the swell of my ass met my torso. "Nothing is going to happen fast. We have plenty of time to get you comfortable with the idea. Just remember how much you loved it when I teased your asshole as I fucked you. The way your eyes rolled back in your head as Gareth worked his dick into this tight hole. Only good things will happen here, I promise."

To distract me, Warrick started to pick up speed, drawing a moan out of me as I dug my nails into his arms, hanging on for dear life. The normally sweet, nutty spice of Warrick's scent changed, drawing on the spice with more heat, adding a little more of a commanding bite to my sweet, fun-loving Alpha. My teeth scraped along his pec muscle until I reached his nipple and flicked with my tongue.

"*Shit*," Warrick growled out, his hands clamping down on my hips. "Watch out, Yun."

I didn't register the warning until Warrick pulled out,

flipped me on my stomach, and felt him ram his cock right back in. No longer was I in control of what was happening as Warrick placed a hand on the back of my neck to hold me in place.

"Sorry, my feisty Care Bear, but I'm going to be the one to mark you first," Warrick announced as he pounded my pussy. "I've been dreaming about this moment since I laid eyes on you. It might seem a little selfish, but you have no idea what you do to me, Bailey-Rose."

Warrick leaned forward, wrapped his arm across my chest, and pulled me up so my back was flush with his chest. I could feel his warm breath on my neck as his lips brushed my ear, all the while never slowing in his movements, pushing me closer and closer to coming. "You're the person I've been looking for all my life. The crayons to my coloring book. The sprinkles on my sundae. The rainbow at the end of a rainy day that promises everything's going to be okay. You are the person I want to wake up to every morning and fall asleep to at the end of every day. There are not enough words to explain my love so you can understand. However, there is one way to convey everything without a single word."

Simultaneously, my building orgasm slammed into me as Warrick's teeth bit down on the flat upper part of my ear. I screamed, not in pain, but in overwhelming pleasure my body didn't know how to process. Once more, my body shed another layer to reveal more depth to my world as that electrifying hum resonated in my chest. There wasn't a full connection since I hadn't left my mark on Warrick yet, but I could feel his emotions with the clarity he wanted.

With a gentle hand pressed to my heart, Warrick just held me, his head resting on my shoulder, relishing in the knowledge I finally understood him. The reverence he held for me was more than I expected, but I could feel a loneliness buried in all the emotions. His family hadn't viewed him as anything other than the third son—a boy who hadn't amounted to much or had the shark mentality needed for the cutthroat world of restaurants and entertainment.

"War..." I whispered, pulling out of his arms so I could face him once more.

Straddling his lap, I reached up and kissed him, my hands clutching his face as my heart broke for the wounds his family left on his heart. "You are all the best notes in my favorite song and the person I know who can always make me laugh. Warrick, there isn't a thing I would change," I shared, nuzzling my cheek against his. "Well, maybe one thing..."

Sinking back down on his cock, I wrapped my legs around his waist as we moved in sync, rocking to a rhythm only we knew. Pressing my head against his chest, I listened to the beat of his heart, smiling as it started to speed up at the same time he changed our movements. When his breathing became more rapid, I had to take the lead as his knot started to swell, ensuring he was buried as deep as I could get him. Rocking faster, I chased after the climax that was looming, but when it seemed I might not get to the finish line, I knew it was time.

Dipping my head, I shoved Warrick back, giving me the room I needed to latch onto the skin over his heart. As my teeth pierced his skin, I could feel the pulse of that treasured organ that gave us life. Each of us had our scars under the surface, and I wanted to place one where it would remind him how loved he was by me.

Warrick tumbled backward as he came with a deep guttural growl, and his knot reached full size, allowing him to shoot his cum deep inside me. This time, I could feel all of it, the stretch that had me questioning if I would break and the heat pooling in the pit of my stomach as I took everything he had to give me. Warrick's hands on my hips shoved me down as he rutted his knot further, sending me over the cliff into another orgasm. A scream tore out of me at the back-to-back climaxes made my body clench even tighter on Warrick's knot.

Finally, my body began to relax ever so slightly with the occasional aftershocks as Warrick's cock twitched. We both lay there panting, sweat coating our bodies, utterly lost in the intoxicating high of a completed bond.

"I love you, Bailey-Rose Thatcher," Warrick stated, kissing my head as he rolled us to lay on our sides.

Tipping my head back, I was given the kiss I was looking for, which had me grinning. *This bond thing could really come in handy for us affection-obsessed Omegas.*

"I love you too, Warrick Shaw," I said, nuzzling my head under his chin as he traced his fingers up and down my back. "Now you have a family who will always see the value you've always had. It's their loss and my gain."

Warrick chuckled, which had us groaning as jolts of bliss sparked along our bodies.

"Okay, no more laughing until this knot has settled down," he muttered. "Holy shit, I had no idea how sensitive it could get."

Fingers combed through my hair, urging me to open my eyes. Gareth gazed down at me with such a tender expression, I melted right on the spot. "Baby girl, let's get some hydration into you while you're resting."

Unsure how he wanted to accomplish that in my current situation, I started to wriggle, but Warrick clamped his arms around my hips. "Care Bear, I'm sorry, but you're gonna have to just relax for a bit."

"Sorry, man, that was my fault," Gareth apologized. "Do you think you can roll on your back again?"

A few deep breaths and a curse or two later, Warrick was on his back, propped up slightly by pillows. Carefully, Gareth assisted me as I sat up, trying to keep my hips as still as possible. Next, he produced a glass with fruit on the rim and a tiny umbrella sticking out of the pineapple.

"We discovered they packed those special electrolyte waters... this one is lime-flavored," Gareth explained as I took a sip.

While the flavor helped, these things would never taste *good,* but I drank the whole thing anyway.

"You hungry?" Yun asked, holding a tray of snacks.

I shook my head. "No, but I was definitely thirsty."

"Want another?" Gareth offered, reaching for the glass.

"Ah..." I considered, tucking some hair behind my ear, feeling a little awkward having such a normal conversation while knotted to Warrick. "Something that's not so healthy."

With a quick kiss, Gareth was hopping off the bed to where our beverage counter was. I glanced down at Warrick, meeting his gaze as he studied me with a moonstruck smile. Immense pride and joy trickled through our bond, telling me what was going on in his mind.

"You're fucking adorable, you know that, right?" Warrick shared, his thumb stroking my thigh.

My cheek burned at his attention, making him smile even wider.

"Just when I thought you couldn't be even more irresistible, you have to go and blush like that," Warrick said with a sigh. "If I didn't have you knotted up already, that would have done the trick."

Trying not to laugh, the sound came out more like a snort, and I quickly covered my mouth.

Warrick snatched me up and flipped us so he was hovering over me, brushing his nose along mine before nuzzling a kiss to my lips.

"Hey, none of that," Gareth scolded, and the sound of a hand slapping bare skin could be heard.

Warrick's head shot up. "Did you just slap my ass?"

"So what if I did? Don't act like a child, and I won't have to treat you like one," Gareth shot back.

The shocked expression on Warrick's face turned into a smile as he burst out laughing. "I can't believe you really did that. Who would have guessed you'd have the balls to make that kind of move?"

Gareth just looked at Warrick with a look of exasperation. "Think whatever you want, man, but you still need to let her back up."

"Well, I'm not sure if it was the shock of your slap or coincidence, but my knot has decided to let my sweet Care Bear free," Warrick informed his grumpy pack brother.

Gingerly, Warrick pulled out of me and gave me one more searing kiss before moving to the side. Gareth scooped me up and headed out on the deck where a full, bubbling tub was waiting. He eased me into the water until I was engulfed by bubbles, making me giggle as I blew some of them in his direction.

"Aren't you going to join me?" I asked.

His answer was to perch on the side of the tub, brushing his fingers along my jaw. "I would love to, baby girl, but I think it best if we give you just a little break."

My lower lip popped out in a pout, not at all pleased with that answer.

Gareth chuckled in a low tone and leaned in to kiss me. "Don't you worry, baby girl, before the sun sets, you'll be fucked, marked, and knotted on my cock. Now relax for the next thirty minutes so the rest of us can ravage you without fear of you passing out on us."

With that instruction and a frosted glass of yummy-tasting juice, I indulged in the best bubble bath I'd ever had while watching the waves in the ocean.

GARETH

With a towel wrapped loosely around my waist, not feeling the need to bare it all when she wasn't looking, I watched our girl enjoying the simple pleasures of a bubble bath. At first, I thought she was going to fight me about taking a little time for herself. Yet all it took was the sweet taste of freshly squeezed fruit juice, and she was convinced.

I grinned as I watched her playing with the bubbles, giving herself a beard, making a hat, and then pretending to be Gandolf.

"You shall not pass," Bailey-Rose declared, pretending her cup was the staff.

Panic set in when she tried to sit back down. and her foot slipped, but thankfully, she was far enough into the squat she didn't hurt herself. An explosion of bubbles and water rushed over the sides of the tub. Waffles scrambled to get up from where he'd been napping and out of the water's way, but the big boy wasn't fast enough. A second later, her head popped up, covered in a mess of bubbles, looking around to ensure no one saw her.

I knew I was safe from being seen since I was standing in a shadow, blocked by a sheer curtain waving in the wind. It hadn't taken me long to figure out if I was going to obsess about her safety, I couldn't let her know I was doing it. The few times I'd been caught in the act, she'd scolded me, but it was hard when she looked so cute all fired up. Watching her dual-colored eyes sparkle with indignation and how she tried to stand as tall as she could, even though she always needed to look up at me, was adorable. Don't get me wrong, I took her anger seriously and heard what she was telling me. However, that didn't mean I would do as she said— it just meant I had to be better about hiding it.

"Did I just hear her quote *Lord of the Rings*?" Ulysses asked, coming to stand beside me, munching on some crackers.

"You sure did." I chuckled. "So much for taking time to relax... she's out there fighting off imaginary evil monsters."

"This is her relaxing," Ulysses commented. "All the times she was stuck in the hospital with only so much TV you could watch, that girl would let her imagination run wild. Once Eli got her into art classes, she'd create whole worlds on paper, bringing them to life."

Hearing that explanation made a whole lot of sense as to why Bailey-Rose put so much detail into her art. She'd shown us all the pieces she'd done for the art installation at her school, and they were breathtaking.

"Seeing her like this tells me we made the right choice to get out of town. I know you didn't want to walk away from the situation, but it was the right thing for her," he reasoned. "All I can feel from her is contentment and joy, which I don't think would be true if we were home."

Turning away from Bailey-Rose, I looked at Ulysses. "It wasn't that I didn't want to leave, but more that I was worried he'd either follow or go back underground if we left. What good is it for us to be gone for the month only to come back to the same shit?"

"I hear you, man, really I do," he assured me, resting a

hand on my shoulder and giving it a quick squeeze. "Eli just messaged Yun and told him he hired a bounty hunter and a private investigator to hunt this bastard down. He seems to think there is something odd about the fact the police haven't been able to find anything yet. Truth be told, I agree with Eli. This shouldn't be hard since Randall isn't that smart. Although if he has help from someone with major pull, it's possible the police will never find him."

Anger and fear churned in my stomach. The cops being dirty was the last thing I wanted to think about.

"Don't move," Bailey-Rose instructed, her voice drifting over to me in the breeze.

We both glanced over to find our Omega hanging half out of the tub putting bubbles on Waffles' head. The dog had refused to get closer to the tub to make it easier for her, but his training kept him from walking away entirely. Nugget, who'd been sleeping on a lounge chair, was there as well, his tail wagging as he sported his own bubble hat. He gave a soft yip as if to tell Waffles to get with the program, which he did, suffering in silence at his charge's antics.

"Do we save them?" Ulysses whispered, popping another cracker into his mouth.

I glanced at the clock and noticed it had been almost an hour since I put her in the tub. "Yeah, probably good to get some more food in her too."

"Want me or Warrick to get her?" he questioned. When I gave him a confused look, he explained. "We're bonded to her now, plus it seems like since you and the other two got a little space from her, you're not running on two brain cells."

My brows shot up. "Wow... and who was the person who fucked her against the wall like an animal?"

"Yeah, which is why I know what I'm saying," he

muttered. "Never mind, you want to risk her not getting a chance to eat, then by all means, go for it."

Out of the corner of my eye, I spotted Yun heading for the tub to collect our girl. "Well, it looks like the matter's settled," I pointed out dryly. "I'm gonna start cutting up some food for her to munch on."

"Gareth, I'm sorry that came out wrong," Ulysses offered.

I waved him off and nodded. "I know, we're all good."

Opening the refrigerator we hadn't noticed since it was designed to look like a cabinet, I pulled out fruit, cheese, packages of pre-sliced meat, and grabbed the box of crackers from the counter. Cooking other than grilling might not be my strong suit, but I rocked at fancy snacks. Pulling together a tropical charcuterie board of sorts, I made sure to have things on there that would stick to your bones, as my mother always said.

Setting it on the coffee table in front of the couch, Yun-Sun walked in with Bailey-Rose wrapped in a fluffy towel. "I got snacks," I announced.

"Oh my gosh, did you pull this together?" She gasped as Yun set her down.

Kissing her forehead, I took a deep inhale of her rose and cherry scent that had my dick rock hard in two seconds. *Fuck, maybe Ulysses had been right about the space.*

"Sure did, baby girl," I murmured. "Eat all you want... there is plenty for all of us."

Vili offered her another glass, and I knew it was one of the special hydration drinks from the wrinkle of her nose. Yet she didn't complain as she ate, knowing it was a battle she'd always be facing to keep hydrated on a good day. Add in large amounts of sex, sun, and heat, and that just created an uphill climb.

Sitting behind Bailey-Rose, Vili, dressed in silk boxers, started to brush out the tangled mess that was her hair and braided it out of the way. "There you go, kitten. Much better."

Leaning back so her head rested between his legs, she smiled up at him. "Thank you for always looking after me and my hair."

After her surgery, it had been hell for Bailey-Rose to lift her arms above her head, so Vili took on the task of hair maintenance. It shocked us all he could manage a ponytail let alone braid. He simply shrugged and said a person who had passed away made sure he knew how to properly take care of an Omega. Even though Bailey-Rose could do her hair now, it had become sort of an intimate moment between them. She loved to have her hair played with, and he wanted nothing more than to spoil *his kitten*.

The comfortable atmosphere amongst us as we snacked and relaxed shifted when Bailey-Rose started to nuzzle Vili's cock. He hissed, gripping the back of the sofa tightly as she rubbed her cheek up and down the silk covering his cock. A wet spot appeared as he groaned, looking skyward as if that would be any help in his current situation. Bailey-Rose shocked us all when she pulled down the band of Vili's boxers, freeing his cock, only to swallow it down as far as she could take it. There was a soft gagging sound, but she pulled back, gripping the base to prevent it from happening again.

Any hope I had of being the bigger man and holding myself back for a third time flew out the window as her towel crumpled to the floor. Dropping to my knees, I parted her legs to see a glistening pussy begging to be fucked. Her scent was intoxicating to the point I felt like I might be drunk off it. Sliding my hands under her ass so I could tilt her hips to the best angle, I dove in. *Fuck,* she tasted like heaven.

My chest rumbled with a purr, making Bailey-Rose squirm in my hands. God, the ego boost you got from knowing you were driving your woman wild was exhilarating. I sucked sharply on her clit, which produced a gargled scream, mouth full of cock. Using her slick, I started to massage my thumb around her asshole, teasing the entrance with the tip, never truly entering her. We all knew that our girl would be double stuffed sooner or later, and we wanted her to feel comfortable with the idea. Yeah, we'd tried it once before, but that had been a moment full of emotions and remnants of her almost heat lingering. I wanted her to love having us buried inside her, no matter what hole it was.

With Omegas, it was more of a mental game because their bodies were created to meet the needs of their pack, not only in being the best match for Alphas to breed but also being able to take a knot or two if the need arises. In some packs, all the Alphas went into rut at the same time, meaning their Omega had to manage two or more hungry dicks at the same time. Yet if the Omega didn't trust their Alphas, the enjoyment of the act was lost even if their body had no problem handling the task.

A small hand fisted a chunk of my hair, forcing me deeper into her pussy with my tongue. It would seem I wasn't giving our little minx what she wanted. Testing a theory, I let my thumb slide into her as far as it would go without using any force. Soon, the whole digit was nestled in her ass, awarding me with another moan and her rocking against my hand.

Pulling back, I languidly fingered her ass with my thumb

as I watched Vili fuck her mouth. "Tell me, baby girl, do you want one of us to fuck your ass?"

Of course, I knew she couldn't answer unless Vili allowed it, but he wasn't looking all that interested in pausing for a chat.

"Hmm... how else can I find out your answer?" I said in a teasing tone. "Oh, I know. If you want your pretty little ass fucked, clench down as hard as you can so it's impossible for me to remove my thumb."

The speed at which she made her feelings known shocked me. She clamped the fuck out of my finger that I seriously wasn't sure I could pull it out of her if I wanted to. I glanced over at Yun-Sun, who I knew wanted a piece of her ass as well. My logic was he'd already gotten the chance to enjoy the hell out of her pussy, so if we were going to do this, then I was happy to be bottom.

"Think you can manage the task, Yun?" I challenged the man.

There weren't many times the cutthroat, domineering Alpha who turned down the job at his father's law firm appeared. However, the smirk he just gave me proved it was hiding just under the surface. "You have her in your lap, and I'll manage the rest," Yun instructed. "Unless Vili is willing to shift this back to the bed?"

In answer, Vili gripped the braid he'd made and pulled Bailey-Rose off his cock. She gasped for air, spit running down her chin, and a blissed-out look of happiness in her glazed-over eyes. "Tell us, kitten. Do we fuck you here or on the bed?"

It took her a second to remember how to speak, but the second I pulled my thumb out, she answered real fast. "The bed... I want to be sandwiched between them as they fuck my pussy and ass while you fuck my mouth."

"You want all three at the same time?" Vili pressed, holding her chin so he could look into her eyes.

"Yeeesss," she pleaded.

That was an answer enough for me, so I scooped her up, threw her over my shoulder, and headed for the bed. I'd waited patiently enough for the other two to claim our Omega, but I wasn't feeling so patient anymore. Dropping into the sunken nest, I pulled one of the angled cushions that padded the circumference of the bed. After cleaning up a little, we discovered they moved and that would certainly come in handy. If Bailey-Rose wanted to manage all three of us, I couldn't be flat on my back, which is where the slight forty-five-degree angle of the cushion was the perfect option to make this comfortable for us all.

Drawing her down my chest as I sank into the mattress, I groaned at the feel of her soft skin rubbing against mine. On the walk over, she'd yanked off my towel so I was once more as naked as she was. I used my thumb to wipe her mouth, not relishing the thought of kissing her covered in Vili's dick slobber. Her pouty lips were even more puffy after the abuse they'd taken from being wrapped around a cock. My kisses started out gentle but quickly shifted into becoming more demanding. I needed this woman like I needed air in my lungs.

"I told you I'd make you mine today, didn't I, baby girl," I whispered against her mouth. "From this day until forever, you're going to bear my mark, and I will never let you go."

Bailey-Rose wrapped her hands around my forearms, her nails digging in slightly. "That's where you're wrong..." she informed me. "I'm the one who's never going to let any of you even *think* about leaving me. I might carry all of your marks, but each of you will only have mine."

Listening to her claim us like that almost had me

coming right then and there. I don't think there could be anything sexier than a possessive Omega when you're their Alpha.

"Damn right, I better have your mouth on me, leaving your mark on my body, or I'm going to make you come so many times you'll pass out," I warned.

"Bring it on," she taunted, sliding her hand between us to grasp my cock. "I think I'll take my punishment now if that's okay with you."

Pushing herself up slightly, I felt the moment the head of my cock found her entrance. She tried to take me all at once, but I wanted this moment to last as long as possible. Grabbing her hips, I forced her body to melt onto my cock, inch by fucking inch until my baby girl was begging.

"Please, Gareth, I want your cock to fill me up," Bailey-Rose whimpered, her head falling to my shoulder.

"At this rate, I won't even need to make you come... seems like a better punishment is to only give you a taste of my cock," I pointed out.

She tried to roll her hips to create some friction, but I pulled her back up and slapped her ass. "Only good girls get cock."

Bailey-Rose gasped, her hot breath on my neck, nails biting into my shoulders. "I'll be good, the goodest girl there ever was. Please just fill me with your cock."

Pleased with her need and submission, I started to purr, letting the tip of my dick vibrate at her opening. However, I had underestimated our girl, and it was too late when I felt her teeth sink into my neck. Unable to control my reaction to her mark, I slammed her down on my cock until there was no more for her to take.

"Motherfucker," I blurted, a dry orgasm slamming into my body, causing every muscle to contract for a split second.

My hands shook slightly as I held Bailey-Rose, my breath sawing in and out of my chest like I'd just run for my life. Sweat broke out on my brow, and I shit you not, I thought I saw stars dancing before my eyes. "Holy fuck, that was incredible."

"Now you know why I wouldn't tell you what it felt like," Warrick commented. "Plus, it's kind of hard to explain if you haven't experienced it yourself."

I flipped off my packmate as I nuzzled the most important person in my world. "You all right?" I asked in a soft voice. "I didn't mean to get that aggressive."

Swiping her tongue over her mark, it sent aftershocks through my body that had me speaking gibberish. "I'm positively perfect," Bailey-Rose answered.

Feeling that I was somehow losing the battle against our feisty Omega, I called in reinforcements. "Guys, am I getting her all to myself, or are we making our Omega's dreams come true?"

Vili stepped up and dropped to his knees before taking Bailey-Rose's hand, guiding it to his cock. "My dream came true... now I return the favor, my kitten."

Yun-Sun positioned himself between my legs with the bottle of heated lube. It was probably unnecessary with how wet our girl was, but again, it was all about the experience. I felt some of the lube drip onto my balls, and I had to admit it was a nice feeling. Yun gave me a nod telling me to start moving before he buried his face in her ass.

Bailey-Rose arched, pulling off Vili's cock to cry out at whatever Yun was doing back there. Vili guided her back where she belonged and took it easy as we found a rhythm. If I thrust too hard, it shoved her too far down his dick. If we thrust together, it was equally a problem, so we alternated, and I kept it shallow while waiting for Yun to join the party.

The man was purring up a storm as he worked her over with his tongue and a finger. I could feel the vibrations through her and now understood why she seemed to lose her fucking mind when we did it. Then the thought of *what it would feel like if both Yun and I purred as we fucked her? Could that possibly be too much?* I suppose there was only one way to find out. Thank God we had the rest of our lives to figure that out.

BAILEY-ROSE

I was going to lose my mind.

Simple as that. My brain was going to break with all the stimulation that was being inflicted on my body. Vili's cock thrusting into my mouth as Gareth glided in and out of me was more than enough to overstimulate me. Add in Yun-Sun's wicked tongue and now two fingers that curled and stroked the inside of my ass, my brain was going to melt.

"Pause for a second, guys... she's ready for me," Yun announced.

Instantly, my eyes popped open, and my breathing picked up ever so slightly. It wasn't that I was afraid or didn't want this because, hell yeah, I wanted Yun's cock buried deep in my ass. What had me a little worried was if I could handle all of this at once. Gareth must have felt me tensing up, so he started to stroke his thumbs over my nipples, distracting me. Vili had pulled back, giving me space to adjust to what was about to happen, but allowed me to groan out my delight at Gareth's touch.

More warm oil was spread over my ass, followed by Yun massaging it into my skin with his strong hands. As I relaxed, he spread me open and eased his cock forward, letting my body accept him as it wanted. The feel of him slowly sinking in was unlike anything I'd experienced. I felt so full and had the urge to push him out, but yet the sensation of his cock rubbing along the walls was mind-altering.

"Such a good girl," Yun-Sun praised, rubbing his thumbs

along the small of my back to keep me from tensing up. "God, watching my cock disappear inside you inch by inch has got to be one of the sexiest things I've ever seen."

His encouragement had me relaxing even further, arching slightly as I wiggled my ass to get more comfortable with the feeling. Yun grunted as that movement brought his hips flush with my ass. This Omega officially had both her holes properly stuffed by her Alphas, and holy fuck, did I feel full. I dropped my head to Gareth's chest as the two men stroked and kissed my skin while I adjusted.

"Oh my God," I muttered. "How is this even possible? I feel like *everything*."

"What do you mean, baby girl?" Gareth questioned, stroking a hand over my head. "Is it too much?"

"Yes, but no," I answered, unsure how to explain what I was feeling. "I can feel both of you so clearly inside me. Like I know which dick is which by the texture and sensation you each have. I wasn't expecting it, is all."

"If you're up for it, *omae*, then I'm going to start moving. Once you're comfortable, then Gareth will join in, and Vili can complete the circle if and only if it's not too much," Yun informed me.

"Aye, aye, captain," I offered with a half-hearted salute. "I'm just the passenger along for the ride of a lifetime."

Yun-Sun leaned down and kissed the corner of my mouth. "You are anything but a passenger, but you are correct on one thing. I do plan on helping give you the fuck of your life."

Shivers of anticipation flickered along my skin as Yun straightened, hands gripping my hips as he pulled back. He gave me one more slow thrust before he got down to business and fell into a steady rhythm. My eyes rolled back in my head as I could feel Yun's cock rubbing over Gareth's, making every sensation even more as it echoed through my entire body. I *needed* to know what it felt like to have them both plunging into me, so I started to rock my hips. The movement was small, but it did exactly what I hoped it would—it got Gareth into the game.

"*Shiiit*," Gareth growled out as he grabbed my hair, pulling me toward his lips. He devoured me as my Alphas used my body, pumping their cocks effortlessly in and out of my holes, owning me for their pleasure.

Breaking the kiss, I shoved up, crying out, needing to expel some of this all-consuming feeling I couldn't even begin to describe. It was as if my body was set on fire, heat licking my skin until I felt like it was burning off any remnants of the broken woman I'd been before these men. Cracking open my eyes, I met Vili's gaze and reached for him.

There was something missing in this almost-perfect moment, and it was my kindred spirit. Of all my Alphas, Vili understood part of me the others struggled with. Yet they fulfilled another part of me that Vili never could, which is what made our pack so beautiful in my eyes. Vili seemed to hesitate, almost as if he didn't think I could handle more. Little did he know this was only the beginning. All this proved to me is I could achieve anything with the right people to experience it with.

"Please, I need you," I pleaded.

With that request, my sweet marshmallow-scented Alpha took my hand. He kissed the back of it, then placed it on the base of his cock as he moved forward. The other two slowed as I kissed the velvet tip of Vili's cock before swallowing it. Learning from doing this with just Gareth thrusting, I kept one hand on Vili's hip to keep from choking on his dick.

It might seem silly to some, but the triumph I felt at the feat of taking three of my Alphas at the same time was thundering in my chest. The surge of confidence had me testing out new ways to tease Vili or rock back into the others, shoving them deeper. Groans and curses filled the air, urging me to find out just what I could do to make it happen again. As if they caught onto my trick, they followed suit as hands groped my breasts and another circled my clit. Their loving assault on my body had me exploding into the first of many orgasms.

"That's one, sweetheart," Yun-Sun murmured. "You need at least two more since there are three of us."

Gareth seemed to love this plan and switched his hands for his mouth. Teeth scraping over my nipple had me screaming around Vili's cock. Then Yun followed up the challenge as he pinched my clit as he thrust in hard and deep. My brain forgot we needed to worry about choking, and my arm gave out, but thankfully, Vili was right there to catch me.

Switching up his grip, Vili brushed away my hands and used both of his to grasp my head. This way, I was held still as he did all the work and fucked my face. I never knew what people meant when you *gawk-gawk* like a champ, but hell, if I wasn't winning that award right now. With all the other sensations going on, I wasn't having any trouble relaxing for Vili to use me as he liked. I was taking him deeper than ever, and it was sexy as hell to feel the tip of his cock slide down the back of my throat. Once or twice I even got to kiss the base of his dick, making me want to ensure this achievement was remembered forever.

Vili's movements started to get slightly more frantic, and he moved to pull back, not wanting to knot in my mouth. However, something feral happened in my brain, and I was unwilling to let him take what I'd claimed as my own. So, of course, I lunged forward, took him *deep,* and bit down.

"*Hva faen,*" Vili barked out. "Ahg. No, Bailey-Rose. Let go, my knot." He hissed, his finger pressing at my jaw.

It was too late, though. His hot cum shot down my throat as Vili's knot swelled rapidly. It was already past the point where I could release my hold, which left me with one option—swallow like a motherfucking queen. The sensation must have been too much for Vili as he tossed back his head, roaring in pleasure as he came again, coating the back of my throat.

Warrick rushed forward and grabbed Vili's shoulders as he started to lean backward, taking me with him. "I got you, buddy. Just take a few deep breaths, and your head should clear in a bit," Warrick assured him.

My heart warmed seeing my pack taking care of each other.

"Now?" Gareth asked, pulling me back to the men who'd paused their thrusting to watch what was happening to Vili.

"Now," Yun-Sun agreed, as he pounded my asshole hard, growling as Gareth did the same to my pussy.

They growled and snarled in their efforts until they both latched on to my neck at the same time. Yun bit just under my jaw while Gareth picked the opposite side lower at the crook of my neck. Just when I thought they were finished, Vili lifted my hand, slipped my ring finger into his mouth, and bit down at the base just like I'd done to him.

There was all of a second where I knew I was screaming, coming, and being knotted as my spirit was sent to heaven. A physical form couldn't comprehend the deluge of endorphins my body was being subjected to. Here in the clouds, among the rainbows and stars, I danced in the euphoria that showered down on me like petals whispering against my skin. Like a butterfly breaking out of their cocoon, the true version of myself had finally emerged.

I was a fully-bonded Omega.

There was no concept of time as I savored the feeling of my bonds. One wasn't complete on my end yet, but I could still trace a finger down each one of them. I smiled as I felt Warrick close by, tracing the lines of my palm and dreaming of our future together. Ulysses was wiping a cool cloth over my body, cleaning up from the foursome I'd just experienced. Ten out of ten would absolutely recommend it. When I reached Gareth, I could sense his worry and the feeling he was blaming himself for something. Since our bond was complete, I reached out with reassurance that I was completely fine.

"The hell?" Gareth gasped. "What was that?"

"Oh, is she checking in on you too?" Warrick asked.

"Wait... how?" Gareth questioned, fumbling for words.

"Welcome to what being a bonded Alpha truly means," Ulysses said, a hint of laughter in his voice. "This is the part they never talk about, the *secret* we're supposed to discover for ourselves."

"She's asleep, though," Gareth challenged.

"I don't know what to tell you, man. This is all new territory," Ulysses offered as he smoothed a hand over my hair. "Maybe her body needed a break, but her mind is awake. She's always been a nosy Nellie."

The guys chuckled at that, but I didn't hear Vili's voice, so I searched through my bonds until I found his. Focusing on his location, I realized he was outside and a little chilled, meaning the sun must have gone down. It was hard to feel his emotions almost as if they were buried under a blanket, muffling their voices. Not wanting to intrude where I wasn't welcome, I started to draw back until he reached out to me, stopping me in my tracks. While I realize this was all happening on some mythical plain of existence, it truly felt like he took my hand and brought me back to where I ran into the barrier.

With a reassuring squeeze, Vili pulled back the curtains and drew me into his innermost thoughts and feelings. Instantly, love and affection swirled around me, hugging me tight, followed by passion and lust as fingers trailed along my body. I got the impression while he enjoyed my mouth, he had every intention of putting his knot to good use elsewhere. Joy bubbled up in my chest, knowing he wasn't upset with me for not letting go. Reassurance flared, shoving everything out of the way, making it clear there were no hard feelings whatsoever.

This was everything I expected to find dwelling in my sweet teddy bear Alpha. It had me curious as to why it was dulled and held back.

Feeling my question, wisps of anger, disgust, and a cold detachment brushed along my skin like echoes of a deeper thought. There was something in Vili's life he was keeping hidden from himself, not me or the guys. He didn't even want to acknowledge this part of himself existed. Sadness welled up in me as I wrapped Vili in all the love and acceptance I could muster. No matter what this dark emotion stemmed from, it would never change how I felt about Vili. The man I fell in love with is the man he was today, and that's all that mattered to me. A sensation of a kiss being pressed to my forehead told me Vili understood. At the sound of a phone ringing, he pulled away from me to answer.

Once back at the nest with my other Alphas, I decided it was time to wake up, reassure my pack, and have us all snuggle in for the night. Ulysses had been right about one thing—my body was definitely tired and for now, sated beyond belief.

My eyes fluttered open, and I hummed at the feel of Ulysses' fingers massaging my head. He must have taken out the braid, although after how rough things got, I'm not sure it would have survived.

Gazing up into his comforting blue eyes, I smiled. "Hi."

"Hi back," he answered, grinning. "Seems we might have overdone it on our first day in paradise. You passed out."

"It was so worth it, though," I shared with a yawn, stretching out. "However, you might be right. I one hundred percent need a nap."

Movement to my left had my head turning. There was Yun-Sun, bent over, wearing only tight black boxer briefs, feeding the dogs their dinner. *Bless that man for giving them dinner and me a show.*

As if he could feel me ogling him, Yun looked back, his gaze landing right on me. "See something you like?"

"What can I say... the dogs are cute," I answered, biting my lip, knowing it was always a risk to tease my serious Alpha.

"Hmm..." Yun-Sun grunted in reply. "Then it wouldn't be a hardship if I chose to sleep outside under the stars while you curl up with them."

Instantly, I shot up and snapped. "Not happening."

The vehemence of my reaction seemed to startle the guys as much as it had me.

"I mean..." I took a second to clear my throat. "It would

be nicer to snuggle up with my pack since we all just bonded."

"Good save there, baby girl," Gareth whispered loudly behind his hand like everyone couldn't hear him.

Warrick just shrugged with a grin. "I thought it was sexy. It's like she turned into Feisty Bear instead of her normal Care Bear mode."

Returning from the deck, Vili set his cell phone aside and regarded us with confusion. "Did I miss something?"

"Just Rosie getting all sassy about Yun threatening to sleep outside," Ulysses explained.

Vili frowned. "Why outside, she's in here?"

That hit my funny bone in just the perfect way, and I started to cackle. Flopping back onto the mattress, I laughed until I cried, then snagged a pillow before rolling onto my stomach. "Oh God, I realize it wasn't that funny, but it kind of was."

Yun-Sun blessed me with an adorable smile as he stepped into the bed with us. "You silly girl, did you really think I would sleep outside? Like Vili said, you're in here. Where else would I rather be?"

Reaching out to him, he caught my hand, letting me drag him down to kneel before me. I crawled up his body until I wrapped my arms around his neck. "Well, now that we've settled that issue, there's just one more thing to do."

"Oh?" Yun asked.

Stroking my fingers over his short, buzzed hair, I kissed him. Drowning in the scent of sweet blueberry muffins, I sucked in his lower lip and completed our bond. Yun's arms crushed me to his body as his hips thrust against my pussy, but his underwear prevented him from ramming home. That didn't stop him from pressing me into the mattress as he used my body to hump against me as I continued to torture him. He finally came, covering my stomach in cum. Gathering it up with his fingers, he boldly shoved those two cum-covered fingers into my pussy.

"I can't be the only one who comes from this moment," Yun explained.

He moved slightly to the side so he could keep his fingers in me but also have access to his mark on me. The feel of Yun-Sun's mouth as he sucked, nipped, and licked his claim on me had me screaming and coming more times than I can even count. Just as I was about to pass out again from the overstimulation, he eased up, giving me one last shattering orgasm before sliding his finger out of me. I watched as he cleaned off his fingers, purring at my taste.

Vili handed over a cloth Yun-Sun used to clean us both up before everyone created a pack, puppy pile with me at the center. A contented sigh escaped my lips as I realized this was our life from now on. I belonged to them, and they belonged to me, each bearing a mark full of love and promise.

BAILEY-ROSE

Three days.

That's how long it got us past the point of needing constant sex.

I'm waking up to find one of them eating me out or fucking me. Then again, it was fair play since I had zero qualms about crawling onto their dicks as they slept if no one else was awake. It didn't take long for everyone to awake and join in, but sometimes, I was ready to go before they were.

Half the time, I wouldn't let them knot me since I knew this wasn't like a heat. My body wasn't looking to breed, it only wanted connection—to feel my Alphas in the most physically intimate way possible, which happened to be a dick in a hole. It didn't matter which one, all three got used regularly and at the same time. If I hadn't gone through my surgery, there would be no fucking way I'd survive this. We never would have been able to bond—the bond itself might have killed me. Yet here I was riding high as I fucked Gareth on the steps leading to the water.

"That's it, baby girl, you take what you need from your Alpha," Gareth encouraged, slapping my ass as he licked his mark.

With a sharp cry, I came, my body shaking as I collapsed against Gareth. Hugging me to his body, he rutted into me hard, groaning as he came, his knot swelling and triggering another orgasm for me.

"God, I love the way it feels to have you knotted in my ass," I sighed, resting my head on his shoulder, fingers combing through his damp hair.

Showering my face in kisses, Gareth brought us down a few more steps so the water mostly covered us as he sat. This way, it would keep us cool since the normal breeze seemed to be lacking today.

"Baby girl, if I could live connected to you like this, I would in a heartbeat," Gareth said, using the tip of his finger to trace his mark on my neck.

It sent shivers through me, but thankfully, we figured out a simple touch wasn't as 'orgasmic' as when their mouth came into contact with it. Warrick thought it had something to do with our saliva, but I wasn't too worried about it. As long as there was no risk of a simple touch causing spontaneous orgasms, I was good.

"Hey, did you forget we were going to the mainland?" Ulysses called from above.

"Shit, I forgot, and now we're knotted," Gareth grumbled.

Grinning, I sat up and squished his face together to make fishy lips. "Maybe don't make that sound like a bad thing while you're stuck with me, hmm?"

"Thots, thot, thawt, I, thent," Gareth managed to say, his brows furrowed.

I kissed his fishy lips before releasing his face. "Really?"

"Yeah, baby girl, really," Gareth stated. "To get to the mainland, we need a boat. The boat is going to be driven by someone. That someone isn't one of your Alphas. Which means you will be wearing clothes, and with my knot in your ass, it's going to be rather hard to get dressed."

It was so easy to get Gareth riled up, and what made it all the more enjoyable was being able to feel his emotions.

The possessiveness pouring off him in moments like this is how we ended up in this situation. I found it sexy as hell, and there was no other option than to jump the man. Of course, now that I'd done that, I might have only made the situation a tiny bit more troublesome.

"Maybe we should start with getting ourselves into the house. Then at least I won't be visible to the strange man," I reasoned. "I already picked out what I was going to wear, so as soon as your knot lets me go, I can cover up."

"She's got a point, better to get inside than sitting right in the line of sight," Lysse agreed.

Gareth groaned, but when his hands gripped my hips, I did my best koala impersonation and latched on. While the guys' knots weren't as sensitive as when we first bonded, they would always be a challenge to work around. Slowly, we made it up the stairs, where Lysse draped a towel over me just to be sure.

"Vili, can you grab the stool?" Lysse called.

I'm sure it's shocking to find out this wasn't the first time a poorly-timed knot happened in the past three days. It's gotten to the point now the guys found a stool that was comfortable to sit on, and we didn't have to worry about getting the nice furniture wet. Gareth popped a squat, and I relaxed, enjoying the one-on-one snuggle time.

A glass of the special hydration was slipped into my hand by Yun, which I dutifully used to take my pills he also brought. Keeping track of time wasn't high on our list of things to worry about, nor was keeping any kind of consistent sleep schedule. This led to me now taking my pills in the middle of the day when nine times out of ten, we were awake and happening.

"Thank you," I said, wiping my mouth with the back of my hand.

Yun-Sun leaned down and kissed my head. "You're welcome, sweetheart. I also got Waffles set in his harness so you just need to worry about you."

My heart was in a constant state of happy pile of goo with how effortlessly these Alphas of mine took care of me. We were still finding a balance of where I could be independent but still allowing them to help. Alphas were wired to be the protectors and caretakers of Omegas, and there was no way I could change that about them. Plus, I was the odd duckling of Omegas who had a fierce need for independence. Logically, I knew it stemmed from believing I wouldn't have a pack, so I needed to be self-sufficient. Yet all that has changed, and these men were my pack—one full of Alphas who desperately wanted to pamper their Omega.

It only took another five minutes before I was free. Kissing Gareth soundly, I climbed off his lap, jumped in the shower to rinse off, and got dressed. Just as I finished tying the bow on my halter top dress, a honk that sounded more like a distressed duck alerted us to the boat's arrival. Snatching up my wide-brimmed hat and sunglasses, I was ready to go.

Vili caught my hand, swinging it between us as we headed to the dock. I was surprised when Warrick hugged the man who'd come to pick us up, slapping him on the back in a friendly manner. Warrick had mentioned that he knew the owners of the resort, but I didn't realize he meant he *knew* them.

"Mitch, I want to introduce you to my pack and our Omega, Bailey-Rose," Warrick said, grinning from ear to ear.

Now that I was closer, I could tell Mitch was closer to our age, with dark, tanned skin and bright green eyes. "Hello to you all," he greeted with a wave. "I hope you guys have been enjoying your time, but I don't blame you for wanting a little time with civilization. It's one reason I choose to live on the mainland… being here all the time would drive me crazy."

Warrick barked out a laugh. "After being his roommate in college, I can vouch for the fact he doesn't do well in confined spaces."

"Well enough about me, let's get this boat headed toward a good time," Mitch announced, clapping his hands together, then gestured toward me. "Ladies first."

The ocean was quiet today without much movement on the water's surface, which made hopping over the gap between the boat and the dock easy. I should have known something was different, seeing the boat was bigger and nicer than the one that picked us up the first day. Heading to the front, I sat near the point of the bow, the breeze ruffling my hair. Waffles settled at my feet, laying as flat as he could, not being the biggest fan of boats. Nugget, however, jumped in my lap, nose in the air, sniffing all there was to be sniffed. I hugged the little guy, peppering his head with kisses he gladly returned.

"You know, I think one day you're going to find a person who really needs you," I whispered to Nugget. "Not that I don't love you to pieces, but I just have a feeling you won't need Waffles or me anymore once that person appears."

Nugget did that adorable head tilt dogs do as he listened, only to sneeze loudly at my prediction.

"Scoff all you want, little man, but don't be surprised if I end up being right," I warned him, kissing his nose.

"What are you right about?" Lysse asked, sliding in beside me and tossing his arm over my shoulders.

"Oh, nothing, just a secret between Nugget and me," I said, leaning against him.

He looked between us and shrugged, deciding it wasn't worth the effort to pull the truth out of me.

Once everyone was on the boat, Mitch released the ties, backed us out of the slip, and gunned it. I squealed in surprise, clamping a hand down on my hat before it flew off. The gentle breeze was no longer with Mitch behind the wheel, looking completely at ease with how fast we were moving across the open water. Ocean mist sprayed around us as we crashed into swells, making me glad I'd chosen the blue dress instead of the white one since I wasn't wearing a bra.

Mitch didn't take us to the same dock we used when we first arrived. Instead, it was further up the coast. Warrick pulled up a map on his phone and showed me where the town we planned to check out was. "You see, Care Bear, they want to keep the tourists in one area near the airport. However, if you want to experience the authentic Prio Gria, you go where the locals hang out."

"Won't they be mad we're there?" I asked.

"Nah, we have Mitch with us. He'll make sure we don't do something stupid," Warrick assured me.

We finally started to slow as Mitch headed for a busy dock full of all kinds of boats. Some were private while others clearly transported goods to and from the area. The atmosphere was lively with people coming and going or hawking their wares. Mitch pulled into an open slip, tossing a rope to a young boy who caught it and tied off the line. It was easy to see how comfortable Mitch was on and off the boat as he leaped off to secure the back of the boat.

"All clear, you guys can come ashore," Mitch called.

Yun-Sun caught me and deposited me on the dock, quickly followed by Waffles, who shook himself from nose to tail with passion.

"*Fuss*," I ordered, bringing him to heel and alerting my companion it was time to go to work.

Instantly, Waffles was alert and ready, standing by my side where he would be until I told him differently.

"Wow, that's one well-trained dog," Mitch commented, regarding my wooly mammoth with a whole new appreciation.

Smiling, I stroked Waffles' head. "Yeah, he's the bestest boy who keeps me safe and alive."

I caught Mitch glance at my scar, but just as quickly, he looked away again. There was nothing I could do about people looking, but what I could control is how it made me feel. The only opinions I cared about were my family's and the five men who held the pieces of my heart. Mitch was a stranger I probably won't ever meet again, so there was no reason to invest time worrying.

"So Warrick says you're our tour guide today?" I asked, changing the topic.

Mitch stuffed his hands into the pockets of his board shorts. "That's the plan. Figured we'll get some food, take you to see the sights, and do a little shopping if that interests you?"

"Sounds like an excellent afternoon," I said, excited to explore this beautiful place.

The small island the resort was on didn't represent the lush splendor that was Prio Gria. Firstly, it was an island fifty times bigger with mountains and a dormant volcano which made the soil incredibly fertile. Mitch brought us into the dockside town where most people were on motorbikes or ATVs with a few trucks full of supplies driving down the main two-lane street. The stores spilled out onto the streets with vendors selling what was fresh for the day before you even entered the shop.

Warrick bought a small sack full of some crazy-looking fruit that he peeled to reveal the bright pink flesh. "Here, Care Bear, take a bite."

Leaning in, I bit down, only to have fruit juice start to run down my chin. Quickly, I took my bite and pulled back, laughing as hot pink juice covered my hand as I tried to wipe it off my face. Warrick's hand shot out, grabbed the back of my neck, fisted my hair, and urged me to look up. My whole body froze as I felt Warrick's tongue glide up my neck.

"Hmm, so sweet," he murmured, then continued to clean up the mess I made.

My hands fisted the fabric of my sundress. I tried to remember we were in public, and I couldn't just fuck him right here on the street, no matter how badly I wanted to.

"There, all clean," Warrick whispered in my ear, his lips brushing over his mark. My body trembled as my underwear was now drenched from the near climax the touch of his lips brought.

Warrick stepped back grinning like a fool and licked off more pink juice from his thumb. "Want some more?"

Scowling, I decided to get my own version of revenge for that stunt. "*Gib laut*," I commanded.

Waffles let out a deep warning bark from behind Warrick, making the Alpha jump and drop the fruit. I gave a triumphant smile. "No, thank you. I think I've had all the sweetness I can handle for now."

The guys tried to hide their laughter but were unsuccessful.

"No worries, Care Bear, I have more if you change your mind," Warrick pointed out, holding up the bag. "I hear they make an excellent late-night snack."

The heat in his eyes told me exactly what he was planning on eating along with that snack—me.

"Are you guys sure you're ready to be out in public?" Mitch asked, eyeing us warily.

Spinning to face Mitch, my skirt swirled around me as I gave him a thumbs-up. "Totally. I just need to make sure they stay away from my marks, and we're good to go. Although I might suggest we do the shopping first to keep us in the public. Just to be safe."

Not completely convinced, Mitch studied the six of us then shrugged. "Ah hell, Prio Grians are a people who embrace the primal love between Alphas and their partners. You guys will fit right in, but just be aware if you guys show them you're comfortable with PDA, they won't hold back with their own lovers."

With that warning lingering in the air, Yun caught my hand and pulled me to his side as we followed after Mitch. Soon, we were lost in a market filled with vendors selling everything from fine silks, jewelry, art, everyday necessities, and any kind of beach wear you could think of. One vendor had funny shirts with food puns, while the man next to them sold handmade leather sandals. It was incredible.

Street food vendors were scattered throughout. Everything smelled and looked so good I had to try it all. My favorite had to be the caramelized banana on a stick. The guys seemed to be more interested in watching me eat it than tasting it. I'm ashamed to admit it took me a second to figure out why, then I just played it up, seductively eating the last few bites then dramatically licking my fingers clean.

"Vili," a man barked out.

Two things happened within the blink of an eye. A strange man grabbed Vili's arm, yanking him away from us. This caused Waffles to lunge, barking at the man since Vili had been standing next to me. Waffles latched onto the man's pant leg and pulled, causing the attacker to land on his back on the ground.

"Waffles, *aus, fass*," I ordered, telling him to let the man go and heel.

While I believed this man wasn't here to do us harm, it was clear his intentions were not all that pure.

"Jonas, why are you here?" Vili demanded, his tone sharp and cold. "How did you find me?"

The man, Jonas, picked himself up off the ground, ignoring Vili's questions as he brushed the dirt off his clothes. As I studied this person who'd appeared out of nowhere, I noticed he had the same strawberry-blond hair Vili did. Even their face shape was similar.

Could this be Vili's father?

Of all my Alphas, Vili's family is the one I knew little about. He never spoke of them other than that day Vili admitted he didn't miss them at all. So why on earth would one of Vili's parents feel the need to track us down during our leave of absence?

Jonas' gaze fell to Waffles, baring his teeth in a silent warning as he angled himself in front of me. "I should sue you for being attacked by your animal," Jonas stated, his tone haughty and full of disdain.

"You could try, but he's a personal guard dog trained to protect his owner after an act of aggression has been initiated," Yun-Sun informed the man. "There are plenty of witnesses around us that will testify you, sir, are the one who attacked first. The ones who should be suing for emotional distress and stalking would be us."

Jonas, while the same height as Yun-Sun, still seemed to find a way to look down his nose at Yun. "Am I to assume you are a lawyer of some kind to speak so confidently?"

"Am I to assume you deserve the right to know that answer?" Yun-Sun shot back, cool, calm, and collected.

The man glared at Yun, taking a step forward but was halted as Vili cut the man off. "Do not ignore me again," Vili warned.

My sweet, smiling Alpha was gone, and in his place was a man I'd never seen before. Vili's whole demeanor had shifted, becoming far more stiff, and the dominance that rolled off him would have rattled me to my core if we weren't bonded. Concern welled up in me as I reached out to him, only to be met with white-hot fury which had me pulling back. A whine slipped out, with Gareth coming up behind me, wrapping his arms around me.

"Shh, baby girl, it's going to be fine," he assured, speaking softly. "Vili's not facing this alone... we've got his back."

Jonas took half a step back and spoke rapidly in Numolandian. You didn't need to speak a word of their language to know this man was pissed the hell off about something. Vili just stood there, appearing to be relaxed, but the aggressive energy coming off him said otherwise.

"Enough," Vili ordered, slashing his hand through the air. "This is no time or place to speak of these matters. I told you so on the phone. Why do you keep pushing?"

"Son—"

"Don't," Vili growled out. "It is beneath you to pretend, speak plainly."

Once more, Jonas started and was yet again cut off.

"So they can understand," Vili instructed. "My pack has no secrets."

"Is that so? Then they know who I am?" Jonas taunted.

Having had quite enough of this man spoiling my packmoon, I answered his question. "You're his father, well... one of them."

Jonas' pale silver-blue eyes met mine. The icky feeling his attention gave me almost got me to drop my gaze, but I wouldn't let this bully win. Clearly, being talked back to wasn't something he was used to. "I am, but who are you?"

Vili sidestepped, blocking his father's view of me. "She's *mine.*"

BAILEY-ROSE

I f my heart could skip a beat without me freaking out about it, that's what it would have done hearing him say that. God, there was nothing sexier than an Alpha staking his claim over you. However, now was not the time for me to be swooning. Something was going on, and none of it was good.

"You've marked her?" Jonas demanded, grabbing a fistful of Vili's shirt. "How could you do that to your family? We haven't approved of this match."

Waffles let out a low, warning growl, but he didn't move from his spot guarding me.

Vili leaned in closer, starting his father down. "You. Are. Not. My. Family."

Breaking his father's hold on him, Vili shoved him back until Jonas stumbled over his own feet, landing once more on his ass. Vili adjusted his shirt and came to stand next to me, wrapping an arm around my waist. "This is my bonded Omega, and these are my pack brothers. They are my family, not you. Bailey-Rose is a superior scent match, one who needs no approval."

Jonas picked himself up, only this time he didn't look quite so haughty. His son had publicly renounced his connection to the Rantala name and claimed us instead. If Vili wanted to, he could legally take any of our last names, and all ties to the Rantala family would be severed.

"Vili, you don't mean that," Jonas argued. "Think of your mother and what it would do to her."

"The mother who allowed me to believe another woman was my mother?" Vili scoffed. "She didn't want me, none of you did. All you needed was an heir. Why care now? There must be something you want for you to come find me."

The fury on Jonas' face had me leaning into Vili, knowing he would keep me safe.

"She is dying," Jonas stated. "Her request was to see you before it was too late."

I gazed up at Vili, trying to read his expression because my emotions were chaotic—anger, sadness, mistrust, and trepidation—almost as if he didn't believe what his father was telling him.

"Why I just hearing about this?" Vili demanded. "If she is so sick, why wait till now?"

"Because you will not speak to us," Jonas accused.

"Well, I'm speaking now," Vili snapped. "See what little effort it took... you just have to show up."

"I will not have this argument here in the middle of the street. Come home, see your mother, and we will then discuss this matter of you being bonded," Jonas instructed. "The jet is ready. We can leave right away."

"Hi, hey, sorry to interrupt," Warrick interjected, waving his hand as he stepped up. "But in case you missed everything Vili just said in this uncomfortable encounter, we are on our bonding leave, and the only thing we're going to do right away is walk away from you. I'm sure Vili knows how to get in touch with you, so when and *if* we decide to go to Numoland, we'll be taking our own jet. So nice to meet one of the in-laws, but we'll be going now."

Taking my hand, Warrick led me away, and since I

wouldn't let go of Vili, he came too. Waffles took up the rear, keeping an eye on Jonas, but I think the man learned his lesson. He wouldn't give Waffles another chance to do real damage this time.

None of us spoke as Mitch led us out of town and to a row of vehicles. These things looked like SUVs that didn't have the top half put on. Instead, there was just a frame so if the thing rolled over, it wasn't going to crush us. Not questioning what we were doing, I climbed up and slid to the opposite side. Vili joined me, holding Nugget as Gareth heaved Waffles into the vehicle.

The engine roared to life, and a puff of black smoke burst out the back, making me jump. Vili placed a comforting hand on my thigh and smiled. Relief flooded me as the man I knew and loved returned, the shadows of his anger gone, leaving only warmth and light behind. I clutched his hand in both of mine and kissed it to share my feelings since I wasn't sure what to even say about the situation.

Leaning down, he nuzzled the hair above my ear. "I'm fine, kitten. No worries, we are here for fun."

That was easier said than done when I knew how upset he'd been to see his father show up. It was clear to me that being around them wasn't good for Vili. However, if his mother really was dying, I wouldn't hold him back if he decided to say goodbye to her.

Mitch got the truck moving and drove into the dense rainforest following a track many had used before him. Enamored by the beauty of where we were, I forgot all about Jonas and whatever issues were tied to the Rantala family. Seeing all of this made my fingers itch to draw or paint— anything I could do to bring a piece of this back with me.

Birds of every color swooped around us, their calls loud and distinctive, filling the air and adding to the experience. The truck was too loud for us to talk, so it forced us to just take in the sights.

Then as we crested a hill, the trees fell away, and a gorgeous stone temple lay before us. It was simply breathtaking with its sweeping arches and peaked roofs. Red and gold paint were used to enhance certain features, making it pop and come to life. Parts of the temple were covered in small square flags in every color you could imagine fluttering in the wind. This place felt like pure magic, and I hoped with everything I had, Mitch planned to let us explore. The gods must have heard my prayers because Mitch parked the vehicle a few feet away so as not to disturb anyone.

"Welcome to the Temple of Erdis," Mitch announced. "This is where all the newly bonded packs of our country come to be blessed by the monks. It is a treasured and sacred tradition of the Prio Gria people that I wanted to share with you. Only those outsiders who are brought here by a native can receive the blessing."

My jaw dropped, having no idea how special this was for us to take part in. "Why us?" I couldn't help but ask.

"That answer will be made clear once you see and hear the story of Erdis," Mitch replied, waving us to follow.

As we entered the temple, I found the walkways were littered with flower petals and strings of tiny little bells hung in the archways. It felt like the wind was playing a special song just for us as we made our way down the walkway to the heart of the temple. Through the arches, I could see gardens filled with flowers and fountains with groups of people just curled up with each other and enjoying the atmosphere.

"Are those all bonded packs?" I asked, keeping my voice soft. To speak any louder felt like it would be jarring in such a tranquil place.

Mitch just nodded and continued farther into the temple grounds. As we entered the center of the temple, I couldn't help but gasp. At the heart of the temple was a statue made out of shimmering polished gold that depicted a woman with four men surrounding her, each tied together by thin gold strings. The men were connected to one another, creating a circle around the woman. Then another string tied the men to the woman at the center like the spokes of a bike. Water swirled around their feet as if some magical current kept it flowing when no source was obvious.

"This is Erdis and her pack," Mitch shared. "It is said she was the first Omega to find men who spoke to her soul and hers to theirs. As a display of that love, trust, and devotion to each other, they wanted a way to display their bond. So mixing red dye and their blood together, they made two marks. One on their hands, a circle around a finger to show they were tied to one another. The second was only for them to see, a mark over their heart to represent they shared their souls willingly to each other and no one else."

As Mitch talked, he guided us along a wall with paintings depicting the story as he explained it. Each image was masterfully created, bringing life to the tale as we learned about this pack.

"Everyone around them became jealous of their love and grew dissatisfied with their lives here on this small island. So Erdis encouraged them to find the people who spoke to their souls, but when they did, to return home so they could share in the celebration. Erdis believed everyone had someone out there who was exactly who they needed to love and be loved by. I suppose you could say she was the original Scent Matcher," Mitch said with a grin.

Having reached the end of the story wall, it led us to another room. In the room was a group of older men dressed in red and gold silks seated on cushions. Beside each of them was a gold bowl, a knife, and a few other tools I didn't recognize. One of the men stood slowly, making his way to us and said something to Mitch in Prio Grian, to which Mitch nodded and shifted to stand beside the older man.

"This is Harta, a descendant of Erdis," Mitch introduced and continued to translate as the man spoke. "He wishes to know if all of you speak to each other's souls?"

Stepping forward, I answered for us all. "Yes, they speak to me as I speak to them."

The older man smiled widely, his eyes getting lost in the wrinkles of his skin. Harta clapped his hands together and bobbed his head as he started to speak again.

"Hearing another's soul is a gift, but that is not all it takes to make a union last. Trust must be given and earned, love must be abundant and grow a little more each day... honesty, clarity, and kindness go hand in hand when speaking the truth to each other. Words prove intention while actions make them true. These are the foundations of a union that will prosper for eternity," Harta explained, taking a moment to stare into each of our eyes as he spoke. "If you commit all that I have said to heart and vow to live by them day by day, then it would be our honor to bless this pack with a physical symbol of this vow."

Confused, I looked to Mitch who simply held up his left hand for me to see the thin red line that circled his finger. My eyes widened as I looked back at my Alphas, having no clue how they would feel about doing this.

"It's up to you, Rosie. I, for one, have zero issues with placing another mark on you telling the world you're ours," Lysse said, answering my questioning gaze.

Gareth jerked his thumb at Ulysses. "I'm with him on this. Sign me up, baby girl, because I'm in this for eternity."

"*Omae*, you are who I chose to spend the rest of my existence with in this life and any other. If there's the slightest chance this helps me to find you no matter where we end up in the afterlife, there's no hesitation on my end," Yun-Sun stated.

Vili took my right hand and gently traced the white-colored scar of his mark on my finger. "I've marked you once, so twice can't hurt."

Stepping up, Warrick caught my chin and stared into my soul, exposing all the emotions he was feeling right now, and it was overwhelming. "Even without the mark on your ear or this blessing on your finger, Bailey-Rose, you are my forever."

There was no holding back the tears that slipped from my eyes at their words. Here, I'd thought we'd gotten through the worst of the mushy, sappy, lovey-dovey stuff over the last three days, but these men were bound and determined to make it so I couldn't survive a moment without them in my heart.

"That's exactly how I feel about each of you," I managed to croak out, my throat tight with emotion. "I thought I could survive without a pack, without all of you, but it turns out I was never truly living until you showed up in my life."

Warrick used his thumb to wipe away my tears before pressing a soft kiss to my lips. Sniffling, I tried to pull myself together as Harta motioned for us to follow him. Six other men stood and approached us with their gold bowls and the knife. With a squeak of surprise, a man pricked the tip of my pointer finger and squeezed a drop of blood into the bowl. Lucky for them, I'm a rather good bleeder these days and didn't have to have another finger poked as I added my drop of blood into the six bowls. Once all of us added a drop, we were guided to cushions in front of the man who was going to do our blessing. Adding in some red dye to the bowl, it was mixed, my finger cleaned with a disinfectant that made my nose hairs burn, and a needle was pulled out of a sterile package.

Taking a deep breath, I closed my eyes only for them to pop open as the men began to sing. Even though I couldn't understand the words, I could feel the intention behind them. It felt like my mother hugged me and kissed me on the forehead, telling me how proud she was of the woman I became. The way the temple was built, it amplified the song in a way I'm sure everyone on the property could hear them sing. *It was amazing.*

The whole thing was over faster than I expected, and I noticed my blessing wasn't just a simple red thread. In the center on the top of my finger was something that resembled a flower with five petals. Realization struck me—he'd made a petal to represent each of my Alphas. I flinched a little as he rubbed in an ointment, but soon it tingled and went numb.

"Petals and promises, good reminder when forget," the man told me, his accent thick, but I understood what he was trying to say.

This blessing was a daily reminder of the promises we made to each other. It would be sitting here on my finger just in case I might ever forget.

"Thank you," I whispered, clasping his hand in both of mine as I smiled. He smiled back and helped me to my feet.

Everyone else was done before me, then again, I was the

only one with the flower so it made sense. Harta gestured for us to follow him, but I didn't see Mitch anywhere and worried we'd be leaving him behind.

A soft touch on my arm pulled my attention back to Harta. "No worry, this for pack only."

Trusting the man, I nodded, following after him as he led us into a garden. If we didn't have a guide, I'm not sure we ever would have found the pavilion Harta brought us to. The air was sweet with all the flowers that bloomed around us, making this moment even more magical. Gauzy curtains fluttered in the breeze, and lanterns were lit, casting light as the sun started to descend. Inside, the pavilion was covered in a soft mat with various pillows scattered around, but in the center was a low table set up with a meal ready and waiting for us. Harta pressed his hands together, bowed, and offered us farewell before he turned back to the temple.

Warrick scooped me up and carried me into the pavilion, setting me down next to the middle spot. He nuzzled the side of my neck, kissing his way up until he reached his mark on my ear. Thankfully, he decided not to torture me and just brushed his lips over it so I shivered in delight. "Well, Mrs. Bailey-Rose, I think it's safe to say you are officially off the market and packed up for life with us."

Grinning, I twisted to give him a quick kiss, knowing anything else would escalate things, and none of us would be eating. "That same goes for you, mister. What will all the girls at The Fat Mule do now that you're mine?"

Warrick let out a heavy sigh. "It's a hard job letting them all down, but somehow, I feel like I got the better end of the deal."

My cheeks started to hurt with how wide I was smiling as I settled cross-legged at the table. Yun-Sun sat to my right as Warrick claimed the seat on my left. However, the table was round, allowing me to easily see and talk to all my Alphas. Each of them seemed to have this glow about them as if the joy we all felt was bursting out, creating a physical difference.

Yun took his plate and started to fill it with a little bit of everything on the table, setting it before me. "Just tell me if you want more of anything, *omae.*"

Everything smelled amazing, but I was a little confused when there was only a spoon to use for the soup. Then I watched Vili using the flatbread to scoop things up along with his spoon. Not one to shy away from using my hands while eating, I dug in, humming and doing a little happy dance at the taste of the food. The guys followed suit, groaning as they ate. Each dish looked so simple, but the flavor and seasonings were out of this world.

"One thing we need to do when we get back home is find where we can get food like this," I decided, shoving another spoonful of rice in my mouth.

"Or we could find a chef who knows how to make these dishes," Yun reasoned. "While I'm sure there are restaurants out there, I doubt they will compare to it being home-cooked."

"I like the way you think, Mr. Lee," I agreed, wagging my spoon at him. He chuckled, sipping at the fruit juice they served with the meal.

As the meal started to wind down, I decided it was time to address the gorilla looming in the background. "Vili," I started, setting down my spoon and meeting his gaze. "Please know that I love you, and I want the best for you, so keep that in mind as I share my thoughts on a matter I don't know much about."

Vili smiled and nodded for me to go on, enveloping me in his reassurance.

"I think you need to see your mother," I stated. "No matter how you feel about her, she is still the woman who gave you life. I realize my family is incredibly close, and I don't know what it feels like to have parents who don't love and support me or my choices. However, I do know what it feels like to lose a parent suddenly. I can't remember the last thing I said to my papa or when I last told him I loved him. You might not have love for your mother, but having closure, good or bad, is a gift you shouldn't take lightly."

Reaching across the table, Vili held his hand open, waiting for me to place my hand in his. Once he curled his fingers around mine, he brushed his thumb just under my new mark. "You speak with wisdom, kitten. There is no love in my heart for the pack who raised me. Yet, as you say, to close door for good is a gift."

"It's not like you'd be doing it alone," Gareth pointed out. "As your family and pack, we will always have your back."

Vili's smile was as bright as the sun hearing Gareth's words. I remember Ulysses once telling me just how important having a pack was to Vili, and now it made all the sense in the world. When the family you were born into fails you, there's always your pack to take their place. Or that's the hope.

"Thank you. I will need my family with me," Vili said, releasing my hand to clap Gareth on the back. "I have someone I can speak to who will be honest about Bianca's health. Once I know how sick, we can choose when to go."

Shortly after our conversation, temple attendants came and cleared away the meal as well as the table. A female attendant returned with a tray full of steaming mugs of a rich drink made from dark chocolate and spices. She also left a bowl of cookies covered in tiny little red petals that melted right on your tongue and paired with the drink perfectly. Arranging the pillows, we all cuddled up and enjoyed watching the stars in the cloudless sky until Mitch came to collect us.

As far as memories go, this was one night I would never forget.

Vili

After talking with Pernilla, my parents' housekeeper and the woman who acted as my nanny growing up, I believed my mother was terminally ill. It seems Bianca was diagnosed shortly after I moved to Preidon but kept it quiet until a year ago when she couldn't hide the fact she was sick any longer. When I explained what I knew to the others, we agreed to finish out the week in Prio Gria, and after those two days, we'd fly to Numoland.

Thankfully, it was still summer in my home country, or else we would need to go shopping for clothes the second we landed. While the tropical wardrobe we all packed wasn't what I would have suggested, it would make do for the short time we will be there. Besides, there was plenty of shopping available since my parents lived in the metropolitan city of Tumie. The flight was long, but the benefit of having a private jet was plenty of space to stretch out.

I gazed at my kitten curled up on the plush sofa, her head in Yun's lap, as he absently combed his fingers through her hair as he read. Every so often, she would start to purr in her sleep just like her namesake would. It had terrified me when we first bonded that she would see the ugly side of myself I kept buried deep. There was no way for me to escape having a bit of my parents' poison in my personality, having been raised around it. Thankfully, we are all our own person and can choose to be different, better versions of what we grew up seeing.

My phone buzzed, and I smiled at seeing the message. If I was going to be forced back to Tumie to deal with my parents, then I was going to do whatever it took to turn this moment into something beautiful. The ballet I'd wanted to take Bailey-Rose to was hosting its last four performances this month. One of those shows happened to be tomorrow night, and as one of Tumie Ballet Company's top patrons, I got tickets and a private box for Bailey-Rose and me.

Ulysses sank into the seat beside me, taking out his phone to snap a picture of Bailey-Rose to send to her parents. We hadn't been able to send many while we were in Prio Gria since most photos we took weren't presentable to share with parents. Last night, we'd made sure to update them on our change in plans, keeping up our end of the deal. My phone buzzed again as Ulysses sent the photo to our family group chat as well. Quickly, I downloaded it and added the picture to my collection.

"Hey," Ulysses said, leaning closer to keep his voice low. "You doing all right?"

"I suppose," I answered, not really sure how I felt.

It wasn't like I hadn't been back to Numoland numerous times since moving and meeting the guys. Only those had been business meetings hosted at a corporate location or one of the stores for a quality check on my designs. It had been ten years since I'd stepped foot in my parents' home. As soon as I could, I moved out and got my own place, needing to be free of their toxic nature.

"I don't know how to feel," I admitted. "Should I be sad? My mother is dying, but I feel nothing."

"No one can tell you how to feel, Vili... that's for you and only you to decide," Ulysses stated. "Like Rosie, I have a good relationship with my parents, so I can't begin to know how you feel, but I'm happy to listen if you need to talk."

Brushing a hand over my jaw, feeling the stubble that was growing in since I decided not to shave during our island vacation, I could hear my mother's voice telling me it was a sloppy look to have facial hair and I should shave every day. The amount of time and effort my parents invested into maintaining their appearances was exhausting. Although I agreed with the sentiment to dress for the success you want to have, there were limits to how far that would take you. If you suck at running a business, nothing you wear could change that fact, but educating yourself could change everything.

"Did I tell you I never finished university?" I asked offhandedly.

"No, I don't think I knew that..." Ulysses frowned, taking a sip of his brandy before his eyes went wide. "Wait, are you telling me you got into one of the most prestigious business schools and didn't graduate?"

"Indeed," I confirmed. "I only needed one more year, but Wilhelm made a call, and I was magically handed a diploma."

"I'm confused, so you did graduate?" he questioned.

"The records say I graduate, but I did not," I explained. "A well-placed donation afforded me a diploma. I tore it up, much to Wilhelm's ire."

"Wooow, that is fucked up," Ulysses muttered.

I hummed in agreement. "Just one of many moments. This is what they do... throw money at the problem, not caring about morals."

Ulysses took another sip before spinning the swivel chair to face me. "Did you really mean it when you told Jonas you want to cut ties?"

I'd thought about doing just that for years, but fear had kept me tied to a family I wanted nothing to do with. Now, there was nothing to be scared of. My pack would support whatever choice I made, and Bailey-Rose would never judge me for turning my back on my lineage. All that mattered to her was that I was happy.

"Yes, I believe it is time to make that happen," I decided. "I am their son in name only. They don't need me, and I don't need them. What is there to hold on to?"

Ulysses nodded, tapping his finger against his glass. "What if you started your own business? Your designs are the ones that sell, so you've already proven you'll have customers. I know with all of our knowledge, we could help get things up and running in no time if that's what you want."

My heart swelled hearing Ulysses' suggestion, and it only confirmed that I was making the right choice. A true family is one who has your back, offers selfless support, and wants to see you achieve greatness. I only hope I could offer the same to each of my pack brothers when the time comes.

"Possibly, I think I'd like to explore the idea," I answered. "Who knows, maybe Bailey-Rose and I team up to build her studio. She does the art, I deal with the people who want to buy."

He chuckled. "Yeah, I don't see Rosie doing well at pricing her work for what it's worth. She'd probably give it away if someone really loved it."

"Or ban the person for life if they don't," I added, knowing how feisty our Omega can get when she's feeling protective.

Snorting as he tried to cover his laughter, Ulysses grinned. "True, but I have a feeling those would be fun interactions to watch."

I glanced at my watch, seeing we still had another three hours to go, so I leaned my chair back and settled in to get some sleep.

Since I refused to stay any longer than necessary in my parents' home, we got the penthouse suite at the Royal Crest Hotel. It was fifteen minutes away from my childhood home but central to everything else in the city. When we landed, it was the middle of the afternoon, and my plan was to see my mother right away. Then the matter would be done and settled so I could enjoy showing my pack around the city I loved.

Looking in the mirror, I adjusted my gold-rimmed glasses I'd designed. My hair shone with a strong red hue after being out in the sun so much. I purposefully didn't shave, leaving the dark blond facial hair that was filling in nicely. Not having a plan for what I was going to do with it, I just liked it was a silent *fuck you* to the values my parents held to so strongly.

However, I did dress nicely in a pair of slacks and a button-down shirt I'd ordered to be sent to the hotel. In fact, all of us were wearing new outfits since I planned to take them to one of my favorite restaurants for dinner. There weren't many places I went to that had a dress code, but the food was so amazing I didn't mind the rule for business attire. Thankfully, they didn't enforce men having to wear a tie anymore since it wasn't mandatory for most companies anymore.

Bailey-Rose wore an adorable lavender button-down dress that hit just below the knee. She paired it with mint-green accents, and the skirt was extra swishy, as she described it. Her hair was curled and full of bounce, making it look like cotton candy. My kitten was the prettiest Omega who ever lived, and I couldn't help but pull her into my arms and kiss her. I tried not to mess up her makeup, but she was going to need more lipstick after I was through with her.

"Vili," she scolded as she wiped the pink lipstick off my mouth. "We can't show up at your parents' house looking like we've been making out."

I nuzzled my face into her hair. "Why is that, kitten?"

"Because," she answered, not really sounding sure of her answer, then rallied, "This is a somber moment, and it seems like your parents are rather serious people."

Sighing, I hugged her tightly, loving how she melted into my arms. The only reason I had the courage to do this now was because of Bailey-Rose. She deserved nothing but rainbows and sunshine in her life, not in-laws who were storm clouds who rained on our parade. Knowing that standing up for myself and my happiness would also bring peace to our lives as a pack was all the motivation I needed.

Taking her hand, I threaded our fingers together and raised it to my lips, brushing over my mark. "Fine, we will behave, but after... I make no promises."

The shiver that ran through her body, followed by the flood of desire and excitement through our bond, I knew we'd have her out of her dress the moment we got home. Grinning, I kissed her forehead for good measure then whistled to get the guys' attention.

"If we want to make dinner, we should leave," I announced.

Gareth looked rather uncomfortable in his new clothes, not one for wearing something so buttoned up. He kept fidgeting with his sleeve or tugging at his shirt collar, frustrated at the fit. Bailey-Rose took pity on him and left my side to undo the top two buttons and roll up his sleeves to just below the elbow.

"There, this is a little more you," she decided, fidgeting with the collar to get it to lay right.

"Oh, thank fuck. I seriously thought I was going to suffocate in this damn shirt," Gareth admitted, running a hand through his curly hair, messing it up into a more natural look.

With a quick kiss on Gareth's cheek and a command to the dogs, my kitten returned to me, wrapping an arm around my waist. "Ready?"

"With you beside me, I'm always ready," I whispered, giving her a teasing wink.

"Stop taking lessons from Warrick. You're cute enough as it is without using pickup lines," she said with a laugh.

I'd hired my normal car service for the few days we'd be here, and the limo was waiting for us as we exited the hotel. The ride over was silent as if the guys knew I would be lost in my thoughts and let me be. Bailey-Rose offered her support as she rested her head on my shoulder and traced the outline of my hand where it rested on her thigh. The touch was soothing and kept me from allowing my anger and frustration with my family to build. Allowing them to have that much power over my mood was something they didn't deserve.

We pulled up to my family's estate, and the driver spoke to the guard stationed at the gate. Once a phone call was put through to the main house, we were given entry. I'd always thought the house was too big—we only ever used about half of it. Yet it was handed down to August, my mother's third and final Alpha, and it had been in his family for generations.

Out of the three men who were supposed to be my paternal influence, August was the lesser of evils. The man simply didn't care about my existence. August had far more important things to do, like travel the world and collect antiquities to sell in his family's auction house. He'd been born rich to a family who had always been rich, so his interpretation of the world was skewed in many ways.

"That is where you grew up?" Warrick asked, gazing at the home which more closely resembled a castle.

"It is," I answered, taking in the dark stone walls, peaked roofs, and wrought iron fencing. "My childhood was as warm and inviting as this home."

A butler I didn't know opened the car door for us and jumped back with a gasp as Waffles emerged. Bailey-Rose decided to hold Nugget so we didn't scare the man further, but I doubted the little dust mop would be as intimidating as Waffles. Taking a deep breath, I prepared myself for the interaction that lay ahead of me and walked up the stone steps. Just inside the door, Perilla was waiting for me, a smile on her wrinkled and welcoming face.

"Ah, my sweet boy has returned for me to lay eyes on once more," Perilla greeted in Numolandian, cupping my face with her hands.

Bending down, I kissed her cheeks before pulling her frail body into a hug. "Perilla, I'm so sorry it's been so long since we've talked. You know my offer to come stay with me in Preidon still stands."

She clucked her tongue and patted my arm. "What would you do with an old woman when you have a family of your own to take care of? No, my place is here, especially with Lady Bianca not long for this world. It is good of you to come, even though they don't deserve it."

Loyalty, that was Perilla in a nutshell. The woman would

never dream of leaving my family's service once she'd given her word to look after them and the rest of the household. How she continued to work at her age was a mystery, but I imagine once my mother passes, that would change.

"Speaking of my family, I'd like to introduce you to them," I said, wrapping an arm around her shoulders and guiding her forward. Switching back to English, I introduced my pack to Perilla and her to them. "We've officially been bonded for about a week now," I added, knowing she'd been praying for me to find the family I deserved.

Bailey-Rose stepped up and pulled Perilla into a hug. "Thank you for looking after Vili until we could find each other. Please know you'd be welcome in our home any time if you'd like to visit."

Perilla blushed, completely flustered by my kitten's warmth. Ignoring the fact they'd just met, Perilla gripped Bailey-Rose's cheeks and cooed at her like a child. *"Sah sott.* You sweet girl, thank you."

Bailey-Rose was a little taken aback but took it all in stride as she smiled, moving to put Waffles between them, took Nugget from Yun, and absently rubbed her cheek.

"Would you lead the way to where Mother is?" I asked, redirecting the conversation. As much as I loved seeing my old nanny, I refused to stay longer than I needed to.

"Yes, follow," she answered, waving her hand, keeping to English for the others' sake even though she didn't speak it well.

The spry older woman marched up the grand staircase like it was nothing, causing us to pick up the pace. For most of my life, our family only used the front half of the house and two of the four floors. Growing up, my parents had a suite on the second floor while I was on the first, leaving the ground floor for entertainment, relaxation, and meals. So when Perilla led me down the hall where my rooms had once been, I was confused.

She rapped softly on a set of double doors that used to lead to my library and study space. A woman dressed in scrubs opened one of the doors. "Yes?"

"Lady Bianca's son is here to see her," Perilla explained, switching back to Numolandian.

The nurse looked back into the room as if unsure. "Today hasn't been a great day, and she just fell asleep."

"Dina, there are no more good days, and she's been waiting to see him," Perilla hissed. "Let him see his mother."

Cowed by the older woman's order, Dina stepped back and opened the door further, allowing us to see the makeshift hospital room they'd created.

"Hey, man," Gareth whispered, placing a hand on my shoulder. "If you want us to wait out here to give you a minute alone with your mom, that's fine. We are here for you, so whatever you need."

"Thank you," I said, patting his hand. "I think that might be a good idea. She might not even wake up. However, will you come with me, kitten?" I asked, holding my hand out.

Instantly, she handed Nugget back to Yun, then took my hand and nodded. "Of course I will."

The nurse tried to close the door on Waffles, but he wasn't having it and body-checked the door nearly knocking the woman over. Giving her a disgusted snort, Waffles trotted over to join us without any further incident.

As I came to stand next to the hospital bed, the woman lying there seemed so foreign to me. Gone was the powerful, self-assured woman who always knew what she wanted out of life. Her head was wrapped in a lavish silk scarf covering her hair. There was no sign of makeup on her sunken, pale skin, her fingernails were bare of polish, and she wore loose silk pajamas that didn't hide how skinny she'd become. An IV was connected to the back of her hand, and she wore an oxygen cannula. The monitors around her whirred, tracking everything there was to know about a person.

"Mother," I said softly, reaching out to place a hand over hers resting on top of five layers of blankets. "Mother, it's Vili."

A groan was her only response, turning her head away from me.

Licking my lips, I spoke a little louder this time. "Mother, I don't know if you can hear me, but I've come to see you. It's your son, Vili."

This time, she turned her head back, and her eyes cracked open. They were clouded, hiding the fact we had matching caramel eyes. Her hand twitched under mine, so I curled my fingers, holding it since it was clear she couldn't.

"Vili," Mother rasped. "Is it really you?"

"Yes, Mother, it's me," I assured her. "Jonas said you were asking for me."

"Water," she requested, trying to lift her hand.

Bailey-Rose moved to the table near the bed and poured some water into a cup with a straw. I left her to help my mother, knowing she'd be the best to know how to help, having been in need of the same help after surgery. Mother seemed surprised as if she hadn't noticed Bailey-Rose before. Then again, I don't know how damaged her sight was—it's possible she hadn't seen her. After a few sips, Mother turned her head away, finished with the drink.

"Who is she," Mother demanded, a frown creasing her brow.

"That is Bailey-Rose, my scent-bonded Omega," I answered. "Jonas didn't tell you?"

"No, but that explains why he was so upset," Mother

said, pausing to lick her cracked lips. "When did you find her?"

"About a month and a half ago," I shared. "But our pack didn't bond until a week ago."

"Hmm," Mother hummed, giving my hand a slight squeeze. "That's good. Now you will have what I could never give you. It never should have been me to get pregnant. Eden was the one who wanted children." Tears started to fall down my mother's cheeks.

Taking my cloth hanky out of my pocket, I dabbed at her face. "Mother, what's done is done. I grew up and found my place in the world, people to love, and who love me in return. Mistakes were made on both sides, but we made our choices."

"All I do these days is look over my life and all the things I did wrong. The two biggest regrets I have that haunt me to this day are how our greed and thirst for power as a pack cost us you and Eden. I stole her from you because I couldn't find the room in my heart to let my Alphas love another woman. They were mine, and she didn't belong with us... or that's what I thought." Mother stopped speaking, falling into a coughing fit that seemed to shatter her whole body.

Bailey-Rose grabbed the water and offered it once more. A few more gulps, and Mother relaxed, taking a moment to collect herself. Dina, the nurse, adjusted the bed so Mother sat up a little more and shifted the pillows to offer better support. Mother hissed through her teeth, flicking her fingers in a manner I'd often seen when she was telling off a staff member. This made it clear to me that while my mother was reflecting on her life, it wouldn't change the woman she was.

Turning her attention back to me, Mother continued with what she had to say, "Vili, I used to hate the fact you kept telling me you wanted to be nothing like us, but I get it. We are awful, selfish people who never think of anyone outside of ourselves. I know it was Eden's influence in your life that saved you and kept you from becoming like your fathers. They want you to sell your share of the business so they can buy the rights to your designs. Promise me you won't do it," Mother begged, gripping my hand as tightly as she could. "Don't let them steal what is yours. Those designs came from your heart, something they will never be able to do. However, that's not all I need you to promise me."

Confused by everything coming out of my mother's mouth, I simply nodded, curious to see what more she felt I needed to do.

"When you leave here today, don't ever come back," Mother ordered. "We will have our goodbyes today, leaving nothing left to say and no reason for you to come to the funeral. I've adjusted my will to give all that is mine to you. You needed a loving mother, but all you got was a cold statue posing as a mother. I might not have been there for you as a child, but I will protect you now. No matter what happens with your fathers, you will be taken care of with the inheritance I've given you. Build a life with that money and raise your children right. I might not be able to atone for what I did to Eden, but I can do something for you, my son."

Tears rolled down my cheeks as I bent to kiss her frail hand. "I forgive you, Mother," I said but continued feeling it was important to be honest. "I might not love you, but I do forgive you so you can be released from that burden in the afterlife. Knowing Eden, she'd tell you the same thing. She wouldn't want to be responsible for torturing you all these years, so take our forgiveness and be at peace."

Mother let out a sob as she nodded. "That is more than I deserve from either of you."

"Goodbye, Mother," I said, with one final squeeze of her hand before releasing it.

"I'm glad I got to meet you, Bailey-Rose, and know my son found love," Mother called as we left the room.

BAILEY-ROSE

The low rumble of Waffles' growl alerted me before I saw Jonas round the corner with two other men. We'd almost made it out of the house, but the expressions on these men's faces told us they weren't going to let us walk out just yet.

"Vili, stop," one of the other men ordered.

He looked like what you'd picture for an older aristocrat with his gray hair, thick black-rimmed glasses, and gray suit with a black turtleneck. It was as if this man had no concept that it was still summer or maybe he didn't leave the walls of this stone building.

"Yes, Wilhelm?" Vili asked, his tone matching the cool, detached nature of his father's.

"Where are you going?" Wilhelm demanded. "I told you there was much we needed to discuss about your place in this company."

Vili pressed a kiss to my temple before he released his hold on my hand, tucking his into his pockets. "There is nothing to say unless to remove me from Preidon location. If so, I won't stop you." He shrugged. "I prefer design to management."

"If that's what you want, then we need to change the contracts," Jonas cut in. "There's no way we can keep things as they are if you won't give more to the company."

Vili scoffed. "Give more? What do you give?"

"Excuse me? We took a small luxury jewelry company

and made it an international success. I think we've done our part," Wilhelm boasted.

Nodding, Vili scratched his jaw as if in thought. "No, the contracts stay. If you no longer want to pay for my designs, then don't buy them... it's simple."

"You can't be serious," the third alpha blurted, an incredulous look on his face. "Just like that, you'd turn your back on us, your family? Your mother is upstairs dying, and you just want to spit on the legacy she helped create?"

Listening to these men who claimed to be Vili's family and the way they twisted everything to make Vili out to be the bad guy was disgusting. While Vili might not be showing it outwardly, each attack chipped away at the shield Vili had placed around himself. A few more blows and they would start tearing into him, and I wasn't going to allow that.

"Seriously, you must be joking with that shit," I interjected with a harsh laugh.

The three men turned to look at me, and I couldn't help but shrink back a little at the weight of their gazes. Waffles was there to remind me that I was perfectly safe as he nudged me forward. Quickly, I collected myself and approached the men who would no longer have a say in Vili's life once we walked out the door.

"Who are you?" Wilhelm asked, looking down his nose at me.

"That's his Omega," Jonas answered as if I was nothing of consequence.

Vili started to speak up, but I gripped his arm. I wanted to handle this. "My name is Bailey-Rose Thatcher, daughter of the oil moguls Rawlins and Adrian Thatcher, owners of Infinery Petroleum Industries. I also happen to be part owner of the billion-dollar company, The Snuggery."

This information instantly transformed the way these men looked at me. No longer was I some riff-raff girl with crazy-colored hair and an eccentric taste in clothes. I'd just proven that I was worth more money than all of them combined.

"Now that I've proven my net worth and have your attention, I'd listen carefully to what I have to say," I informed them. "Vili is no longer your son, nor does he have the last name Rantala. Instead, he's a Thatcher, my bonded Alpha and a valued member of our pack. As for what his mother would think... she's the one who told him to get the hell away from *you*. Now, Vili has told you he's not changing his contracts, but should you have any further questions about them, feel free to speak to our lawyer."

As if on cue, Yun-Sun walked up to Wilhelm and handed him a card. "Just so you know who you'd be going up against, my father is In-Su Lee of Lee, Holt, and McNeil. I'm sure you've heard of his skills in corporate law, and while I might not like the man, he taught me well. I look forward to hearing from you, but we need to be on our way. We have important dinner reservations."

Vili's fathers just stared at us as I walked out hand in hand with Vili and Yun-Sun, a little pep in my step as we climbed back into the limo. God, I don't know that I'd ever had a moment where I went toe to toe with *three* Alphas and spanked them good. The shock and disbelief written all over their faces was something I would treasure, knowing it would be the last time I ever saw those assholes.

I gasped in surprise as Vili pulled me over to straddle his legs. With a hand holding the back of my neck, his lips crashed against mine. Instantly, I was purring as I wrapped my arms around his neck. All too soon, he pulled back to rest his forehead against mine.

"Did you mean it?" he asked. "Can I really take your last name?"

Grinning with delight, I nuzzled his nose. "Vili Thatcher has a nice ring to it, don't you think?"

"I love you to the moon and back, Bailey-Rose," Vili whispered, pulling me into another passionate kiss.

Dinner was a fantastic experience, and the food was as wonderful as Vili promised. The chef even came out and greeted us, bringing a dessert he made especially for Vili, knowing it was his favorite. This man had no idea the day Vili had gone through or how perfect his kind gesture was, but I could feel how much it meant to Vili.

After dinner, Vili walked us to the arboretum behind the restaurant. He truly wanted us to see the beauty of Tumie and Numoland, ignoring the dark stain his family had left on the day. Finally, we made it back to the hotel, stuffed and jetlagged, making it easy to fall asleep curled up in the arms of my Alphas.

We spent the following day exploring the city, Vili showing us all his favorite places and childhood haunts. Learning about him was truly an amazing gift since he'd been so closed-lipped about his life here. Now, even if we never came back to Tumie, I would have experienced everything there was to Vili's time here.

This was the most walking I'd done in a while, but I wasn't willing to tell the guys I was getting tired. However, I forgot that now we're bonded, they all knew the truth anyway. Ulysses stopped in the middle of the sidewalk, dropped to one knee, and looked over his shoulder at me.

"Hop on, Rosie," he instructed.

"What?"

He rolled his eyes and gestured with his hands. "Come on, hurry up. I'm blocking traffic."

That got me moving since he knew how much I hated it when people stopped for no reason, becoming an obstacle to the flow of foot traffic. Hopping up on his back, I wrapped my arms around his neck as he secured my legs. Waffles watched us, seeming a little unsure about this situation, but Nugget jumped on Lysse's leg as if he wanted to be picked up too.

"Sorry, Nug, I can only carry one of you," Lysse said.

Nugget gave a frustrated sneeze, shaking his whole body but fell in step alongside Waffles as we continued on. I peppered the side of Lysse's face with kisses then nuzzled his neck. "You're pretty amazing, you know that?"

"I wouldn't go that far, but I'll take it." Lysse chuckled. "Why didn't you just tell us you were getting tired?"

"Because I didn't want this day to end," I admitted. "If I said I was tired, then you guys would overcorrect and make us go back to the hotel."

He grunted at that, unable to deny the truth of my words. Vili spun around and walked backward as he spoke. "Not this time," he announced with a grin. "I have surprise planned."

"You do?" I gasped excitedly.

"Two, in fact," Vili answered, holding up his fingers in a peace sign as we came to a stop. "The first is here."

Looking to my left, I saw a shop full of stunning dresses ranging from what you'd wear for a fancy date night to ball-gowns that would fulfill any woman's dreams. Yun-Sun held open the door for Lysse to enter, ducking slightly so I didn't hit my head. Once we reached the center of the store, he let me slide down.

The shop looked like a fairy garden vomited all over the place. Lush velvet chairs in jewel tones were scattered around the space. The walls were brick but covered in ivy and other flowering greenery. Wisteria hung from the ceiling, and the lights were all crystal chandeliers sending glittering rainbow light all over the store. When I finally got to absorbing the fact there were racks of dresses in every color I could think of, I almost fainted with excitement. Waffles took up position behind me, offering his support and giving me something to lean on.

"Whoa," I managed to say, covering my mouth with my hands, feeling so overwhelmed.

Vili, grinning like a cat who'd just been given a bowl of cream, bowed and extended a hand to me. "Mrs. Thatcher, would you go to the ballet with me tonight?"

A squeal of joy burst out of me as I did a little happy dance before leaping into Vili's arms. "*Yes*, oh my God, yes. I would love to go to the ballet with you."

Vili cuddled me close, purring his delight before setting me down. "Then, my kitten, pick your dress."

Gawking at him, I tried to say something but instead just impersonated that silly signing fish as I flapped about. "I-I get to pick a dress from here?"

"Of course, why else would we come?" Vili questioned, trying not to laugh at my reaction.

"This is like that moment in all those romantic movies every woman dreams of," I blurted as I looked around the shop. "I don't even know where to start."

"Maybe I can be of some help," a woman around my age offered as she approached us.

She looked like an elf with her delicate bone structure,

bright tawny-brown eyes, and shoulder-length cotton-candy pink hair. Instantly, I wanted to be her best friend.

"Zelly," Vili greeted eagerly. "I didn't know you were in town. Is Elora here too?"

"No, big sis is home doing some interviews for her new album that's releasing in two weeks. Since the music is done and she didn't need me for a while, I decided to visit Mom and Dad. Mom mentioned you'd be stopping by with your new bonded Omega and figured it would be fun to help," Zelly explained.

She then turned to me with a giant grin blooming on her face as she held out her hand. "Name's Zelia, but most people call me Zelly."

I took her hand, impressed with the strong grip she had. "Bailey-Rose, it's so nice to meet you, Zelly."

"God, you have amazing style," Zelly added, twirling me around. "This is going to be so much fun. Come on, B-Rose, let's find you some dresses."

And like that, I was swept away in the current that is Zelly. Every so often, she'd pull out a dress and hold it up to me then shake her head or toss it on the rack she dragged with us. In a matter of minutes, I had twenty different dresses to try on, and that was only looking through half the shop. Zelly hurried me into the large dressing room and, without batting an eye, helped me undress.

"Um, Zelly..." I started to say, only to have a face full of tulle as she dropped a dress over my head.

"Sorry, what was that?" Zelly asked, pulling the dress into place.

"I'm fine to try these on myself," I shared as she spun me around so she could zip up the dress.

Zelly looked at me in the mirror, cocking her head as she took in the dress. "It's no big deal. I help my sister when she's on tour for outfit changes. I promise I'm not a creepy creeper, and you'd need help with the zipper anyway."

It was clear this was a losing battle, so I just let the matter drop and focused on the dress. It was a pretty shade of purple with gauzy sleeves and lace stitched on to make it look like it was covered in white ivy. "It's nice..."

"Only if you were trying to get your baby brother back from the Goblin King," Zelly commented as she started to unzip me.

"Oh my God, you know the *Labyrinth*?" I asked, shoving the dress down and stepping out. "I love that movie."

"Of course you do because whimsical fairies like ourselves eat up that shit." Zelly chuckled. "Let's go more *Stardust* this time."

This dress had more of a fitted bodice and loose skirt for more of that vintage look. We both looked at it, and instantly, I was kicking it off. Five more dresses of various styles later, Zelly sat down on the mushroom puff stool, cross-legged, tapping her chin as she stared at the dresses left. I sorted through the options, but none of them called to me.

"Of course," Zelly exclaimed. "You're Alice."

"I'm what?" I questioned, but she was already racing out of the dressing room.

"Ah... Care Bear, you two doing okay in here?" Warrick asked, peeking behind the curtain. "Holy shit, it looks like pageant queen hurricane blew through here."

That had me giggling as I took in the disaster of dresses thrown all over the place.

"Wait, Care Bear, where is Waffles?" he asked.

A mound of dresses rose up, and Waffles crawled out from under the bench, giving a scolding woof.

"Poor guy," Warrick said, brushing glitter off his head.

"Why don't you come out here and hang with us dudes? It might be safer."

Waffles looked back at me, and I gave his release command, allowing him the freedom to leave. "I'll be fine to manage on my own for a little while, I promise." With a wag of his tail, Waffles fled the dressing room just as Zelly burst back into the room.

"I've got it," she cheered. "You need simple fantasy, something that adds to the adorableness of your tiny size. I present to you Drink Me."

With a flourish, Zelly presented a knee-length dress made from a satin material, which started out a light blue and faded into a beautiful lilac. The crowning feature was the giant bow on the back that added to the dress' silhouette. Throwing my arms up in the air as a signal I was ready to try it on, Zelly dropped it over my head. The back laced up, which was amazing since it was strapless.

When I looked in the mirror, I couldn't help but do a little tip-toe dance and throw my arms around Zelly. "This is perfect."

"Now the question is, are you wearing your hair up or down?" Zelly asked as she turned me back to face the mirror. "I think doing something like a cute messy ponytail with loose, wispy strands to play up the mood of the dress."

"I don't think I could do that..." I said, trying to process how that would even happen.

Zelly took my hand and dragged me out of the dressing room, through the store, and shoved me into a seat before a makeup station. "Didn't I mention we are full service here at Dreams Do Come Tulle?"

"You could have, and I doubt I'd remember with how distracted I was," I admitted.

"No worries, I'll have you glammed out in no time,"

Zelly assured me as she looked over the makeup. "Now, where did I put the glitter?"

Time flew by as Zelly and I chatted. To my delight, I learned she lives in Preidon with her older sister who just happened to be one of the biggest names in music right now. Like me, she was also an Omega but hadn't been interested in finding a pack as of yet.

"Don't get me wrong, I absolutely want that in my life at some point," she said, leaning in to add highlight powder to the tip of my nose. "I'm a lot to handle. My personality is big, my style is a little out there, I'm used to traveling all over with my sister, and I don't want a group of people I'm matched with to change me."

Reaching up, I clasped my hand around her wrist, pulling the brush away from my face so I could look her in the eyes. "If they are truly your scent-matched pack, that won't happen. I was rejected from the program because of my heart condition, and when I stumbled upon them, it was perfect. My Alphas were the first to ever look at me and see the real Bailey-Rose, and that's who they fell in love with. All I'm saying is when it's right, you'll know."

Zelly smiled sweetly and surprised me when she nuzzled her nose against mine. "Well then, B-Rose, it's a good thing we met today because I could use a friend who gets where I'm coming from. I think I'll keep you."

That had me burst into laughter since I felt the same way about her. I hadn't had much luck with friends in the past, but somehow, I knew Zelly and I would stay in touch.

"All right, my adorable little Polly Pocket, what do you think?" she asked, twisting the chair around so I could see what she'd done.

Stunned, I looked at my reflection, amazed at her talents. Matching the dress' colors, for my eyeshadow, she used one on each eye, drawing attention to the fact I had mismatched eyes.

"I couldn't help myself. You have such a unique appearance, I had tocelebrate that," Zelly shared, resting her arms on the back of the chair, peering over my shoulder. "What's that saying... if you're born to stand out, why the hell would you want to blend in?"

"Thank you, Zelly. You have no idea how much this means to me," I said with a sniff.

"Hold up there, B-Rose, there is no crying allowed," Zelly ordered as she quickly lunged for a bottle and proceeded to mist my face. "This stuff will lock in this makeup look that even a whore sweating in church will come out looking sexy as hell. It's what my sister uses for her live performances, so I know what I'm talking about." Leaning close, she whispered. "It's absolutely sex-proof as well. So get your freak on, girl, and no one will be the wiser."

Winking, she pulled off the cape she'd used to cover the dress and helped me to stand.

"Now, I just need shoes to complete the look," I noted, glancing at my sandaled feet.

"Pff, easy-peasy," Zelly said, waving off my worry. "You a heel or wedgie girl? Never mind, I have the perfect pair for you to try."

Giving my dress a twirl in the mirror, I felt giddy with how special I felt. While I might be going to the ballet with Vili, all my guys were here and had been in on the plan. How could a girl not feel like the luckiest woman in the world when they'd sacrifice their time to hang out in a dress shop?

"Tell me these aren't perfect for you," Zelly challenged, holding up a pair of wedge heels that looked like sprinkled doughnuts. "We just got these in from a local designer, and you would be the first person to wear them."

"Hell yes," I agreed, holding out my hands grabbing for them. "I need to put these on now."

My foot fit perfectly, which was surprising since I normally needed to buy from the kids' section. It completed the outfit to perfection. "This is the most amazing fashion moment of my life."

"Damn straight, sister. We alternative girls need to stick by each other," Zelly agreed, giving me a side hug. "Now, it's time to show the men and watch them drool over how fantastic you look."

Grinning, I channeled my inner Kate Moss and strutted my stuff. The guys cheered and whistled as I did my runway walk until I almost fell off from laughing, but Yun was there to catch me. Zelly had been right about that spray. I can personally confirm my makeup was indeed make-out proof times five.

BAILEY-ROSE

We had dinner together as a pack, but afterward, Vili and I split off from the group to head to the theater. I loved how easy it was for us all to be together as a family, but I was thrilled to get a little one-on-one time with Vili. Solo dates with my Alphas were something I wanted to keep as a common occurrence in our lives. There would be times in our lives when someone might need more from me, and the others would have to understand, which is why creating moments like this would make it easier for everyone since it was already part of our routine.

The theater was decked out for the event, but Vili had refused to tell me the name of the ballet. Yet when I saw the giant decorated pile of whipped cream, center focus in the lobby, I connected the dots. However, my excitement was cut short as a man in a red suit jacket with the theater logo on it was pointing at Waffles and yelling at me. I'd planned on learning Numolandian, but this moment had me putting that higher on the list of priorities.

Vili cut the man off, saying only three words in a threatening tone, which had the man backing off. There were a few more words exchanged before another man approached us, shooing the angry man away.

"Mr. Rantala," the man dressed in the fancy suit greeted, shaking Vili's hand. He continued to speak in Numolandian in a manner that had me guessing he was apologizing for the interaction.

Vili raised a hand so the man paused long enough for Vili to get a word in. "Gustaf, allow me to introduce you to Bailey-Rose, my bonded Omega, and her service dog, Waffles. She's here with me from Preidon."

Gustaf placed a hand over his heart and gave me a small bow. "A pleasure, madam," he said in flawless English. "Vili, I was simply thrilled when I got word you were coming tonight, and now I get to congratulate you on your bonding in person. Mrs. Rantala, you're in for a wondrous evening, and I applaud you for dressing so beautifully to match tonight's performance."

"Thank you. I'm incredibly excited to be here," I offered. "However, I would like to mention it's not Rantala but Thatcher."

Gustaf blinked, not following my train of thought since, in his mind, that conversation was five minutes ago. Vili gave my hand a reassuring squeeze and pressed a kiss to my hair.

"When we bonded, I took her last name of Thatcher," Vili explained. "We are Mr. and Mrs. Thatcher."

"Forgive me," Gustaf gasped, looking horrified, and flipped open the tablet he'd been holding. "I will make the adjustments to your file at once. Please forgive my mistake, Mr. Thatcher."

"No need for apologies, you couldn't know," Vili assured the man. "I think it is best we head to our seats, no?"

"Certainly, follow me right this way," Gustaf said, jumping into action.

He led us to an elevator, brought us to the second floor, past a security guard who nodded at us, then pulled back a thick red velvet curtain to reveal the private box. Vili used a hand on my waist and urged me forward as he hung back to say something to Gustaf, but I was too in awe to pay any attention. The theater was exquisite, having retained its original beauty and architecture. Everywhere you looked, there was something to take in. Craftsmanship like this didn't exist anymore, but this building held onto it like a secret, revealing the treasure within to those who took the time to appreciate the arts.

Our box was dead center, allowing us to see the full span of the stage. Beautiful brass opera binoculars were resting on the plush velvet seats for us to use if needed. I spotted what looked like a champagne bottle in an ice bucket and dismissed it since I couldn't drink. At least Vili could enjoy it as we watched the show. Waffles found a place out of the way and settled down, sighing as if he was as tired as I'd been earlier.

A warm body pressed up against mine as I looked over the railing. Vili's sweet marshmallow scent had me dreaming of s'mores and licking the melty, gooey goodness off his body. He placed his hands over mine, letting his fingers slide into place between mine like puzzle pieces that fit together perfectly.

"Finally, a moment alone with my kitten," Vili murmured, kissing my neck. "You look radiant tonight, Mrs. Thatcher."

Tilting my head back, I looked into his caramel-colored eyes to see the love I felt for him reflected there. "Thank you, Mr. Thatcher, you look pretty dashing yourself. I like this moss-green color on you. It brings out all your best features."

He chuckled. "You should thank Zelly... she picked it. Said I had to match your level, although I don't understand what that means."

"It means you need to look as pretty as me so you don't look like the odd man out," I explained.

"Ah, but I don't think I can be as pretty as you, kitten,"

Vili teased, stepping back. "But I can try to make pretty things that match your beauty."

Twisting to face him, I gasped when I saw the necklace he'd revealed. It lay on black velvet, making the gold coloring stand out. The chain was made of delicate links, and one end had the outline of a puffy cloud in blue gems. Threaded through the cloud was the other side of the necklace that ended with a rainbow colored with gems that matched the real thing.

"Vili..." I breathed in awe.

"This is the first of my collection titled *Clouds and Daydreams*," he shared. "They are all inspired by you."

Unable to speak, I stood there as he placed the necklace around my neck and held up the mirror tucked inside the jewelry box. It was the perfect length so you could see both charms no matter what I was wearing.

"It's absolutely perfect, Vili," I said, pulling him into a kiss. "I love you so much."

"I love you too, kitten."

Taking my hand, he gathered up the opera glasses, and we settled into our seats. I was impressed to see the chair's wooden arm could be lifted, creating one large space for us to cuddle on. With Vili's arm wrapped around my waist, the lights dimmed, and the conductor came out. The audience applauded as he took his bow before facing his orchestra. While the theater was massive and being where we were, I didn't feel the need for the glasses.

Soon, I was swept up in the beautiful melodies of the score as a little boy ate too much whipped cream and had to go to the doctor. Unable to help the boy naturally, the doctor provided medication to ease his suffering. Only this led to vivid nightmares full of every sweet imaginable coming to life. The music swept you along, immersing you in this colorful, decadent world of confection.

The stage was full of stunning dancers dressed in costumes of cupcakes, ice cream covered in chocolate with a cherry on top, candy cane snakes, and fluffy adorable animals with overexaggerated features. Nothing was to be taken seriously—this performance was all about indulging in the fanciful, and I was enamored. When the intermission was called and the theater lights came on, I couldn't believe it was halfway over already.

"Come, kitten, let's get something to drink," Vili urged as he untangled himself and stood offering his hand. "I forgot to say no champagne."

"If you want to have some, I won't be bothered. It's not like I don't like the stuff... I just can't drink it," I pointed out.

"I don't care for it, too dry," he admitted. "They have hot chocolate, not as good as mine, but lots of whipped cream."

"Sold," I answered, looping my arm through his as we left the box.

There was a bar down the hall meant only for those sitting in the box seats, so we got our drinks and a yummy-looking cookie without any trouble. I could only imagine the lines downstairs for the general audience. To me, it wouldn't be worth it—I would hate to miss a second of this performance just to get a drink or snack.

"I'm going to the ladies' room, just to be safe," I whispered, handing Vili my cup.

He nodded and kissed my cheek. "I'll meet you at our box, number six."

Smiling and flashing him a thumbs-up, I hurried to the restroom. It was as opulent as the rest of the place. There was even a lady in the room who had everything you needed to refresh yourself before returning to your seat. Once I'd taken care of business, I returned to our box, double-checking to make sure I'd picked the right one. Pulling back the curtain, I noticed the space was different. An easel was set up with a pad of sketching paper and bright-colored chalk to sketch with.

"Oh, sorry, wrong spot," I mumbled, ducking out of the box, only to be stopped as someone grabbed my wrist.

"Kitten," Vili called, pulling me back. "You are where you should be."

Confused, I looked at the art supplies and how the chairs had been pushed all the way back to give more space. There was also a small table with our drinks, cookies, and chocolate-covered strawberries.

"I... I don't understand," I whispered.

Vili chuckled and, with a hand on my waist, guided me to the easel. "If you are like me, seeing creativity brings out ideas that make your fingers itch. So now you can dream your own dream and let the magic dance on the page."

Hands on my hips, he stood behind me pressing slow, lingering kisses along my bare shoulders. Attached to the easel was a soft glow that gave me just enough light to work by as the theater lights dimmed once more. My fingers traced over the chalk until I landed on the first color I wanted to use. Once more, the music swelled as the second act commenced with Princess Praline coming to rescue the boy from the evil doctor who trapped the boy in the hospital. During their harrowing escape, the doctor and nurses became drunk, stumbling about the stage, thwarted by the alcohol come to life doing their part to help the boy.

Soon, I was lost in the fantasy of it all, my hands moving across the paper, sketching, smudging the pigment, and creating my version of a character that would be part of this world. My attention was instantly pulled back to the present as I felt Vili slowly untying the back of my dress. Slowly, it inched down my body until my breasts were exposed, only to be covered by his hands as he gently kneaded them.

"Don't focus on me, kitten, keep drawing," Vili instructed as his fingers rolled my nipples between his fingers.

I tried to take a deep breath, but it was more of a shudder as I tried to keep my legs from buckling. Vili must have noticed because he tugged on my dress until it pooled around my feet and pulled over a stool that had been placed next to the easel. Feeling the cool air of the theater on my skin, I shivered, goose bumps rising as I felt my slick soaking the new pair of lace panties I wore.

"Tell me, kitten, does it excite you to know only an easel blocks people from seeing you?" Vili asked, a purr rumbling in his chest. "Or is it that your Alpha can't wait any longer and must have you now?"

Yelping in surprise, Vili hoisted me onto the stool, drew my legs apart, and stroked his fingers over the damp lace covering my clit. When he pressed down, I let out a moan and fell boneless against him.

"Kitten, you must be quiet," Vili warned. "We can't have people checking in on us."

Turning my face, he kissed me, feasting on my mouth as if he could swallow the sounds I was making. Freeing my lips, he directed my attention back to my drawing. "This drawing is too beautiful to leave unfinished. The more you draw, I will give immense pleasure. Stop drawing, I stop touching, leaving you incomplete."

Inching the stool closer so I could reach, Vili waited to see what my choice would be. Like any Omega worth her heat, I picked up my chalk and got to drawing. Never in my life did I think it would be this hard for me to focus on my art. Typically, it was all-consuming once I got started, but now I just wanted to chuck the whole thing away so I could be bent over the stool and fucked. However, Vili wasn't one to set rules unless he intended to keep them, and right now, I wanted that finger teasing my clit to make good on his promises.

Eventually, I found a balance once I realized Vili wasn't on a quest to make me come immediately. His plan was to use it as my reward—when I finished it, he finished me. A strangled cry burst from me as he slipped two fingers inside my pussy and just let them sit there. After a few deep breaths, I got back to the drawing, and he timed his fingers to the strokes of my shading.

"I would hurry, kitten. There are only thirty minutes left of the ballet," Vili shared, using his other hand to trace around my nipple.

Thankfully, I was nearly done. Only a few more bits of shading, and I could call it good enough. This was nowhere near as detailed as I would have made it under different conditions, but to hell with that—this Omega needed to get her reward. I went to grab the color I wanted but dropped it as Vili slipped a finger in my ass. Gasping for air, I had to brace myself on the easel before slipping off the stool. Bending at the waist, I grabbed the chalk which gave Vili the perfect chance to remove his fingers and swipe his tongue over my pussy.

"Oh fuck," I swore as quietly as I could, followed by a whimper.

One more color. Come on, girl, you can do it. Just stand up, add the depth, smudge it out, then you can assume the position.

Gritting my teeth, I did just that at a speed I didn't know I possessed. Flinging the chalk away, I twisted to grip the railing of our balcony and wiggled my ass.

"The drawing's done, now fuck me, Vili. I earned my reward," I demanded.

Vili cocked a brow at me with a smirk that told me he rather liked my sass. "Truly, it's done?"

"Yes, I swear on my new heart, the drawing is done."

Two seconds later, Vili stuffed my pussy with his cock, and I had to bite my lip to keep from screaming. The Alpha didn't waste any time and got right down to business. I was glad that in this position, I could watch the ending of the ballet as the boy decided to live in this fantasyland forever. Honestly, I couldn't blame him. If I could live in a world filled with dancing sweets and all was right with the world, I'd stay too. However, If you were to ask me at this moment, I'd tell you to kick rocks because this right here was pure heaven.

Vili reached around and started to rub my clit as his hips slapped against my ass. This wasn't about making love or enjoying each other's bodies. Right now, we were slaves to our lust for one another. I reveled in the fact my body could handle down and dirty, rough and raw sex like this.

With a solid slam and a perfectly timed pinch of the clit, I exploded. Turning my head, I latched onto my arm, trying to keep my voice from being heard. Vili buried his head in my neck as he pulled back slightly so his knot didn't lock us together as he came inside me. Hearing his soft grunts as he thrust against my pussy, his knot prevented him from thrusting deeper. It had me wishing Vili had risked it and locked us together.

Gathering me up in his arms, without letting his cock

slip out, Vili sat us down on the velvet seats. We just sat there cuddled together, each of us purring up a storm as the orgasm afterglow resonated around us. When the crowd started cheering, we knew time was up, and I had to get back in my dress. There was nothing to be done about the cum which soaked my underwear, but in a way, I enjoyed feeling it, knowing what we'd done up here wasn't a dream.

Finally dressed with my drawing in hand, Vili and I left the theater, grinning at each other like two kids who got away with stealing cookies out of the cookie jar. The driver took us back to the hotel, and Lysse immediately escorted me to the waiting bubble bath.

"How..." I started to ask, then remembered Vili texting someone on the ride home.

Lysse stripped me out of my clothes but struggled just a bit when it came to removing my underwear. "Fuck, Rosie, your scent is driving me crazy."

Before I could say anything, Lysse grabbed my hips and locked his mouth around my nipple, lavishing his mark with attention. My lust still hadn't completely cooled since the theater, which meant I was rocketed over the cliff and orgasmed right where I stood. A scream burst from me as my fingers curled around Lysse's hair, ensuring he wouldn't move from that spot.

I shouldn't have been worried—the last thing my Alpha wanted to do was let go. Lust roared through my body as our bond amplified our feelings. Seconds later, fingers were in my pussy, scooping out Vili's cum. Part of me started to worry, but that went out the window the moment I felt those same fingers smear that cum over my asshole. My needy Alpha was going to use it as lube, not that he needed to since I was more than ready to take him in either hole.

"Rosie, I'm going to fill your perfect little ass with my

cock, then we're going to sit in the tub so I can clean you up," Lysse informed me.

The only response I had was a whimper as I nodded my agreement.

This wasn't the first time something like this had happened. During our three days of mindless sex, I'd noticed how much they enjoyed it when I kept their cock warm. There were a few times when they'd fallen asleep with their dicks still hard inside me, but I wasn't complaining. The feeling of being connected to them so intimately without it being about sex was utterly romantic to me.

Lysse picked me up, splayed my legs, and slowly lowered me down on his cock. We both groaned as he entered, allowing my body to take him as it pleased, letting Lysse sink into me. Once he was balls deep, arms wrapped tightly around my middle, he sat on the wide edge of the sunken bathtub. Swinging around to drop our legs in the water, I sighed at how warm and inviting it felt. Finally submerged in milky water, Lysse got to work washing every single inch of my body.

By the time he was done, I was wiped, barely keeping my eyes open. Another pair of hands helped to dry me off, causing me to focus long enough to see it was Yun-Sun. I reached out and ran a hand over his short, buzzed hair. Yun took my hand, dried it, then kissed my palm before nuzzling it. Neither bothered to put me in a nightgown as I was placed in the large, fluffy bed.

"Rosie," Lysse whispered, filling my ass once more with his cock. "It's okay, you can fall asleep, but I won't be able to settle down until I've knotted you, my love. Don't you worry about a thing, I'll do all the work. I just need to fill my Omega with my cum."

As he whispered to me, his voice lulled me into a state of

being half asleep. Through our bond, I made sure he knew I had zero issues with him fucking me to sleep or finishing if I ended up passing out before he came. My body was theirs to love, and I trusted each of them with my life, sleeping or awake. Plus, it made for fantastic dreams to fall asleep to.

BAILEY-ROSE

Today was a do-nothing day where we ordered room service and didn't bother to get out of bed. Yesterday had been a little bit too much for me on the physical side as I continued to build up my endurance. So, as a pack, we made the executive choice to be as lazy as we were productive yesterday.

We were watching some random, trashy reality show about city people being sent to work on a farm. Depending on where they were shooting the show, there were different types of farms. Just like a train wreck, it was so bad it was hard to stop watching. The episode we were currently watching had three guys who were trust fund babies and had never been forced to do manual labor work on a cattle ranch. It happened to be castrating day, and they were tasked with getting the young bulls through the chute and into the crush.

I lay on my stomach draped over Gareth's back as I munched on crackers, utterly invested in what was going on. Flinching as one of the young bulls slammed the side of the chute, it knocked one of the prissy boys off the fencing, landing him in the mud.

"Baby girl, I love you, but you're somehow managing to get more cracker on me than in your mouth," Gareth commented.

Looking down at my hand, I realized the cracker I was holding was now crumbled into dust from how tight I was fisting my hand. "Oh shit, sorry," I mumbled as I brushed the crumbs off him onto the plate.

"What has you all stressed out?" Gareth questioned, twisting to lay on his back so he could pull me closer. "The only time I see you waste food is when you're upset or anxious."

"Is that what it's really like to live and work on a cattle ranch?" I asked, sweeping a rogue curl out of his face.

He studied me for a moment before answering like he was deciding how best to answer me. "Most things are true, but like any good TV show, it's a bit dramatic. Sure, any time you work with animals, there's a chance for things to go wrong. They have a mind of their own, and if they decide they don't want to do something, it's not that easy to change their mind. However, cattle have a prey mindset, unlike dogs which have a predatory way of thinking."

"I don't see how that has anything to do with safety?" I pointed out.

Gareth chuckled, snuggling me tight to his chest. "Oh, is that what this is really about? You want to know if I'll be safe when I go back to work?"

"Look, I didn't really know what was involved in the rancher life, but now I do," I reasoned.

"Baby girl, for the love of God, please do not take this show as the metric to base your ranching knowledge on," Gareth pleaded, cupping my face in his hands. "These men have no idea what they're doing, and I'll bet you anything the ranch hands have been instructed not to help those idiots. The goal here is to show just how dumb these silver-spoon candidates are by putting them in situations they aren't prepared for. If they were on our ranch, there's no way we'd let them do half this shit without someone right beside them."

"So you're telling me this show makes everything look more dangerous than it really is?" I countered.

He started to answer, then paused, changing his mind at the last second. "You know what, instead of answering that for you, why don't we all go to Watson Ranch, and I'll show you firsthand what it's *really* like to be a rancher?"

I blinked at him for a second, letting that offer sink in. "Seriously?"

"One hundred percent serious, baby girl. What do you say? I don't make this offer to just anyone," Gareth teased.

Looking over at the others, I raised a questioning brow. "What about you guys? Any interest in learning to be a rancher?"

"Oh, I'm so down. Unlike our rebel country boy, I look *good* in a cowboy hat and can rock a mean pair of boots," Warrick said, pretending to tip his imaginary hat at me.

Yun-Sun shrugged with a smile on his face. "We don't have anything else planned, so why not?"

"He makes a good point," Lysse agreed. "If there was ever a time for spontaneous travels, it would be now."

"Yes, I would very much like to be cowboy," Vili decided, giving two thumbs-up.

Gareth rolled up into a sitting position, taking me with him so I ended up in his lap. "This will be perfect. My mom's been bugging me about meeting you guys, and I can introduce her to Bailey-Rose as well."

"What about your dads or your brothers?" I asked.

"My dads, maybe," he answered off-handedly. "Depends on if they feel there are more important things to do in the city. As for my older brothers, they don't ever come to see my mom. Once they were bonded and building their own families, they pretty much forgot about her. It's sad because she'd love to be a bigger part of her grandkids' lives."

For some reason, that shocked me. "You're an uncle?"

"In the literal sense that my one brother had two kids, yeah. Although I've only seen them a few times for big family moments. I'm not really in their lives," Gareth admitted.

"Huh, well then, it sounds like us making a surprise visit to the ranch will be exciting for your mom," I reasoned. "We might need to do a little shopping, though."

Yun-Sun held up the tablet he'd been reading on. "We can just order things to be sent ahead. The flight's gonna be about ten hours, but we'll be going backward in time so that should work out just perfectly."

Crawling out of Gareth's lap, I tossed my arms around Yun, smacking a kiss on his lips. "You're brilliant, did you know that?"

"I might have heard it a time or two in my life, but somehow, it means more coming from you," Yun-Sun answered and pulled me in for another kiss. "Now, let's see what Ranch Depot has for us to buy."

Gareth groaned, falling back onto the bed. "You don't have to buy from there, any place that sells jeans and T-shirts is fine."

"Nope, sorry, pal, but we want this to be a true immersive experience," Warrick countered. "Did you want me to pick you out a new hat?" The only answer he got was a middle finger which only had us all laughing.

By the time the day was coming to an end, we'd packed, ordered our new clothes, and alerted the pilot we'd be flying out in the morning. Thankfully, they were merciful to me and scheduled take off at ten, allowing me to sleep until nine, which was good because the guys didn't let me get to sleep until almost two in the morning. Gareth spun some story about this being the last night we had not to worry about being heard. Apparently, they seemed to think I was incapable of being quiet during sex. Well, Vili and I both know that's not true.

Watson Ranch was located in Molis, a mountainous state in Preidon and a four-hour flight from Windermere. Even disembarking from the plane, I knew this place was unlike anywhere I'd been before. Mountains could be seen on the horizon no matter where you looked. The sky was a bright blue with picturesque puffy clouds floating overhead. Even the air seemed cleaner and smelled better, full of a rich pine scent.

Waiting for us outside the plane was a woman with chin-length silver hair that had a slight natural wave to it. She was dressed in a lovely flowing dress with a bright, bold flower pattern and a rhinestone-covered belt accentuating her waist. The moment she saw Gareth, her face lit up, telling me what I'd suspected—it was his mother.

"Oh, it's my baby boy come home to visit," she gushed as she hugged Gareth tightly. "I've missed you so much... phone calls just don't beat getting to see you face to face, sugar."

"*Mom*," Gareth grumbled, but he didn't even try to refuse her affection.

"Hush, this is what you get for not showing your face for four years," she scolded, rocking him from side to side in her excitement.

Once she released her hold on Gareth, her attention shifted to us. When her gaze landed on me, her smile only got bigger. "You must be Bailey-Rose. I'm Deanna, but everyone just calls me Dee. I suppose you can call me Mom too, if you like."

Taking a step forward, I reached out my hand to my mother-in-law. "It's so nice to meet you, Dee."

She took one look at my hand, then used it to pull me into a tight hug. "Sorry, darling, but around here, we give each other proper hugs, especially when they're family."

It was hard not to like Deanna—she had a warm personality and made you feel at ease. This only confused me even more as to why Gareth and his brothers didn't come home to spend time with her. I grinned as each guy got their own welcoming hug, suffering as the woman seemed determined to crush them with her excitement.

"How on earth do you have suitcases with you? Everything you ordered arrived about an hour ago. What more could you possibly need?" Dee asked, watching the staff unload our luggage.

"Mom, don't smother," Gareth warned. "We decided to come visit at the last minute and originally packed for a tropical island. Shorts and sandals don't really work when it comes to ranch life."

Deanna just took his grouchy behavior in stride and shrugged. "I don't see why they wouldn't. It's not like we expect them to work for their supper. We have hired hands for all that."

"Actually," I cut in, shutting Gareth up. "I was hoping to learn what it's like to live and work on a real ranch. You know, to understand what life was like for him growing up."

"Really?" Deanna asked, surprised. "Huh... I suppose that would be of interest to someone who hadn't grown up in the country. What is it that your family does?"

"Oh, ah, my family is in the oil business," I answered, feeling odd about admitting that for some reason.

Deanna's eyes went wide. "Well, *shiiit*, you're one of *those* Thatchers? Lord have mercy, how did I not figure that out before now?"

At the surprise of this news, I noticed her slight accent became much thicker, and it made me like her even more.

"Dee, it's fine, really. I don't have much, if anything, to do with my parents' business. That's all been left to my oldest brother, Eli. I spend my days in an art studio covered in paint," I assured her.

"It is what it is," Deanna agreed, then clapped her hands. "I have the cars waiting out front, but be sure to use the bathroom. It's about an hour's drive to the ranch."

"Mom, I already warned them on the plane. We're adults and can take care of ourselves," Gareth pointed out.

His mother just gave him a dubious look then brushed off his words with a shoulder shrug. "Suit yourself, but I don't want to hear anyone crying when they can't hold it any longer, and the only option is to drop trou on the side of the road."

I covered my mouth with a hand to keep them from seeing me snickering, but Yun caught me and winked. Knowing the guys had been pushing water on me the whole flight, worried I was going to have trouble with the altitude, I made sure to relieve myself. Finally, we piled into the two SUVs and were off. I'd been placed in the car with Deanna, Gareth, Waffles, Nugget, and Warrick. The others and the luggage were in the second vehicle, where I'm sure it was much quieter.

It didn't take me long to figure out Deanna didn't get much chance to talk with anyone outside the ranch staff. At first, I tried to keep up, be engaged, and ask questions until I realized what Deanna really wanted was to be listened to. She didn't need anyone to say a word or participate—you just needed to be someone who hadn't heard the story before. By the time we reached the ranch, I knew all the local and ranch gossip, every embarrassing story she could think of about Gareth and his brothers, and how thrilled Dee was to have us staying for a few days.

"Please tell me she will eventually run out of things to talk about," I whispered to Gareth.

He smirked and shook his head, patting my knee in sympathy. "Not in the years that I've been alive."

Then the main gates to the ranch appeared, and I tuned everything out at the sight of them. It wasn't that they were grandiose or anything, but their sheer size was impressive. The side columns were made out of a sandy-colored brick. Pitch-black wrought iron made up the gate in a picture of a massive steer with horns and the name Watson Ranch arching over the steer. Slowly, they opened, giving me time to take in the other details of the mountains, trees, and birds carved into the metal, turning it into a mural.

"That was a gift from the Governor of Molis on the ranch's hundred-year anniversary. Stunning, isn't it?" Dee sighed.

"Is that what the hundred written on there was for?" I questioned.

"No, that's actually the address. We're one hundred Creek Valley Trail," Dee answered. "The governor thought it would be a fitting gift to mark the occasion."

"I'll say," Warrick muttered. "How long did that take to even make? The whole thing had to take months to weld together."

"That's the coolest thing about the gate. It only took a month since they used this new laser-cutting technique the governor's brother created. Since the news article about our gate was published, the man's simply been slammed with work," Dee interjected.

Something told me that gate wasn't just a gift out of the kindness of the governor's heart, but I wasn't going to rain on her parade. After the longest driveway I'd ever seen, we arrived at the house. I'd been picturing a typical two-story farmhouse with the wraparound porch you always see in the movies, but this was anything but that. Gareth's childhood home was a single-story ranch-style house that seemed to be the size of three houses connected together. It was made out of river stone and dark wood with lots of flowers surrounding the front of the house. There was even a pond with a pier for fishing or possibly swimming. A fountain was in the middle of the pond, adding to the liveliness of the property. Off to the right, if you continued to follow the gravel road, you'd end up at what I would guess to be one of the barns. With horses grazing in the pasture, I made a good guess it was where they were kept.

Gareth had said many of the farm hands still preferred to work with horses over ATVs, needing sharper turns and faster responses to situations. The only horse I'd ever been on was a pony at the carnival that walked in circles. I loved all animals and couldn't wait to slip them all some carrots or a sugar cube or two. Taking everything in, my body practically vibrated with excitement, so much so it had my two Alphas grinning from ear to ear.

"God, you're the cutest thing ever, Care Bear," Warrick said, wrapping his arms around me from behind and kissing my head. "I never knew how amazing it would be to feel the world through your emotions."

I caught Gareth's mother looking back at us as she pretended to check her makeup in the visor mirror. Deanna had a twinkle in her eyes that only pure joy could create. Yet

I could also see a shadow of wistfulness as she watched Warrick nuzzling his face into my hair.

How lonely this life must be for her not to have her pack or kids around to keep her company.

If I hadn't been sure about making this trip, I was now. Deanna seemed like a wonderful woman who deserved more than what she was getting out of life right now. There had to be a reason she wouldn't leave the ranch to see her grandkids. Surely, they wouldn't turn her away if she made the trip into the city to see them, right?

The vehicles stopped at the front door under the awning that shaded us from the bright sun. It wasn't overly hot, but I knew being at a higher elevation meant the sun was much stronger. Thankfully, I had a bit of a glow after the week on the beach. Most of the guys had turned into bronze super-models, leaving Vili and me looking like ghosts with our fair complexion. Poor Vili seemed to become pinker rather than golden.

"Come in, come in," Dee urged, gesturing us to follow her into the house. "I'll have the ranch hands set your luggage in the back rooms. I'm sorry I don't have a space big enough for all of you to stay in one room, but I think the two guest suites will work out well. There's always Gareth's room too, if needed. I made sure to keep his room just as it was in case he ever needed it. Looks like all my worrying was for nothing, but that's what we mothers do."

Deanna led us into a large family room with vaulted ceilings, a giant stone fireplace, and lovely artwork hanging on the walls. It perfectly blended masculine and feminine energy with leather, dark wood, fluffy pillows, and plants filling the space.

"Sit, I'll get some sweet tea for us to sip on," Dee instructed.

"Mom," Gareth called, following after her. "Let me help… that tray will be heavy."

Deanna gave her son an adoring look, cupping his cheek before they disappeared down the hall.

"This place is amazing," I said softly as I looked around. "Did you see the pond? How could you not want to live in a place like this? It's paradise."

Lysse tucked some hair behind my ear in a subtle effort to draw my attention. "So tell me, Rosie, you've been to the beach, experienced international city life, and now here we are on a ranch in the middle of nowhere. What is your favorite?"

Leaning forward, I rested my chin on my hand, mulling that over. Everything we'd done so far had been amazing, each place having its special something. How could I possibly choose?

"Don't roll your eyes as I give you this answer, okay?" I warned, knowing even if he agreed, chances were he'd still do it.

Lysse drew an X over his heart. "Promise… even crossed my heart."

"This is going to be the most cheese ball thing ever to be said, *but*… I think any place would be my favorite as long as I was there with all of you," I admitted.

Not only did Lysse roll his eyes, but the others even groaned at my sappy response. Thankfully, Warrick scooped me up as I started to pout and snuggled me close. "Don't mind them, Care Bear. I personally love that you are so damn cheesy. This way, I'm not the only one who says shit like that in this family."

We were all distracted when Deanna and Gareth rejoined us, carrying a tray of filled glasses and another full of daintily cut sandwiches. There was no way she'd done that just now, seeing there were four different types to choose from. *Just how much had she done to prepare for us to visit?*

"Bailey-Rose, the lemonade is for you," Dee pointed out. "Gareth wrote down the list of things to avoid so I can make sure we have something for you to enjoy. I make my tea strong and sweet, so I think that might be a little too much for you, darling. As for the sandwiches, I didn't know what everyone would like, so I did a little of everything. We have ham and cheese, egg salad, hummus and cucumber if anyone is a veggie lover, and my famous chicken salad."

"Thank you, Mrs. ... I mean, Dee," Yun-Sun said, catching himself. "You didn't have to go to all this trouble for us."

"Nonsense, meeting my sugar bear's pack for the first time is a major deal," Dee argued, sitting in a well-loved armchair. "Now help yourself... there's plenty to go around. I've got more in the kitchen."

GARETH

For the next few hours, we chatted and filled my mom in on how we met, Bailey-Rose's surgery, and the adventures we'd been on for the past few weeks. I'd been worried that coming home after so long, Mom would start in about how I'm never around and worry over every little thing I do. What I hadn't expected was for her to be so absolutely invested in getting to know my pack. Granted, once my brothers found their packs and matched with their Omegas, they didn't bother coming home anymore.

I knew she worried about me more because of what happened with Callie and the fact it hit me so hard. It was another reason I didn't want to be here in this house that reminded me of my little sister, not that you'd know I had one since there wasn't a picture to be found. My fathers decided it was best to remove all traces of her from the home so Mom wasn't tortured by Callie's ghost, which was one of the many things I viewed differently than my fathers.

Through our bond, I could tell that while Bailey-Rose was enjoying the social time, she was anxious to do something else. I glanced at my watch, seeing it was getting close to dinner time for the animals and us.

"Hey, baby girl," I said once the conversation fell to a natural lull. "If you want, it's almost time to feed the horses. Any interest in helping me?"

Instantly, her eyes lit up. "Yes, one hundred percent yes."

Grinning, I stood and held out my hand to her. "Then

let's go see what you ordered from Ranch Depot. You'll need something other than sandals to wear out to the barn."

The guys excused themselves as well since it would be a good chance to get settled and figure out rooms. One of the rooms was larger and had a king-size bed with a futon that pulled out into a queen bed. This meant we either agreed to snuggle up to all be in the same room or split it three and three. We decided to split the rooms, and we'd rotate who slept with Bailey-Rose.

"It's only for a short time," Vili pointed out. "We will manage until going home."

When we decided to come here, we decided to stay for three days so we had a week at home before our leave ended. Of course, for most of us, nothing really changed after that, but Ulysses and Yun-Sun still hadn't decided what they were going to do for the long term. Either way, we had a little over a week before we had to worry about all that.

Once the rooms were sorted, the boxes were opened, and our girl was decked out in jeans, boots, and a T-shirt, we headed to the barn. The moment we entered, I was hit with every scent that reminded me of home and fond memories of growing up here. Guys were tossing hay down from the loft, prepping for feeding, filling the air with its sweet scent. *God, I'd missed this.*

"Gareth... Gareth Watson, is that you?" an older gentleman asked, walking over to us.

It took me a moment, but I recognized the man as Tripp Carson. He'd been brought on as ranch manager a few years after Callie's death. My father, Jonathan, had concluded we needed someone who didn't know our family trauma to run the ranch. So he fired the man who'd been working for our family since I was born and brought on Tripp.

"Mr. Carson, it's nice to see you," I greeted, shaking the

man's hand and gestured to my right. "This is my bonded Omega, Bailey-Rose."

"Nice to meet you, ma'am," Tripp said with a tip of his hat. "What brings you two out here...getting a little dark for a ride."

"Actually, we were looking to help with feeding," I explained. "Do you still use the annex barn as the old folks' home?"

Tripp grinned and nodded. "Sure do,... best-looking lawn ornaments in all four counties that I know of. If you two want to handle those four, we'll settle up here in the big barn."

"Sure thing, you still keep your notes in the same place?" I asked.

"You bet, no point in changing a system when it works," Tripp answered. "Oh, while you're out there, could you take a look at the water trough? Your mother decided to try a new idea and add goldfish to the tanks. Something about keeping them from getting green so fast in this summer heat. Told her we'd try it out there before adding them to all the water troughs."

I sighed, shaking my head. "No problem."

"Oh, and make sure to keep the little dog away from Titon. He don't take well to them," Tripp added as we headed for the barn.

Pulling open the barn door, I let Bailey-Rose and the dogs in before shutting it. "First, we have to open the stall doors since they're trained to walk right in from the pasture to their spot." I showed her how the lock worked, and she took care of the two on her side.

"Now, we put a little grain in a bucket and shake it," I explained, stepping into the small feed room where the grain and other everyday supplies were kept. "Those hungry beasts will come running no matter how far away they are. I've never met a horse who wasn't eager to get their dinner when there was a promise of sweet, sweet grain."

"How come these horses are kept separate?" Bailey-Rose asked.

"It was a Watson family rule that no horse who's worked the land will ever get sold when they can't work anymore. They've earned the right to retire here for their years of service. So the seniors got their own pasture and small barn to themselves where they didn't need to compete with the youngsters," I shared, handing her the bucket. "Care to do the honors?"

She nodded eagerly and followed me to the main gate. "Waffles, Nugget, stay," she instructed, ensuring they were out of the way.

I watched the woman, who was teaching me to enjoy life again despite the dangers that lurked around every corner, shake the bucket. She shook that thing like it was her purpose in life and some of the grain even spilled out. That was one thing I loved most about Bailey-Rose—she did nothing half-assed. If she was going to do it, then dammit, she was going to give it her all.

A whinny rang out, and I knew it was Bandit—he had always been a vocal guy about pretty much everything. However, when it came to food of any kind, that boy wouldn't miss an opportunity. Titon was leading the way with Bandit right behind him, and the other two picking up the rear, took their time, knowing dinner wasn't going anywhere. Bailey-Rose laughed as the two geldings shoved each other, trying to be the first one in the barn.

Titon was what you thought of as the perfect specimen of a working horse—even in his old age, he held his form well. His bay coloring also made him quite eye-catching as well. Bandit was an ornery yet mischievous, flaxen-colored Haflinger that had been Callie's best friend. While the ATV had been a special gift for Callie, the thing she loved most was this naughty horse that wasn't really a pony but not quite a horse. Those two got into all kinds of trouble as they roamed the lower pastures. I know one thing—if Callie had been with Bandit instead of on that ATV, she would be alive today because there was no way that horse would let anything happen to her.

With everyone in their stall, Bailey-Rose and I slid the stall doors closed, ensuring they'd stay there. "Come here, baby girl... let me show you what each of these old fogies are gonna be eating tonight."

Drawing her back into the feed room, I showed her the chart Tripp created and hung above the feed bins. "Can you read this section off for me while I pull it all together? These guys are special and get a fair amount of supplements. It's one of the reasons none of the stable hands like feeding out here. It takes just as long to feed these four horses as it does half the other barn," I joked.

"Yeah, well, it will be the same for them when they get old," she pointed out. "Wonder if they realize the nurses will be grumbling just as much handing out their medication."

Laughing, I shook my head as I pulled together four buckets of feed. With Bailey-Rose's help, I got all four serv-ings settled in no time. The final step was to add a bit of oil for Candy to mix it all up, and then we were good to go.

"Hey, there's a note on Bandit's column that if he's limping or looking sore, to give him something for pain management," Bailey-Rose pointed out. "He seemed fine when he ran in."

"Let's feed the other three real quick then I can look in on him. Once that feed is clipped into place, no one is able to get close to him until he's finished," I explained, handing her a bucket. "That's for Candy, the white one."

Candy was a sweet girl, always had been, probably why my mother picked her. She'd be perfectly safe for Bailey-Rose to interact with first. Titon, like his owner, was a bit of a prick, and Diego, the other gelding, was hit or miss on how he interacted with strangers. I doubt he had gotten better in his old age.

Done with the other three, Bailey-Rose pulled back the stall door enough for us to look in on Bandit. Looking at the fella, I couldn't see anything wrong, but I decided not to take a risk and ran a hand down his legs.

"What are you looking for?" she asked as Bandit snuffled her pockets in the hope there could be food hidden there.

"Heat, when horses get sore or something is inflamed, it gets hot," I answered. "Although it looks like he's totally fine. I didn't find a hot spot, so he's probably good to go."

Before I could stop her, Bailey-Rose grabbed the bucket and walked in to clip it to the hook. Other than Callie, Bandit always charged at the person, so we installed a second hook close to the door so no one had to get body checked into a stall door. However, to my amazement, Bandit waited for my girl to clip the bucket, pat him sweetly on the neck, and step back before he dove into his meal.

I moved to grab her and instantly, Bandit lifted his head and pinned his ears, warning me not to get any closer to his food. "Take a step back for me, okay, baby girl," I whispered. "Bandit isn't all that friendly when it comes to anything getting close to his grain."

"Oh, really? He doesn't seem to mind me," she commented but did as I asked.

"Either way, we still need to grab hay for these guys, and

then they'll be settled for the night," I said, wrapping an arm around her waist to keep her close.

The guys might make fun of me for being overprotective, but I'll be damned if I ever let anything happen to Bailey-Rose, especially here at the ranch. Hay was the easy part, and we got the horses settled in no time. Bailey-Rose lingered watching Bandit as the hellion tossed around his hay, searching for the bits he liked best before eating the rest.

Turning to look at me, she searched my face as if looking for something. "Can I ask you something?"

"Baby girl, you can ask me anything. I have no secrets from you," I told her.

"Was Bandit Callie's horse? I only ask because when you look at him, I feel this sadness from you, and it's the only reason I could think of," she explained.

Stepping up behind her, I rested my hands on her hips as I peered over her head at the horse. "Yeah, Bandit was Callie's partner in crime. He's a pain in the ass to everyone else, but he loved my sister."

"You know, if you ever want to talk about her, I'd love to listen. She sounds like someone who would have great stories," Bailey-Rose commented. "When Papa Addy died, it helped to share how amazing he was, to keep his memory alive. People always tell you to move on or get over it, and things will pass. How can you simply move on from the pain of losing someone you loved? It doesn't make any sense."

A bitter laugh escaped me as I rested my head on hers. "My fathers are those people. After Callie's funeral, they demanded the housekeeper pack up all her things and remove any pictures that would have my little sister in them. I know people grieve differently, but they had no right to dictate that when they didn't even live here five days out of the week. No one asked my mom what she wanted or hell, even me since I still lived in the house full time. My relationship with my fathers hasn't ever been great, but that was the moment I knew we'd never be able to see eye to eye."

Bailey-Rose turned to face me, resting her head on my chest as she wrapped her arms around me. "Grief makes you selfish and lash out at those around you. It's no excuse for what they did, but sometimes it helps to understand their actions. When things don't make sense, we stew on them, trying to unravel the reasoning behind it all."

When she started to purr, offering me all the comfort she could, I closed my eyes and held onto this amazing woman who loved me for some reason. There were no words, just feelings drifting between us as we let our bond do the communicating. *How could my fathers not have known how much pain my mother was in when they have a direct connection to her soul? Or could it be they didn't care?*

"Will you tell me about Callie?" Bailey-Rose asked in such a soft voice I almost missed it.

"You two would have been best friends, I know it. She was wild, but only because she loved to live life to the max. I don't think there was a single thing she was afraid of... well, except for shots," I remembered, grinning. "There was one time Mom forgot to tell Callie she had a doctor's appointment, and the three of us had been running errands. So there we are, Callie lost in her own world playing on her tablet when she looks up and finds out we're in a clinic waiting room. To make matters worse, it was the appointment to get her school shots. I swear if I hadn't been there to calm her down, she would have decked the nurse for coming near her with a needle."

Bailey-Rose chuckled as she took a step back. "Was she really going to punch the nurse?"

"One thousand percent yes, she was," I stated without question. "Callie was a country girl through and through. She knew how to hold her own against just about anyone or anything that tried to get in her way. Hell, for the fun of it, she trained one of the bulls to charge up to her and tap her outstretched hand before she'd give him his grain. I about pissed myself watching it happen, but Callie just laughed her ass off, telling me I looked as white as a ghost."

Taking my girl's hand, we headed back to the house. Mom would want us all to sit down together for dinner—it was her one rule. No matter what, if you were home on the ranch, dinner would be eaten together as a family. It also made me realize how lonely Mom must be out here all by herself during the week. I'd half expected her to move to the city when I left the house, but here she was living life as she always had.

"Oh good, I was just about to send one of the others out to get you," Mom said as we walked in. "Come on, dinner's ready. Oh, don't forget to take off your boots. I hate when shavings get tracked through the house."

The dining room was dressed to the max with candles, fine crystal goblets, and china my mother got as a wedding present from her mother. Such was the honor bestowed upon guests. Once the six of us were seated, Mom hurried back to the kitchen and helped the staff bring out the platters of food. My mouth watered at the sight of the country chicken and biscuits in the casserole dish Mom carried out. It was my favorite meal she made, and no one else could match the taste, so I gave up trying. Why mess with perfection when you can get it from the source?

"Now, I didn't know what everyone liked so I did chicken biscuits and a beef stew," Mom shared. "Don't be shy about taking what you want either. I've never known how to cook for anything less than an army."

Soon, the table was full of delicious-smelling food, but no one touched a thing until Yun-Sun walked around the table filling a plate for our Omega. At least, I thought that's what he was doing, but I noticed two plates being prepared. When he set one down in front of Bailey-Rose and the other in front of Mom, I about smacked myself. *Idiot.* Of course, he would do the same for my mom. She's an Omega too, with none of her pack here to provide for her needs. *I lost some major favorite son points, that's for sure.*

"Thank you, Yun-Sun, but you didn't have to do that. How precious are you," Mom gushed.

Now that the ladies had been served, the rest of us dug in. The dining room was filled with the sounds of us men groaning over how good the food was. Bailey-Rose was doing a happy dance in her chair with each bite she took, making me just want to kiss the hell out of her. Most of us went back for seconds, and I prayed there was a whole ass other dish of chicken biscuits so I could have it for lunch tomorrow.

"So, dearest, how did you enjoy feeding the horses?" Mom asked Bailey-Rose since we were useless for conversation.

Our girl scrambled to guzzle down some water to clear her mouth before answering. "It was fun. I've never been around horses like that. Living in the city doesn't give you many chances to interact with animals that aren't pigeons."

Mom covered her mouth with her napkin, trying not to laugh, but her crinkled eyes gave it away.

"Oh, there's no need to hold back on my account. I laugh at myself roughly ten times a day," Bailey-Rose assured her. "You can't take life too seriously, or else you'll miss all the fun of living it. Something I hear Callie and I might have had in common."

Mom's eyes grew wide at the mention of Callie's name. It had been an unspoken rule that once my sister's things were boxed up, we didn't talk about her anymore.

"Ah... Callie..." Mom paused to clear her throat and blink rapidly. "Yes, that girl certainly loved to take life by the horns, as we say. You know, I remember one time while Callie and I were out riding, we came across a hill covered in puffy white dandelions. She took off like a bat out of hell, sending Bandit up the hill, dismounted, and rolled all the way down. It almost looked like it should have been snowing the way those seeds filled the air. Then she popped up, hands on her hips..." Mom stood and replicated the stance for everyone. "Looked me dead in the eye, and said, 'your turn, Mom.' "

Everyone chuckled at that as Mom took her seat and dabbed at her eyes. "I go back every year once the dandelions change and look at that hill, remembering that day. I can't ever bring myself to roll down the hill without her, but God, it was one of the best days."

"I would love to see that hill so I could draw that moment for you to remember that day." Bailey-Rose offered.

Mom clutched her napkin to her heart, lip quivering as she tried to hold it together. "I could never ask that of you, and the hill is just a hill."

That response smacked of my father, Hank, and the way he looked at life—always practical, never sentimental. How the hell they ended up with an Omega like my mom makes no sense. I knew they loved each other but were polar opposites on so many things.

"I have an idea... why don't we all go for a ride tomorrow, and I can show you," I volunteered.

Something in my gut told me having a painting from Bailey-Rose recreating that moment would mean the world to my mom. My fathers couldn't tell her to get rid of it since it was a hand-crafted gift from their son's Omega.

"One problem," Warrick interjected. "None of us know how to ride horses."

"Oh, that's not a problem," Mom assured. "We have more than enough ATVs for you all to use. There's no training needed for that."

Panic rolled in my gut at the thought of Bailey-Rose on an ATV. I hadn't used one since Callie's accident, choosing to drive a truck, walk, or take a horse. Rationally, I knew what happened to Callie was a one-in-a-million situation, but lightning can strike the same place twice if you wait long enough.

Bailey-Rose grabbed my arm, digging her nails into it, causing me to hiss in pain and yank it away. "What the hell, baby girl?"

BAILEY-ROSE

Watching as Gareth slowly became consumed by fear and being able to feel it at the same time sent my head spinning. Nugget barked and gently tugged on my jeans, trying to get my attention. The little guy could feel my anxiety, but the truth of the matter is, it wasn't mine. Gareth was so consumed with fear, it bled out of him and into me. One therapist had told me if I began to spiral, I needed to trigger my brain into focusing on something else. She'd suggested sour candy or something extremely cold placed on my stomach. Well, I didn't have either of those things, but I had to act fast.

Praying Gareth would forgive me, I drove my nails into the soft skin of his forearm near the wrist. Seconds later, he was yanking his arm away from me. "What the hell, baby girl?"

"I can't believe that worked," I blurted.

Grumpy Gareth was in full form as he scowled at me. "What worked, and how does that have anything to do with you clawing me?"

Flinging myself at him, he reacted immediately to ensure I was safe, protecting me from hitting the table or falling to the floor. "Okay, Bailey-Rose, that's enough. What is happening right now?" Gareth demanded.

"You got lost in the darkness for a moment, but I brought you back," I answered. "Don't ever scare me like that again."

Through our bond, I could tell he was still utterly

confused. *Could it be that he had no idea just how dark and defeated he'd just been?*

Tugging me off him so I was back in my chair, Gareth boxed me in. "I am so lost right now I couldn't tell you which way is up. Pretend I have no idea what you're talking about and explain it to me from the beginning."

"Your mom suggested we use a motorized steed instead of a horse since no one but you knows how to ride. Then you turned to look at me, and a tidal wave of fear, anger, and despair slammed into me from you. I tried to shake you, called your name, but there was no response, which is when I decided drastic measures needed to be taken," I said, breaking it down for him. "Was it the word that triggered you? Is being here too hard? Oh God, was it because I asked you to tell me about her in the barn?"

Gareth's whole body slumped forward, and he rested his head on my lap. "It's not your fault, baby girl, and it has nothing to do with being here or talking about Callie. Since she died, I haven't ridden one of those things. Picturing you riding one suddenly turned into you ending up like my sister. It's irrational, and I have no reason to think that way, but I can't help it."

Deanna got up from her chair and wrapped her arms around her son. "I had no idea. I'm so sorry, sugar bear."

Gareth gave in to the affection from his mother instead of pulling away like I feared. He hated to look or feel weak in front of people, but then, your mother isn't people.

"It's not your fault, Mom. I thought I'd be better about it after all these years. Doesn't stop me from driving any other vehicle, recreational or not. Seems this reaction is tied directly to ATVs, which, other than here, I never interact with," Gareth explained.

Deanna pulled her chair over to sit closer to her son,

patting his hand in a comforting gesture. "Still, you used to be able to talk to me about things like this. I know after Callie's death, you changed, and I tried to find a way to make you understand we never blamed you. It was a tragic accident that no one could have foreseen."

I felt a jolt of anger flash through Gareth. "If you don't blame me, then why did you let them wipe her from existence? There is nothing left of her in this house. It's like they wanted to forget, and neither of them could even look at me after that."

Tears rolled down Deanna's cheeks, and she did nothing to stop them. "I'm so sorry, Gareth, we made you feel that way. I know she meant the world to you. The two of you were thick as thieves, and I should have guessed you'd shoulder the blame. As for your fathers, well, I wasn't supposed to be able to have any more kids after you. Yet by some miracle, Callie defied all the odds, and I brought her to full term. I'd prayed for it to be a baby girl, and there she was, my little miracle."

Deanna paused to lick her lips and brush at the tears which had stopped. "They would never come out and say it, but your fathers believed Callie wasn't theirs, that I'd cheated. Batty fools forget the only time an Omega can get pregnant is during a heat. Trust me, there was no one hiding in the closet for three days just to try and get me pregnant. When she was born, it was obvious she was Hank's... the girl was his clone. They tried to make up for everything they said and did, but there's a reason I live here and they live in the city. Removing Callie from the home after she passed was an act of shame on their part. Hide the reminder of what they accused me of and maybe, just maybe, I would forgive them. Yet they seem to forget it happened over our anniversary, a constant reminder they were trying to woo me back at the same time our daughter tumbled to her death."

No one said a word. You could hear a pin drop with how quiet the room was after hearing that bomb drop.

Deanna shoved to her feet and held out a hand to Gareth. "Come with me. I want to show you something."

He did as she requested and stood but hesitated looking back at us.

"Oh no, they are coming too," Deanna announced. "I'm going to need their help. It's time to stop hiding things away. Callie would be pissed if she found out the family tried to forget about her."

As a group, we followed Deanna as she weaved through the house then stopped in front of a set of double doors. Pulling out a key attached to her necklace, Deanna unlocked the room and shoved open the doors. Tucked away in this room, farthest away from where it seems the family spends time together, was a Callie time capsule. The room was set up as I imagined it was when she was alive. It was clean and tidy, making it apparent Deanna took special care of every single thing. Pictures of a happy, smiling girl hung on the walls, some just by herself, others with one family member or another.

I was drawn to a picture of Gareth hoisting Callie up, looking as if he was going to toss her into a giant pile of leaves. The love and happiness shown in that one captured moment told me everything I needed to know. Gareth didn't see Callie just as his sister, but almost like a father to a daughter. He'd shared before that he was one of the only people who spent time with her with the age gap between the brothers. This helped me to understand the weight of responsibility he'd placed on himself and why her loss changed the way he viewed the world.

"You kept it... you kept everything," Gareth whispered, his voice choked up with emotion. "How... how long has this been here?"

I shifted slightly so I could look at Deanna as she sat on Callie's bed, waiting for her answer. "I was *never* going to let them throw away the last connection I had with Callie. Instead, I had them put it in storage, and once you left home, I was alone. Your fathers come once or twice a month to check in on me, but what they'd managed to repair between us was lost forever when my sweet angel died. So I had everything brought back where it should be, in her home, where she belonged. When I feel lonely, I come in here and talk to Callie, share my day, the town gossip, whatever I think might have interested her. However, I didn't realize how selfish I was for keeping this all to myself when you were hurting just as much. So, moving forward, I would like to bring Callie back into this home because she will always be part of this family."

Now, I was the one who had tears streaming down my face. None of them had gotten to heal from Callie's loss. They'd never been given the chance, and I, for one, believed this was the first step toward tending to those old wounds. This wouldn't fix everything, but it would be a start, and that's all anyone needs to start moving forward.

"Gareth, will you and one of your packmates please grab that family painting off the wall?" Deanna requested. "I want to put it back in its rightful place in the living room over the fireplace."

Lysse stepped up to help as the rest of us were instructed to grab this or that photo from around the room. We spent the rest of the evening bringing Callie out of hiding and proudly displayed all the Watson family members throughout the house. When all the pictures were dispersed, Deanna called it a night and herded us to the movie room.

"You guys enjoy yourself and stay up as late as you like," Deanna said as one of the staff brought in a tray full of drinks and snacks. "I'm a country girl at heart, early to bed, early to rise, as they say. Don't worry about any kind of schedule. You're all still on leave, take advantage of every moment you have just to be together. Sweet dreams, and I'll see you all tomorrow." Blowing us a kiss goodnight, Deanna headed off to her room.

It didn't take long before we were all cuddled up on the couch eating bowls of chocolate pudding. Vili chuckled at me as I licked the bowl clean, but it tasted *so* damn good. I glanced up at him with a scowl until he leaned down and licked a bit of pudding off the tip of my nose.

"Messy little kitten," he murmured, cuddling me closer and started to purr.

Gareth stood and collected everyone's bowls, then faced us with his arms crossed. "So about tomorrow..." He paused, then started again. "I would like to try for us all to go out on the ATVs. I'm not sure I can do it, but if that's the case, I'll take one of the horses out with you guys. The best way to see the ranch and the real beauty of it is to get out into the pasture lands."

"Don't stress, man. We'll figure out a way to explore the place so we all enjoy the day," Lysse assured him.

Warrick nodded. "Darn tootin'."

"Don't do that," Gareth muttered, rolling his eyes. "No one talks like that... it's just for the movies. Someone might think you're making fun of them and shoot your ass."

"What?" Warrick blurted, looking horrified.

"Yeah, everyone around here has a gun, and it's legal to openly carry. Trust me, it makes for incredibly safe neighborhoods, but there's a downside to everything like what could happen if they lose their temper," Gareth explained.

As the boys went back and forth about their feelings on the matter of guns, I poked Yun-Sun with my toe. He turned his attention to me with a questioning brow.

"Can I use your phone to send my mom an email?" I requested.

Without hesitation, Yun pulled out his phone and handed it over. Since everything with Randall had gone down, the police wanted to keep my phone to track any messages he might still be sending me. So, in the meantime, I used one of the guys' phones to keep in contact with my family. Pressing my thumb to the sensor, it unlocked, and I pulled up my emails, glancing over the junk. Then I spotted one that was from my school, which was odd since there wasn't any reason they should be contacting me.

MISS THATCHER,
THIS EMAIL IS BEING SENT AS CONFIRMATION
THAT THE PAINTINGS YOU SUBMITTED FOR
YOUR FINAL ART PROJECT HAVE BEEN
COLLECTED BY A MR. RANDALL STEELE.
THANK YOU FOR CHOOSING OUR SCHOOL TO
FURTHER YOUR EDUCATION, AND
CONGRATULATIONS AGAIN ON GRADUATING.
PROFESSOR ROBERTS, DEAN OF ARTS
GOLDEN OAKS UNIVERSITY OF FINE ARTS

I read the email twice, trying to figure out what the hell was going on. Looking at the date, I realized it had been sent four days ago. With traveling and time changes, I forgot to look at my email, but I hadn't realized it had been four days. Then another email appeared as I refreshed the inbox, and I froze—it was from Randall.

PAINTINGS - RANDALL STEELE
HI BUMBLEBEE,
I WENT BY YOUR HOME TODAY BUT DIDN'T SEE
ANY SIGN OF YOU, SO I GUESSED THOSE
ALPHAS MUST BE KEEPING YOU LOCKED AWAY
AT THEIR HOUSE. DO YOU KNOW WHAT I
FOUND WHEN I WENT THERE? SECURITY
GUARDS WITH ATTACK DOGS WALKING THE
PROPERTY. MY SWEET, FRAGILE BUMBLEBEE, I
TOLD YOU THEY WERE NO GOOD. NOW YOU'RE
TRAPPED, AND THEY'VE HIRED PEOPLE TO
PREVENT YOU FROM LEAVING.
GOD, I MISS YOU SO MUCH, BUMBLEBEE.
I NEEDED TO HAVE A PIECE OF YOU CLOSE, SO
I WENT TO YOUR SCHOOL. WHEN I CALLED,
THEY SAID YOUR PAINTINGS WERE STILL
THERE, AND I COULD PICK THEM UP FOR YOU.
YOUR TALENT IS AMAZING, AND I NAILED THE
ONE YOU DID OF US TO MY BEDROOM CEILING.
MOTHER WASN'T HAPPY ABOUT THAT, BUT
SHE'S THE REASON YOU WERE TAKEN FROM
ME IN THE FIRST PLACE. SHE TOLD ME I
NEEDED TO MOVE ON AND FIND A NEW OMEGA
TO LOVE, BUT I ONLY WANT MY BUMBLEBEE.
JUST KEEP HOLDING ON. I WILL FIND A WAY TO
GET YOU FREE FROM THOSE BASTARDS. THEN
WE CAN RUN AWAY WHEREVER WE WANT TO
GO AND START OUR LIFE.
P.S. YOU NEVER SAID THANK YOU FOR
HELPING YOU GET THAT SURGERY YOU
NEEDED. THAT'S A LITTLE RUDE, DON'T YOU
THINK?
YOUR REAL ALPHA, RANDALL

I froze, unable to speak, move, or do anything but stare at the words on the screen. My hand started to shake, and I lost my grip on the phone so it tumbled to my lap. The sound of my pulse in my ears roared so loud I couldn't hear anything else.

Randall had gone to my home, both my homes, looking for me. What would have happened if we weren't out of town?

"Bailey-Rose," Yun-Sun snapped, using his Alpha bark to force a reaction out of me. "Breathe, take a deep breath in for me, sweetheart."

Only then did I realize I'd been holding my breath.

Submitting to his command, I gasped for air as my whole body started to shake. Or maybe I'd already been shaking and didn't notice in my terror-filled state.

Lysse appeared before me, cupping my face in his hands and forcing me to look up at him. "Rosie, you are safe. We are thousands of miles away from home, and the only people who know we are here are your family and Gareth's. Randall cannot hurt you while you're here with us and Waffles to watch over you. Now you say it with me," Lysse instructed.

"I am safe," I managed to get out with a shaky voice. "I am not alone, my pack and Waffles are here to keep me safe."

"Good, that's good, Rosie," Lysse murmured, using his thumbs to wipe away my tears before releasing my face. "There's one other important thing you need to remember about all this... you fought back and won. Did you hear me?"

"Yes," I whispered, feeling my panic start to ebb, but I was nowhere near being all right.

"I want to hear you say it," he pressed. "Bailey-Rose Thatcher, tell me what you're not."

My lower lip quivered as I tried to keep my emotions from overwhelming me. "I-I'm not a victim. When he tried to take me, I fought like hell and survived."

"Damn straight, Care Bear," Warrick agreed from where he was standing behind the couch. "You are the bravest person I know, and no one can take that from you. Randall is a fucking bug under your heel and doesn't deserve to breathe the same air you do."

"Hey, man, you might want to tone it just a bit," Gareth murmured. "Anger isn't going to help us take care of her right now."

At some point during my meltdown, Vili had wrapped himself around me like a human blanket. It made me realize how Gareth had gotten so lost in his fear and panic about the ATV ride he couldn't hear me. Soft lips pressed against the back of my neck as a flood of emotions finally made their way through my mental block. All of my Alphas were mainlining every version of love and support you could describe in the spoken language to fight against the fear that still lingered.

"Sweetheart," Yun-Sun said, drawing my attention. "I need to make a call to the police and your brother about this. Do you want me to make that call in another room or stay here?"

Instantly, my hand shot out to grab his arm. "Here, stay here, please."

"Okay, *omae*, I'm not going anywhere... none of us will," Yun assured me.

The sound of ringing soon filled the room as Yun-Sun placed the call on speaker. I appreciated his efforts not to keep what was said hidden from me. There was no doubt in my mind that Eli and my Alphas hadn't told me everything, but I trusted it was for a good reason.

"Yun-Sun, good evening," Eli answered.

"Well, it was a good evening until a few minutes ago... the bastard sent Bailey-Rose an email," Yun explained.

There was a momentary pause, and I could feel Eli's anger emanating through the phone. "Am I on speaker?"

"You are, and she's right here," Yun answered.

"B, are you all right?" Eli asked.

"Yeah," I said, my voice cracking, but I cleared my throat and tried again. "I'm okay."

"I'm so sorry, little B. I thought for sure by now we'd have found him. The two men I hired have gotten way more leads than the police, but there's still something we're missing about this. Can one of you send me the email?" Eli asked.

"It should be in your inbox," Yun-Sun interjected. "I set it to you and the police. They might not be doing much, but we need to follow the letter of the law if he has someone powerful enough to protect him this long."

"Agreed," Eli grumbled. "You're back in Preidon, correct?"

"We're at my family's ranch in Molis. We planned to be here for the next two days, but if you think it's better for us to come back, we can," Gareth answered.

"No, I think it's best you stay, especially since he tried to sneak into both houses," Eli determined, clearly having read the email. "B, what painting is he referring to? When we find him, it will help to prove he's the one who wrote these emails."

Licking my lips since my mouth had gone bone dry, I tried to remember just what pieces I'd entered. We'd only been required to do four paintings showing various skills we'd learned throughout the four years, but I'd done double that, unsure which ones I wanted to submit. Then again, I left all eight with the school since I was so excited to return home. Then I remembered I'd used our picnic lunch date as inspiration for one of the paintings. The couple was sitting on a blanket in a field of wildflowers. That had to be the one Randall was talking about since none of the others had a couple pictured.

"Eli, ask Mom for emails I sent her about which painting to choose for my final grade. I took pictures of them all, and if I remember correctly, there will be one with a couple on a picnic. This way, they have proof the painting is mine, and it was last seen at my school," I instructed. "Oh, and Professor

Roberts sent me an email confirming the paintings were picked up by Randall."

"Got it, little B, that will help immensely," Eli said. "Did you also notice he mentioned staying with his mother? He didn't ever talk about her, did he?"

"No, he never talked about his parents, only to say they were well-off and high-profile," I offered.

I could hear the sound of Eli typing on his computer and muttering to himself about how clueless the police were. "Is there anything else I should know?"

Shrugging, I looked at the guys. "Not on my end... what about you guys?"

There was a chorus of no's, making me feel better. If they had known something, they would have admitted it even if they'd originally planned to keep me out of the loop.

"If that changes, call any time. I'll always answer," Eli stated.

When Eli said things like that, it wasn't just words—he meant it. That was my big brother in a nutshell—a man of unwavering loyalty and the person I would forever want in my corner.

"Don't worry about filling in the police... let me worry about that. You guys are still on bond leave and should be enjoying this time together, not having to deal with bullshit like this," Eli added. Hearing him swear had me raising a brow since that was rather unlike him.

"Thank you, Eli," Lysse said. "You have been invaluable in all this, and I hope you know how grateful we are."

Eli huffed out a laugh. "Here I was thinking you guys might resent me for taking charge. There are no thanks needed, not when it comes to family or my baby sister. They are the most important things to me."

"Until you find your own pack, you mean," I said, cutting

in. "It's time for you to think about yourself for once, big bro. You can't use me as an excuse anymore."

"*Bailey*..." Eli said in a warning tone. "This is not a topic I'm willing to discuss with you over the phone in front of your pack. Crew might let you get away with pulling that kind of stunt, but I won't. Now I'm going to hang up while you're going to behave for your Alphas and let them take care of you. I'll reach out if I have any updates on the situation. Goodnight."

BAILEY-ROSE

The screen blinked, alerting them that the call had ended and making it so Eli got the last word—like always.

"Ug, he always has to do things like that," I grumbled. "I'm just trying to look out for the man. The way he talks, you'd think I was asking about his sex life, which I do not want to know anything about."

Vili's body started to shake as he laughed silently behind me. "Oh, kitten, you are precious."

"What? I can't help but feel responsible for my brothers not having their own packs. They gave up everything to be there for me, and I just want to return the favor," I reasoned.

Lysse just shook his head and reached down to scoop me up. "Come on, you little troublemaker, let's get ready for bed. I think we've all had enough emotional upheavals for one day."

"Uh-huh, you're just trying to change the topic and shut me up with snuggles," I accused.

He glanced down at me. "I could think of something else to keep you quiet if you're not interested in snuggles."

My jaw literally dropped. "Ulysses, are you saying what I think you're saying?"

"I don't know, Rosie, what do you think I'm saying? The blush on your cheeks tells me it's something dirty," he teased as we headed down the hall to our rooms.

"Nope, your punishment is I'm not telling," I sniffed.

Lysse came to a stop and shifted his hold so when he pressed me against the wall, his hips kept me from sliding down. "I'm sorry, did I just hear that right? My Omega is going to punish *me*?"

Hearing the low tone of his voice with a hint of a growl in it had me instantly wet. "Y-yes," I managed to say unconvincingly.

"That won't do, Rosie, not at all," Lysse scolded, reaching up to hook two fingers at the point of my V-neck shirt. "Seems to me that you're the one in trouble here."

With a hard yank, Lysse ripped my shirt, pulled the cup of my bra down, and exposed my breast. I gasped as he latched his mouth over my nipple, then clamped my hands over my mouth to keep from moaning as I orgasmed right there in the hallway. Lysse knew what he was doing, freeing his mark so he could torture me with it. The way I was trapped against the wall prevented me from getting any stimulation on my clit. Even though Lysse was causing me to come over and over again, it didn't give the relief only a physical touch would bring.

Shuddering, my eyes rolled back in my head as a fourth orgasm rolled through my body. It was a struggle to keep my hands over my mouth, but if I didn't, I knew I'd wake the whole house up. *Maybe they were right, and I wasn't the best at keeping quiet.* Finally, Lysse released my nipple and grinned wolfishly, rather proud of himself for turning me into a puddle of pudding. He tugged at my hands, and the moment my lips were revealed, he dove in, urging me to open for him. There was no muffling my moans now as I melted against Lysse, surrendering to his claim over my body.

"Are you going to be good now, or do you need to be

punished further?" Lysse asked as he placed soft kisses along my neck.

"I'll be good," I answered and wrapped my arms around his neck. "I think you need to take me to bed now."

"We're not having sex when we get there," Lysse informed me.

That had me snapping to attention. "*What?*"

"It wouldn't be much of a punishment if I rewarded you after, now would it?" he reasoned.

Gaping at him like a fish, I didn't even know what to say to him. I looked around to see if the others would be on my side, but they were nowhere to be seen—*traitors.*

Flopping dejectedly against Lysse, I let him carry me the rest of the way to the bedroom. When he set me on the bed, I fell backward, making no effort to hide how I was feeling about this punishment.

Vili appeared above me and looked rather confused. "Kitten, why are you pouting?"

"Lysse said no sex," I answered.

"Ah." Vili nodded, then pulled me up into a sitting position. "Arms up."

Fearing they would extend my punishment, I did as I was asked. Swiftly, Vili removed my shirt and bra then slipped my silk nightie over my head so it fell into place. With a playful shove, I was once more lying on the bed as Vili tugged off my pants, quickly following up with removing my socks. The bed shifted, and Yun-Sun pulled me into his lap so we were nose to nose.

"Sweetheart, there is no reason to pout. Sex isn't the only way to show love and to receive comfort from your pack," Yun commented, brushing his nose along mine before kissing me in an unhurried fashion as if he was savoring every second. "You are looking for the easy way out, knowing if you get us all riled up, we'll fuck you till you pass out, and you won't have to fear your sleep."

I jerked back, looking at him. "How..."

"*Omae*, you are not one to be a brat for no reason," Yun countered. "Lysse is the one you know the best, so it was easy to find the buttons to push. However, you forgot he knows you just as well, and instead of him playing into your trap, he turned the tables."

Sighing, I touched Yun-Sun's chest and admitted the truth. "I didn't even realize I was purposefully doing that until you came out and said it. What if my nightmares come back? I've been doing so well since we left for this trip."

"If they do, we will be right here with you," he whispered, leaning his forehead against mine. "It was hard for us all when we couldn't hold you in our arms to keep the nightmares at bay. Now, nothing is preventing your Alphas from coming to your rescue."

There was a bark from Nugget, who'd joined us on the bed, his fluffy tail wagging. Grinning at him, I held out a hand—all the encouragement he needed to leap into my arms. "Nugget will be there too, just in case you need backup, right?"

He let out another bark before attacking my face with kisses, which had me laughing. Waffles, feeling like he was being left out of the recognition, added his two cents with a deep *woof*. Nugget wriggled out of my arms and bounced across the large bed to where Waffles rested his head. It was adorable to see the two of them interact as polar opposites as possible.

I shivered as Yun kissed his mark on my neck. Through our bond, I could tell he wasn't trying to start anything—he just loved seeing his claim on my body. "I love you too," I whispered.

"Does that mean you're not upset with us anymore?" Yun asked, a smirk tugging at his lips.

Letting out a dramatic sigh, I pressed my hand to my forehead like I was going to faint. "I might waste away with a serious case of bluevaries, but I'll soldier on."

"How brave of you, Care Bear," Warrick teased as he walked over to the bed, then tackled me out of Yun's lap to tickle me. "I'm not sure I would be as forgiving if you left me with blue balls. It just shows how magnanimous you really are."

Refusing to surrender, I waited to call 'uncle' until I was crying and out of breath. "Uncle, uncle, uncle. I give up."

Instantly, Warrick stopped his assault on my ribs and flipped us over so I was sprawled against his chest. I could hear his heart beating almost as fast as mine was as we gasped for breath. "That was just mean, Warrick," I managed to say, poking him in the side.

The strangled cry and convulsion that came as a response to that had me sitting up. "Oh my God, you're super sensitive to tickling too, aren't you?"

"I don't know what you mean?" Warrick countered, trying to play off his reaction.

Before I could test out my theory, a hand grabbed me and pulled me off my potential victim. "Baby girl, this is the opposite of getting ready for bed," Gareth pointed out.

"He started it," I argued.

Gareth just gave me a look, telling me he wasn't falling for the bait. Instead, he grabbed the covers and pulled them back before plopping me down. Then he slid under the covers, got comfortable, and tugged me onto his chest. As if to ensure I wasn't going anywhere, he wrapped his arms around me and closed his eyes, letting out a contented sigh. "This is perfect."

"You sure about that?" I questioned. "It can't be comfortable having me lay on you like this."

"Oh, it's fantastic having you sprawled out on my chest," Gareth countered. "Plus, if you have a nightmare, I'll know right away so I can wake you up."

Clearly, I wasn't going to win this fight, so I did the next best thing—I wriggled up his body so I could get to my mark on his neck and let my teeth scrape over it nice and slow. Before my mind could register the sound, the sting on my ass told me I'd just been spanked.

"Try that again, Bailey-Rose, and I promise your night won't end as you think it will," Gareth warned, pinning me with his gray-blue eyes.

Biting my lip, I nodded and slid back down so I could rest my head on his chest. Instantly, he started to purr and combed his fingers through my hair, rewarding me for my choice. Damn them for always knowing what I really needed, even if I didn't. Unable to fight against the skills of an Alpha, I drifted off to sleep.

Thankfully, I slept soundly without any nightmares and woke up to the sight of all my guys clumped together on the bed. It was more than a tight fit, but they'd made it work so they could all be here for me. These men never ceased to amaze me with the lengths they would go to ensure I was safe and happy.

Deanna had already eaten breakfast but left us a note she was out working in her garden. The house staff got us settled at the table and brought out a feast of breakfast foods. Many of the things were not on the heart-healthy diet, but I decided that since this was vacation, it wouldn't hurt to indulge.

"Gareth, did your mom make all of this, or do you have a cook?" Ulysses asked, shoving his face with a second helping of biscuits and gravy.

Lysse had caught Gareth just as he'd taken a bite and hurried to swallow, using his coffee to help wash it down. "We have a cook that Mom will call in if we need help for a party or something. Otherwise, you're eating the real deal, all home-cooked by the master chef herself."

"Seriously, this is the best food I've ever eaten," Warrick mumbled, his mouth full of eggs.

I poked at the grits, unsure what to make of the stuff. "I have to agree with you on that, but I'm not sure grits are on my list of favorites. Why is it so... gravelly?"

"It not gravel, it cornmeal," Vili corrected, scooping up a large spoonful of the stuff. "I find it very tasty."

This was just going to be one of those things I was willing to give a chance but wouldn't be something I'd try again. Not wanting it to go to waste, I slid the bowl over to Vili, who was more than happy to finish it off. My favorite thing had to be the blueberry muffins, reminding me of the ones my mother and I made.

"Those are made with berries from her garden," Gareth shared as I grabbed my third one out of the basket. "Mom believes the best food starts with the best ingredients, so she likes to grow all she can to control the quality. Guess it's not surprising she ended up bonded with a pack who runs a cattle ranch."

Once we finished stuffing our faces, Gareth took us out to the garden. Now, when I think of a home garden, my mind pictures a small plot of land with vegetables and such growing. Deanna had other visions of what she wanted from a garden. The woman had a damn greenhouse that you could fit an entire house in. I suppose if you wanted to have fresh food through the winter, this was the way to do it.

"Oh, you're all up and happening, I see," Deanna called, waving at us with a gloved hand.

We walked down the path between the corn and tomatoes to reach her. Deanna tugged off her gloves and gave us all big hugs.

"Did you sleep well? The beds were comfortable? It's been so long since anyone has used them... I wasn't sure," Deanna asked.

"I slept like a rock," I answered, then jerked my thumb at the guys. "Not sure about them since they all decided to sleep in the big bed with me."

"Oh?" she questioned, cocking her head slightly, reaching out to brush my cheek. "Are you all right, darling? That sounds like you had your Alphas rather worried about you."

Unsure how to answer, I looked at Yun-Sun for guidance. He took the hint and gently gripped the back of my neck, rubbing a thumb over his mark as he explained about Randall. Deanna looked absolutely horrified and pulled me into another hug.

"You poor thing, how could someone be so awful?" Deanna demanded, squeezing me so tight I was worried I wouldn't be able to breathe. Finally, she let me go, holding me at arm's length, a serious expression on her face. "You are more than welcome to stay here as long as you like. We can change up the guest room to make it more comfortable for you all. It's no trouble at all."

Smiling at my mother-in-law, I leaned in to hug her this time. "It means the world to me you offered that to us. My hope is that he will be caught soon, and my life will find a new normal with my family. Either way, I refuse to let him keep me from my home, even if it scares me to return, knowing he's still out there."

Deanna sniffed, cupping my face in her hands. "What a brave, beautiful soul you are, Bailey-Rose. My son is a lucky man, and I'm so relieved to know he has you to look after him."

"Lately, it's been them looking after me, but I will always be there for him," I assured her.

Quickly, Deanna brushed away a tear as she turned away from us to collect herself. "I don't want to keep you if you plan on exploring the ranch. They said it's probably going to rain later today, so you best get a move on. Oh," she called out as she spun around. "Sugar bear, there's a present for you in the machine shed. I hope I picked out the right thing. It was a bit of a rush to get it here before you got up."

Gareth looked puzzled. "You didn't have to get me anything, Mom."

"Yes, I did. Once you see it, you'll understand," Deanna assured him.

"Dee," I cut in, resting a hand on Waffles' big head. "Would you mind if I left these two here with you? I promise they won't cause any trouble, but there's no way we can take them with us."

Deanna smiled and clapped her hands. "I'd be glad for the company. Don't you fret. I'll make sure these two are looked after. You go have fun."

Giving Waffles his commands, he laid down right where he was with a heavy sigh. I had no doubt he'd be asleep in no time—it was his favorite hobby when he was off duty. Nugget, on the other hand, would happily be Deanna's shadow for the foreseeable future. Gareth kissed his mother's cheek before leading the way out of the greenhouse.

The machine shed wasn't really a shed. It was a barn full of equipment they needed to run things around the ranch. Massive tractors and trailers meant to be filled with hay took up most of the space. However, it wasn't hard to figure out what Deanna had delivered since it had a giant red bow on the hood.

"Holy shit," Gareth swore as he walked around the shiny new off-road vehicle. "This is amazing. Look, it has a roll cage and a harness so even if the thing gets flipped, I'll be fine. Not to mention it's a two-seater so I can call dibs on getting Bailey-Rose to ride with me."

I could feel his excitement as he explored his new toy's features. Deanna had not only given Gareth more than a new ride but the ability to enjoy a hobby he'd lost the day Callie died. Now he could relax, knowing this vehicle would protect against the same tragedy happening again.

"So, are you just going to drool all over it, or are you going for a ride?" I asked.

Gareth scooped me up and twirled around before setting me on the hood. "Oh, we're going for a ride, all right, but first, we need to get your helmet on."

"Helmet? Why would I need one of those?" I questioned, looking at the thing. "I'm going to be strapped in, so I doubt that's a necessary step."

"Baby girl, keeping you safe is always a necessary step," Gareth pointed out, pressing a quick kiss to my lips. "If you want to come on this ride, you're going to wear a helmet, and not just you, but all of us will be wearing them."

Sighing, I gave in because there was no way I was going to miss out on this adventure. It would appear that Deanna not only had the off-road vehicle dropped off but new helmets for us as well. She'd gotten black for all the guys and a purple one for me that was small enough to fit just right. Glancing at the label, I noticed it said child's size—figures. Now that everyone was suited up, Gareth helped me climb in and get buckled up. With how snug the harness fit, I wasn't going anywhere, no matter what the hell happened on this ride.

"Okay, so follow my lead. I'm going to take us all the way out to the back pastures then head back in. This way, if or when it rains, we'll be heading home instead of having to turn around," Gareth explained. The guys all gave him a thumbs-up and started up their rides.

Seeing the grin on Gareth's face as he flipped a few levers and hit the start button made up for how damn loud this thing was. The other part I didn't count on was how bumpy it would be, but then again, I'd never been off-roading. Whoops of joy came from the guys as we finally made it to open pasture land and gunned it. Once I overcame the slight terror of how narrow the track was and how close the massive pine trees were on either side, I started to enjoy myself.

I was finding it was harder than I realized not to panic and worry over things like I'd had to for my whole life. Taking the world by the horns and living it up took work. Every instinct I had was to protect myself from anything that might cause my heart harm. Six weeks ago, this ride would have sent me to the hospital, but now I'm giggling and tossing my hands in the air as we flew over a bunny hill.

"We got air on that one," Gareth yelled. "God, I forgot just how much fun this was."

Just as we turned, breaking free from the forested area of the ranch and out on the open grazing, the wind shifted. The temperature dropped ten degrees, making me shiver, and the once bright blue sky turned gray. Gareth slowed to a stop, waiting for the others to catch up, shutting off the engine so we could talk.

"Well, it looks like the weatherman was wrong, but that happens this far into the mountains. If the storm is blowing in this fast, it will leave just as quickly, but we need to get to shelter now. There is an annex hay barn not too far from here that will be our best bet," Gareth explained.

The guys all nodded, and engines started up once more. This time, there was no zooming off. Gareth drove more cautiously as he navigated his way to the hay barn. I was a little worried when I noticed it was made of metal, but the chances of it getting hit by lightning was low, right?

"I'm gonna open the doors. Don't move," Gareth ordered.

Offering him a thumbs-up, he gave me another warning look then took off. Ulysses pulled up and hopped off, helping Gareth wrestle open the massive doors. It didn't look like this place was used for anything more than storage, and the doors weren't willing to slide open. Warrick had to help out, and the air was filled with the shrill shriek of scraping metal. They'd only gotten one side open, but it was more than enough space to get the ATVs inside. Yun was the last one in, and as if in perfect timing, the clouds unleashed the rain.

BAILEY-ROSE

The rain sounded so loud in the metal building I had to cover my ears. Then the ground shook with the rumble of the thunder, making me panic just a little that we might never make it out of this hay barn. Arms wrapped around me, and I was engulfed in the sweet, nutty scent of Warrick.

"It's okay, Care Bear, we'll be just fine," he murmured, his lips brushing my ear.

I nodded, taking in slow, deep breaths of his soothing scent, letting it help calm my anxiety. After a few minutes, the rain started to lighten up so it wasn't quite as loud in the barn. Lightning still crackled through the sky, followed by the booming thunder, but it didn't seem as ominous.

"Hey, come over here. I found a few saddle blankets left out here," Gareth called from the far corner. "Looks like some of the workers have been using this place to take naps or something."

Warrick kept me tucked under his arm as we made our way over. I had to agree with Gareth. It looked like someone had made a small area with old hay piled up with some woven blankets covering it. The space appeared to fit maybe three people lying down but probably only two comfortably. Warrick sat, pulled me onto his lap, settled me close, and rested his chin on my shoulder.

"So, how far out are we?" Yun-Sun asked as he sat against the giant wall of hay that took up half the barn.

Gareth sprawled out next to Warrick, looking up at the metal roof. "About as far out as we can get. That's why we have this barn here. We keep some backup hay out here just in case there's ever a drought or something else that causes the grass not to grow well. This way we can keep the cattle fed but still say they are free-range. I was just about to have us start heading back through the grazing areas when the storm hit."

"That was pretty amazing timing," Lysse commented, pulling a piece of hay out of the bail to chew on, only to scowl then toss it aside.

"Weather here like Numoland," Vili pointed out. "In the mountains, things change fast. One minute sunny and bright, then *bam,* it goes dark. Only for us it's with blizzards, not rain."

"I've never been in a blizzard," I shared. "Windermere doesn't really get them. We're lucky if we get actual snow with the cold fronts."

"This why I like Windermere, mild weather, no natural disasters... it is good," Vili said, nodding.

Gareth sat up and turned to look at me. "Have you ever been somewhere with enough snow to cover everything, turning the world completely white?"

I shook my head. "Nope, only seen pictures."

"Oh, then we are definitely coming back out here in the winter. I'll teach you how to ski or snowboard... you'll love it," Gareth assured me. "Not to mention it's the best feeling to come back inside with a fire burning and curled up in a blanket with some hot cocoa."

"I would be fine with that right about now," I mumbled, feeling a little chilled in my jeans and tank top.

Warrick dropped a kiss on my shoulder as his hands slid

up my ribs to cup my breasts. "I can think of something else we could do to warm you up."

My breath hitched as his fingers found my nipples already hard from being chilled. It would seem that my efforts to get them to fuck me last night weren't a total waste. I could see the simmering lust and need in all their gazes as they watched Warrick slip his hands under my shirt.

He groaned loudly. "You naughty girl, how did I miss you weren't wearing a bra?"

"I guess you weren't paying attention, distracted by food and off-roading," I teased.

As if Warrick needed to prove to everyone I wasn't wearing a bra, he rucked up my shirt, exposing me to my Alphas. "God, why are you so fucking perfect? I mean, look at these tits so hard and ready, begging to be touched and sucked."

Gareth leaned in and shoved one of Warrick's hands out of the way so he could wrap his lips around my nipple. Moaning, I arched, giving him better access as my fingers sank into his thick, curly hair.

"*Yeees*," I cried as I felt Gareth's teeth scrap over the tip of my nipple.

"I wonder... do you think you could come just from us playing with your nipples?" Warrick asked, his nose rubbing against his mark on my ear. "No way to know unless we try, right, Gareth?"

Releasing my nipple with a pop, Gareth grinned at me. "Oh, I'm more than happy to test out that theory. It's not like we have much else to do while waiting for the rain to stop."

"Good point," Warrick agreed, tracing his finger around the outline of my areola. "The pursuit of knowledge is always a worthy way to spend your time, and I want to be an expert in Bailey-Roseology."

Hearing Warrick talk like that, I wanted to laugh, but my breath was stolen away when Gareth pulled on both my nipples. He wasn't rough—it was more the tension he kept on them as he kissed his mark on my neck. Slowly, he released them, massaging the whole breast, letting his thumbs flick over the taut nipple. I could tell I was sopping wet as my pussy begged for the attention to shift downward.

"What do you think, baby girl... can you stand to only have us touching your tits until you come? The way you're whimpering right now tells me you're becoming very needy," Gareth commented as he rolled the hardened buds between his fingers.

No words came out of my mouth, only sounds that no one would mistake for anything other than desperation. Dipping his head, Gareth stroked his tongue over my sensitive flesh. Faster, slower, faster, slower, driving me to the edge and keeping me there. My head rested on Warrick's shoulder with my eyes closed as I willed my body to just let me have my release, but it refused to listen.

Then I felt hands undo my jeans button and heard the telltale sound of the zipper being pulled down. My whole body shivered as that hand slipped past my underwear and cupped my pussy. Feeling his hand there was torture as he refused to apply any pressure to my clit or slide a finger into my wanton pussy.

"Please, please let me come," I begged, opening my eyes to meet Warrick's. "One touch, that's all I need, one finger to press against my clit. *Please*," I whined.

At first, it looked like Warrick was going to fight against the pull of my whine, but just like an Alpha's bark, some things you just couldn't ignore. So he did just as I asked and pressed a finger right to the magic 'O' button. A scream tore out of me as I came. It felt like my body was erupting with pleasure as Gareth continued to torture my nipples. Soon, my body was shaking as Warrick made slow circles around my clit, drawing out the climax as long as he could. When I couldn't take anymore, I slumped, turning boneless in his lap.

Fuck, that was amazing.

"Holy shit," Lysse swore. "That has got to be one of the sexiest things I've ever seen."

Cracking open an eye, I found him kneeling nearby with his hand wrapped around his dick. In fact, Yun and Vili were in roughly the same position, each eagerly watching as their packmates tortured their Omega with pleasure.

In the beginning, I'd been a little self-conscious about them all being around when I was having sex with any of my other Alphas, but I got over that rather quickly. I'd been afraid it was the beach house packmoon effect, but seeing them like this and how turned on I was told me not to worry. Being watched and feeling the need and desire of each of my guys added a whole other level to our intimacy.

"So, how many licks do we think it will take to get me to orgasm?" I asked. "Since it's for science and all."

"Gareth, out the way," Warrick ordered as he lifted me off his lap and placed me on all fours.

Before I could question what he was doing, my pants were yanked down, and Warrick's mouth was on my pussy. A sharp moan burst from me as I fought back the urge to cry. Finally, my pussy was getting the attention she deserved. Pausing, Warrick used both hands to spread my cheeks to give him better access to both my holes. He'd found a new way to edge me, playing with one until I was ready to pop, only to switch to the other. When I felt his thumb slide into my ass, my arms gave out, and I crumpled. Only his hands on my hips kept my ass in the air as he feasted.

"Come here, sweetheart. You can rest your head on my lap," Yun offered as he maneuvered me so my head rested on one of his bare thighs. Of course, this put me face-to-face with his dick as it stood watching, ready for action whenever it was called onto the field.

Unable to just lay there and leave this faithful friend who'd given me many, many happy moments, I reached out and started to stroke that velvety fella. Yun hissed as he sucked in a breath, his hand fisting my hair he'd been stroking. I ran into a small problem, though—things were a little dry, and I was worried about how sensitive the skin was. So I pulled his cock down so I could suck on it as I rested in his lap.

"Fuuck, your mouth feels like heaven," Yun-Sun bit out between clenched teeth. "Good girl, take that dick nice and deep, and let me feel your throat wrap around my cock."

Over the past few weeks, I'd become a *huge* fan of dirty talk, especially when it was tied in with them praising me. I would stretch the limits of what I could do to please them and be rewarded with praise and orgasms.

"I can't hold back anymore. I need to be inside her," Warrick announced.

Everything paused as I was stripped out of my clothes. The guys had it easy—they just let their pants fall to their ankles and were ready to bump and grind. Warrick picked me up and slowly impaled me on his dick, which had us both moaning and groaning. The feel of him sliding into my wet, needy pussy was pure fucking bliss. Once he'd filled me with his cock, I felt someone step up behind me.

"*Omae*, I'm going to fill your perfect ass with my cock. Then Warrick and I are going to fuck you till you scream and pump you full with our cum," Yun-Sun informed me as he slid two fingers in my ass, making sure I was ready for him. "Don't hold back. We're all alone out here with no one to hear your sexy moans."

He didn't need to worry about me holding back. I was so damn turned on, there was nothing anyone could do to keep me from voicing my pleasure as he thrust into me.

"That's it, sing for us, Care Bear," Warrick urged as he and Yun found a rhythm.

With my legs wrapped around Warrick's waist and their hands gripping me tightly, I wasn't worried in the slightest about being dropped. Showing that trust, I leaned back into Yun and curled an arm around his neck, drawing him down so I could kiss him. I was more than happy to oblige Yun-Sun feasting on my mouth while Warrick took the opportunity to suck on my nipples. They were sensitive from Gareth's attention, but it was a good pain, making the pleasure I was feeling even better.

It wasn't long before I was coming again, shattering in their arms and clamping down on their cocks. Now, all three of us were crying out as they continued to fuck me through my climax. Neither of them lasted much longer as their knots began to swell.

"What do you want, sweetheart? Do you want us to fuck our knots deep inside you, or would you rather be ravaged by your other Alphas right away?" Yun asked.

How the hell was I supposed to be able to answer that right now?

"No knot," I managed to get out in time for them both to pull back.

Yun's mouth latched onto his mark on my neck, rocketing me into another orgasm as their hot cum shot into me. I milked them for all they were worth as Yun forced me to come over and over again. When they were finally finished with me, I was shaking at the slightest touch from being overstimulated.

"Come here, kitten," Vili cooed, taking me from Warrick and Yun.

Someone had put one of the blankets over the hay bale, making a seat. Vili cuddled me on his lap, letting me sink on his cock. Whimpering, I nuzzled into his neck, clinging to him as he gently stroked my back.

"Shh, my precious kitten," he soothed. "Just relax and let your body adjust."

My sweet, sensitive Alpha just held me as I collected myself, enjoying the feeling of him inside me. I started to rock my hips, not anything major, almost as if we were on a boat rocking back and forth. Vili's hands cupped my ass, urging me to move a little faster as he thrust up as I rocked to create the perfect tempo.

"Rosie, is it okay if I join in?" Lysse asked.

I lifted my head and smiled, reaching out to him. "My Alphas are always welcome."

He cupped my face and kissed me deeply before releasing me to drop to his knees. Vili widened his legs, giving Lysse more room to get closer. I rested my head back on Vili's shoulder, taking a deep breath and relaxing as Lysse found his way. Something felt a little off, but it wasn't until the head of Lysse's cock slipped into my already full pussy I realized what had happened.

"Wait," I gasped, slapping a hand to his chest.

"Shit, I'm sorry, Rosie," Lysse swore. "Take a deep breath and I'll pull out."

"Hold on, just give me a second," I said.

There was a slight ache at first as my pussy stretched, but it subsided. The first time I'd been truly knotted, the same thing had happened. My body hadn't expected the feeling, but once it understood what was going on, I'd managed just fine. This was a little more than any of their knots, but I knew my body could take it. I was fucking drenched with slick and Warrick's cum, so lubrication wasn't going to be an issue.

"We can try it if you two are okay being this... close," I offered.

Vili and Lysse looked at each other, but neither were bothered by what happened. I could tell through our bond they'd been more worried about me.

"Kitten, if you are fine, that is what matters," Vili answered. "I am happy to try new things."

Lysse wrapped his arms around me so he could cup my breasts. "Here, let me help you relax."

With a gentle touch, Lysse slowly traced the spot where he claimed me. The sensation went straight to my clit, pulling a long, deep moan from me. It was a sensation unlike anything else when my guys interacted with their marks, and there was no good way to describe the feeling of this kind of intimacy.

"That's it, good girl, just relax and let us take care of you," Lysse praised, kissing along my shoulder. "I'm going to stay just like this as Vili starts to move. We're going to ease our way into this, all right?"

I hummed my agreement as I closed my eyes, allowing myself just to feel. Vili resumed his gentle rocking, but because I was sitting on his lap, it moved me as well. This meant he was thrusting me onto Lysse's cock bit by bit.

"Oh my God," I whimpered, feeling so full and over-whelmed by the sensation of feeling them both inside. "Don't stop, it's okay. I can take more."

"Are you sure?" Vili pressed. "There is no need to do this now. We can take time, build up."

Gingerly, I removed Vili's glasses and nuzzled my nose against his. "Don't stop," I reiterated before claiming his lips to keep him from arguing further.

In an effort to stop further argument, I took matters into my own hands and sat up, forcing more of Lysse's cock into my greedy pussy. There was a chorus of swearing from them as Lysse was now balls deep, nestled nicely against Vili's cock.

I spotted Gareth watching, eyes wide, burning with need as he watched. Pre-cum was leaking out of his dick as it bobbed, desperate for someone to offer it some relief. Crooking a finger, I called him over, never wanting one of my Alphas to be in as much discomfort as he looked to be.

"Can I help with that?" I asked once he reached us.

Gareth seemed to glitch at that question, unable to answer, but that could have been caused by my hand wrapping around his needy dick. Tugging him a little closer so he was right behind Vili's shoulder, I took him in my mouth.

"Ahg," Gareth cried out, his hips thrusting forward, hitting the back of my throat. "Fuck yes, I love the feel of your mouth, so warm and wet, begging for my cock."

The warmth flooded me as I felt how pleased these three Alphas were, and I started to purr.

"Shit, shit, shit," Lysse cursed as his hips bucked, thrusting into me. "Rosie, if you keep that up, I'm not going to last much longer."

Vili's fingers dug into my hips as he tried to find some coordination with Lysse, but they were all too far gone. As they rutted into me, sending me crashing into orgasm after orgasm, I struggled to remember my name. Gareth fisted my hair and used it to angle my head the way he wanted, fucking my mouth with abandon. I'd experienced what I thought was rough sex with my guys, but the blissed-out sensation I was experiencing now told me they'd been holding back. I choked a few times on Gareth's dick but managed to recover and was glad I hadn't worn any makeup.

"Ah, shit, I can't hold it, I'm coming," Lysse roared and yanked himself out of me. The next moment, I felt something warm spilling onto my back.

However, my attention was pulled away from that as Gareth slammed his cock down my throat. I felt his knot starting to swell, so I shoved him back enough that I wasn't face-locked to his cock. It's happened on occasion, but I learned that while I can do it, my jaw ached for a full day after. As I swallowed Gareth's cum, Vili's fingers worked my clit as his knot swelled, locking us together. Having been bombarded with sensations and orgasms, I shouldn't have been surprised when I came once more then passed the hell out.

Ulysses

The storm didn't end as quickly as Gareth assumed it would. Thankfully, there was a break in the rain, and we booked it back to the house as quickly as we could. It ended up working out for the best since we'd worn our girl out. I can't blame her for passing out after taking on all five of us guys, who'd been a little pent-up. Going from having sex all day every day and having to adjust to a more realistic expectation was hard.

I now understood why people talked about their bonding leave and how they wished they could go back to those days. All you needed to worry about was you, your Omega, and your pack— that's it. Everything else could be put on the back burner to deal with once you came down out of the bonding haze. The thing was, that haze lasted a lot longer than one month. It was fucking hard to keep my hands off Rosie and not resent her clothes for being closer to her body than I was. Yet we were in someone else's house, and walking around naked wasn't going to fly. I suppose I would want the same respect from a guest staying with us, so I couldn't be that upset.

However, that didn't keep me from slipping my hand under Rosie's shirt so I could rest my hand on her stomach while we watched a movie. A fluffy blanket covered her, so it wasn't like I was flaunting her bare skin to the room. She giggled as my thumb brushed over her belly button, and I couldn't help but grin. God, that sound did something to me in a primal way. It fulfilled a need deep down fueled by my Alpha instincts, which constantly pushed me to ensure our Omega was happy and safe.

"Lysse, stop," Rosie whispered.

"Stop what?" I asked, this time purposefully tracing her belly button, knowing full well she was super ticklish there.

Slapping her hand over mine to keep it from moving, I snorted, trying to keep my laughter to myself. Waffles lifted his head, looking up at me with a warning in his expression. You wouldn't think a dog could communicate that clearly with a look alone, but Waffles wasn't just any dog. He wasn't like Nugget, who wanted pets and cuddles from Rosie, but there was no doubt in my mind that Waffles adored Bailey-Rose. The silent suffering he endured as Rosie put his fur in pigtails or painted his nails was enough to prove it.

Another thing we Alphas figured out was when it came to Waffles, he would always put Rosie first. Something I didn't know I would value as much as I do. Knowing we were nearing the end of our leave and I'd have to go back to work, I was comforted to know he was with her. Yes, Gareth got Waffles because of the Randall situation. Yet the reality was with as big of a heart as Bailey-Rose had, she could easily end up in a situation she didn't anticipate and might need a little backup.

The vibration from my phone jolted me out of my thoughts as I pulled it out of my back pocket. Seeing it was Eli, I instantly answered and waved for the guys to pause the movie. "Hey, Eli," I answered.

"Do you have a minute? Are the others with you?" Eli asked.

"Yeah, we're just hanging out watching movies. Give me a sec, and I'll put you on speaker," I said, sitting up and turning up the speaker volume. "Okay, go ahead."

"The cops just arrested Randall Steele," Eli announced.

Everyone erupted in cheers at hearing the news. Vili stood and clapped with how excited he was.

"Guys, there's a catch," Eli said loudly, cutting off any further excitement. "Steele isn't his real last name, or I suppose it's not his legal last name, which is why it was so hard to find him."

"I don't understand. Why does that matter?" I questioned. "Legal or not, it doesn't change what he did."

"Yeah, well, when your mother is the highly regarded Scent Matcher, Mira Chambers, it matters," Eli stated.

Shock slammed into me hearing the name of the woman we'd met with on the day of the attack. "*What*?" I snapped. "His mother is a fucking Scent Matcher?"

"Hoooly shiiit," Warrick said, drawing out the words.

"Wait, you mean that bitch we met with is his fucking mother?" Gareth demanded. "I knew that whole thing was a bunch of bullshit. The last thing she expected us to do was fight to keep Bailey-Rose. What, did she plan to give Randall our leftovers if we did reject our Omega?"

"Eli," Yun-Sun cut in, waving for everyone else to shut up. "What haven't you told us yet?"

There was a slight pause, and I could feel Rosie's panic building the longer the silence went on. "His mother is claiming we have the wrong person. That Randall couldn't have been the one to attack Bailey-Rose or to be stalking her. Claims that Randall Steele and Randall Chambers are two different people, and we've got the wrong man arrested. She's demanding the police let him go at once."

"No, they can't do that, Eli," Rosie blurted. "We have video proof it was him, not to mention all the phone records and texts."

"Yes, we have all that for a man named Randall Steele.

Mrs. Chambers' lawyer is demanding proof be shown that Randall Chambers is Randall Steele," Eli explained, his tone gentle, trying not to upset her even more.

Rosie looked at me with desperation, begging for me or anyone to find a solution. Her head whipped around to Yun. "Wait, what about the pack he told me about? Could those records be under his legal name, and that's why nothing came up? If they come forward about him assaulting their Omega, it wouldn't matter if we could prove what he did to me."

Yun frowned as he processed that idea. "Eli, do you know if the cops found anything on Randall Chambers?"

"As far as they can tell, he's been a model citizen. Although, with a mother as powerful as his, I wouldn't be surprised if she got his record wiped or paid people to keep things off his record. They'd have to get a court order to look at the Scent Matchers' official records."

Yun scoffed at that. "No one has ever been able to get a judge to approve one of those." Leaning forward, he rubbed his head with both hands before shooting to his feet and pacing.

"How long can they hold him?" I asked.

"Twenty-four hours," Eli sighed. "If they don't have proof by then, they'll have to let him go."

"Wait," Yun shouted. "What if Bailey-Rose picked him out of a lineup? They can't deny an eye-witness, especially when it's the victim of the crime."

"No," Eli barked. "Bailey-Rose is not going anywhere near him."

"I don't like the idea either, but I would much rather get this man put in jail," Yun argued. "All right. What if we could have your investigator look at the hospital records and see if there's anything about his previous pack? There can't be many Omegas who were admitted for being attacked."

"Oh, there might be a report about a fight too," Rosie added. "He attacked one of the other Alphas when they refused to let him see her. They called security, but he ran off which is when he met me."

"It's worth a try, but I don't know if they can find that information in time. Hospitals are not known for giving out information," Eli warned.

Bailey-Rose's hands were curled tightly around the blanket in her lap as if she were trying to hold herself together. It was hard to get a feel for her emotions since they were changing faster than I could track them. Then she started to chew on her bottom lip as her brows furrowed. I knew that look. I'd seen it on her face anytime she needed to face up to something that scared her. As if to echo what I already knew, a tidal wave of determination poured out of her.

"Eli," Rosie said, cutting off the conversation between her brother and Yun. "We're coming home, I'm getting off the plane, and I'm going to the police station."

"I said no, Bailey-Rose, that's not going to happen," Eli stated.

There haven't been many times that I've seen these two siblings fight, but from what Crew told me, it was legendary.

"Eli, I love you, and I know you want what's best for me, but you can no longer dictate what I do. I am a bonded Omega, and the only people who can keep me from doing this are them," Bailey-Rose countered and took a deep breath, trying to calm the adrenaline flowing through her. "I'm not asking… I'm telling you that's what we're doing."

Before I could even think to stop her, Rosie reached out and ended the call. While I understood they were siblings, I somehow got the feeling *no one* hung up on Eli Thatcher. Instantly, my phone was ringing, and Eli's name popped up on the screen. I went to answer, but Rosie hit the fuck-off button and turned on the do-not-disturb mode.

"He will stop calling eventually," Rosie commented as she got up from the couch.

"Kitten, I think we need to talk," Vili pointed out, catching her wrist as she passed by. "No, do not glare at me. This affects us all, so we will take a moment to talk as a family."

"He's right, baby girl, and before you get all fired up, none of us are saying no," Gareth reasoned. "Please, just let us walk through what this means for you to do this. There is nothing we want more than for this to be over, but not at the expense of your well-being."

She relented and let Vili tug her to sit next to him. "Tell us why."

Rosie frowned. "What?"

"Why you? Why not find other pack and arrest him again for that crime?" Vili clarified.

Not expecting that question, she needed to sit with that a moment before she answered. "Because if I can do something that will get him off the streets and put away so he can't do this to me or anyone else ever again, then that's what I'll do. I would never be able to look myself in the mirror if I didn't. What if he did this to another Omega, and they couldn't or didn't fight back? Part of the blame would be on me."

Vili nodded but didn't say anything, so the rest of us followed his lead, trusting he knew what he was doing. Rosie's eyes welled up with tears, and it took all my willpower not to go to her. I could feel her pain, fear, and sadness swirling like a hurricane in her emotions.

"You keep telling me I was brave, I fought back, and I survived," she started, pausing to sniff and wipe at a tear that slipped out. "None of that is how I feel about that day. Yes, I survived, but in doing so, I also put my life on the line. There was no way I could know if the ambulance would make it there in time or if the surgery would work. Yet everything turned out for the better, but I don't feel like I survived. Randall still haunts my dreams, and I fear when I have to look at a phone his name might pop up with a text or something telling me I belong to him. Going to that police station, looking him in the eyes, and sealing his fate to be locked away... that's when I know I've fought back and earned the right to say I was brave."

Hearing Rosie say she didn't think she was brave tore at my heart. How could she not see the truth? Bailey-Rose Thatcher was one of the bravest fucking people I've ever known, and it had nothing to do with what happened with Randall. For twenty-five years of her life, Rosie faced death every goddamn day, having a ticking time bomb of a heart living inside her. Even though I could see that clear as day, it was obvious that she didn't, and no one but her could change that.

"Thank you, my brave, sweet kitten, for being honest," Vili praised, pulling Rosie onto his lap, cuddling her close, and kissing the top of her head. "If this is something you need, then we will be right at your side. You will not face this fear alone."

Warrick stood, pulled out his phone, and kissed Rosie's nose. "Hi, Captain... change of plans. We're flying back home in the morning. Yup, what's the earliest we can take off? Seven..." Warrick glanced at Rosie, knowing she wasn't a fan of early mornings. She nodded and blew him a kiss as he finalized things with our pilot.

"Well, looks like we should go pack. It's gonna be an early morning," I announced.

Everyone got up and headed for the bedroom except for Gareth, who went to talk to his mother. I felt bad for changing plans on her, but this was important, and we could always come back.

It was noon by the time we got to the police station and found a disgruntled Eli along with a smiling Crew waiting for us. Crew hugged Rosie, picking her up off the floor in his excitement. Then he and I bro-hugged it out before Detective Vogal and Detective Kelsen came out to greet us.

"Thank you guys for making the trip back, especially on the last few days of your leave," Kelsen said. "We're all set for the lineup if you are, Mrs. Thatcher?"

Bailey-Rose nodded as she tugged the sleeves of her dinosaur sweater over her hands. Yun-Sun cupped the back of her neck, offering her his support as we were led down a hall into a room with a large glass window. The area the men would walk into was empty, but Detective Vogal walked up to the intercom and notified them we were ready.

"Now, Mrs. Thatcher, five men will enter the room, each holding numbers. I will ask them to step forward one at a time. Once you have seen all the men and the person who attacked you is there, just tell us the number he's holding," Vogal instructed. "Mr. Lee, are you acting as her legal counsel in this matter? I want to make sure we have all the details flushed out so there's no surprises later."

"Yes, I am her lawyer in this matter and will act as a witness to this lineup," Yun assured the detective.

None of us had ever seen Randall in person, only on the video recording from the studio. However, the second he entered the room, Bailey-Rose stiffened, and her anxiety shot through the roof. Rosie and Yun-Sun stepped closer to the window, and Vogal called up each person.

"It's number three," Rosie announced once all five had been called forward. "The man who attacked me in my studio, Randall Steele or Chambers, whatever you want to call him, is the one."

"Thank you. Please clear the room," Vogal ordered, and all five men were escorted out.

Kelsen offered Rosie a chair, but she declined and chose to lean into Yun-Sun instead. "You have been an immense help, Mrs. Thatcher. Now that you've ID'd him, there are no grounds to the argument his lawyer has been trying to use."

"So it's all over now?" Eli questioned.

Kelsen's gaze flicked to Vogal, who shoved his hands into his pockets. "There's one last request that we'd like to make. You are not obligated to say yes. You've more than done your part to help put this man in jail for a solid ten years, maybe fifteen. However, Randall has indicated to us that he's willing to admit to an assault on another Omega if he can explain it to Mrs. Thatcher."

"I'm sorry, are you asking if our Omega, who's been through hell and back, is willing to be in the same room as that fucking bastard?" Gareth demanded, getting right up into Vogal's face. "Are you out of your mind?"

"Sir, I would please ask that you take a step back," Vogal requested, but his tone didn't give the impression he was asking.

Rosie grabbed Gareth's hand and drew him back. "Gareth, we talked about this. If I can help put him away for longer, then I should try, right?"

I think we all regretted agreeing to any of this now that the situation had changed. Having her stand in a room with Randall on the other side of the glass was one thing, but having her breathing the same air as him was a whole different ball game.

"Baby girl, you don't need to do this," Gareth argued. "You did what you said you were going to do, and the fucker is going to jail."

"Yeah, but what if they find a way to get them to drop the charges?" she countered. "The woman hid her son from the police for *weeks.* Do you really think she couldn't find a way for him to avoid jail time?"

"I hate to interject, but Mrs. Thatcher isn't wrong," Detective Kelsen said. "If we have him on two accounts of assault toward an Omega, it will seal his fate for good. Omegas are a protected classification, but we need to prove there's a pattern of behavior and it's not a one-time occurrence. Not to mention, if Mr. Chambers admits guilt himself and signs a confession, they can't just throw it out."

"How do you expect this confession to happen? There's not a chance in hell his lawyer will let him confess," Yun-Sun challenged

"If she asked him to fire his lawyer, he would. I've never seen a man more desperate to clear the air than he is about talking to Mrs. Thatcher," Vogal muttered.

"Fine, if we do this, then she's not going in alone," I announced.

"The guard dog can't accompany her... it's too big a risk," Vogal countered.

I shrugged and crossed my arms. "All right, then two of us will go in with her. We'll stand near the door, but there's not a chance in hell I'm trusting anyone but us to keep her safe."

The detectives looked at each other and nodded. "We can work with that, but it can't be him or the brother," Vogal said, glaring at Gareth. "The last thing we need is for this to turn into a counter-suit for brutality in the police station."

"I can agree with that," I answered. "It will be me and Yun-Sun. This way, we make sure none of us do something they can legally use against us."

The detectives left to get things sorted, and the moment the door was closed, Eli was slamming me against the wall. "What the fuck are you thinking? How dare you call yourself an Alpha."

There was a lot I could take from someone who I considered family, but he crossed the line. "Eli, you better get your damn hand off me before I do something both of us will regret."

Eli started to say something, but Bailey-Rose beat him to it. "Eli Bartholomew Thatcher, if you don't back the hell up and find the marbles you've clearly lost, then we've got a bigger problem than Randall to deal with."

More than the words coming out of Bailey-Rose's mouth, I think the tone is what shocked us the most. If flames or rage could have come out of her ears like in cartoons, they would have. One thing that was never talked about as often as it should be wasn't a pissed-off Alpha but an enraged Omega. I would rather fight a bear or a lion than face off with Rosie right now.

Slowly, Eli released his hold on my shirt and stepped back with his hands held in surrender. Detective Kelsen entered the room and paused, feeling the energy coming off our girl. Unsure if she should leave, the detective looked to us for help. "Ah… is this a bad time?"

"No, it's perfect timing," Bailey-Rose answered, shoving

up her sleeve past her elbows. "Let's get this over with before my brother or I end up in a cell."

Marching out the door, the rest of us scrambled to follow. Two doors down, Vogal waited outside the door and watched as Rosie gave Waffles his marching orders. She looked over her shoulder at Yun and me. "Coming?"

"Bet your ass we are," I grumbled, stepping into the interrogation room.

Randall was cuffed to the metal bar on the table, and when I glanced at his feet, they were cuffed to the floor. It seems they made an extra effort to ensure Rosie would be safe. Detective Vogal held out a chair for Rosie and then sat beside her, pulling out a notebook. Using his pen, he hit the record button on the microphone attached to the center of the table.

"All right, Randall, I've managed to convince Mrs. Thatcher to be here, and now you have to hold up your end of the deal," Vogal stated. "What was the name of the Omega who rejected you?"

Randall wasn't paying any attention to what the detective was saying. He had eyes only for Bailey-Rose. I watched as he studied her, and his eyes narrowed when his gaze fell on the bonding mark on her neck.

"You let them mark you?" Randall hissed. "Bumblebee, how could you allow yourself to be defiled like that?"

"I didn't come here to talk about me, besides, you're one to talk. I hear you have another Omega," Rosie countered. "What happened to me being the only one for you?"

That's my girl.

"No, Bumblebee, they are lying to you," Randall gasped, lunging forward. "Don't believe them, there is no one but you, I promise. That bitch said she loved me, told me we were meant for each other, but she lied. The night we were supposed to bond our pack together, I was handed a letter telling me I was no longer part of their pack. They'd rejected me... *me*, Bumblebee. So I had to punish her for lying. It's not good to lie about something so important. The bitch wouldn't admit the truth, so I had to keep punishing her. Then the others showed up and tossed me out of the house, said they'd call the police. Mother would be upset with me if the police got involved, so I left and went right to her office."

"What happened then?" Vogal asked.

Randall acted as if he hadn't heard what the man said, so Rosie repeated the question. "What did your mother have to say about all of her lies?"

"She told me that cunt wasn't worth it, that she would find me someone else, someone better. In fact, she printed out a whole list of people I could pick from. I wasn't ready to give up yet, not until I made Crystal admit she lied," Randall explained.

"Crystal, is that her name?" Rosie asked. "Just so I know who not to listen to since it's all lies."

"Yes, that's the bitch, Crystal Declan, but I don't know if she kept her last name or not. Safer just not to trust any Crystals... they're all liars," Randall decided, nodding to himself. "Liars are bad, the worst kind of people. You don't lie at all, do you, Bumblebee? No, you've always been honest with me... that's what I love most about you."

"That's right, Randall, I've never lied to you, and I won't ever say anything untrue. Do you want to know why?" Rosie asked, cocking her head with a sweet smile on her face.

"Tell me, please. I want to know what makes you so special," Randall urged, a look of excitement on his face.

Rosie stood and rested her hands on the table. "I will never tell you a lie because I *need* to know you believe me when I tell you something. The most important thing in a relationship is trust and honesty, don't you agree?"

"Yes, yes, I couldn't have said it better. No secrets, none... they are like poison," Randall agreed emphatically.

"No secrets," Rosie murmured. "Now, I have something important to tell you, one of the most important things ever."

Randall gazed at her with rapt attention. "I'm listening, my dearest Bumblebee."

"You. Are. Not. My. Fucking. Alpha," Bailey-Rose stated bluntly, making sure every word was crystal clear for the man to hear. "I do not love you. In fact, I have no feelings toward you that are even remotely affectionate. We will never see each other again because I have a pack and five Alphas I love more than anything in the world. They treasure me like I'm the eleventh wonder of the world, and you would never ever be able to come close to giving me that kind of love. I hope you rot all alone in your cell, destined to be rejected forever."

"*You fucking whore,*" Randall bellowed, shoving the table so it crashed into her.

Yun-Sun darted forward and scooped her up just as Randall flipped the table, nearly hitting them both with the metal legs. Vogal hadn't been so lucky and got clocked in the jaw, knocking him onto the floor. Feeling that this was an acceptable moment for physical force, I dragged the detective out of the way and faced off with the raging Alpha.

"Hey, jackass," I shouted, drawing his attention.

Randall tried to throw the table he was still attached to at me, but instead of moving away like he thought, I got right up close and personal. Putting every ounce of strength I had, my fist slammed into his face. Stunned, he stood motionless, so I took the chance to follow it up with my other fist. This time, he crashed to the floor, and I may or may not have helped the table land squarely on his chest, pinning him to the tile floor.

"Stay the fuck away from Bailey-Rose, or next time you won't be going to jail... I'll bury you six feet under," I snarled. Vogal, now on his feet, just stared at me, eyes wide. "What? The bastard attacked us first. I had every right to defend myself. Saved your ass too, didn't I?"

Not waiting for a response, I marched out of the room and made a beeline for the only person I needed right now. Without even stopping, I picked up my Omega, who instantly wrapped herself around me and headed for the door.

"Where are we going?" Rosie asked.

"Home, we're going home to start the rest of our lives together. That sound good to you?" I asked as I kicked open the front doors of the station.

"Sounds like a dream come true," Bailey-Rose answered, snuggling her face into my neck.

BAILEY-ROSE

With everything that happened with Randall, we decided as a family that we needed one more additional week of leave. We were down to the last two days with Lysse and Yun-Sun returning to work on Monday. However, my mother decided it was the perfect time to host a party at their house and invite *everyone*. Well, everyone but Vili's fathers since this party celebrated our bonding and Vili legally changing his last name to Thatcher.

"We have to do something," Mother argued. "This is a big deal, one that should be celebrated. After everything you've told me his family put him through, he deserves to know what it truly means to have loving parents."

There was no way to change Jolene Thatcher's mind once it was made up. I suppose I might have inherited a slight bit of that, or so the guys tell me.

"Care Bear, we need to go. The pack of honor can't be late," Warrick pointed out.

"I know, I know, but Deanna is going to be there, and I really wanted to give this to her while she was in town," I muttered, adding the last few dots of white. "There, now it's done."

Stepping back, I gazed at the masterpiece I'd been working on off and on for the past week and a half. It was my interpretation of that day Deanna had told us about with Callie. Only in my version, Gareth was there with them. I wanted her to look at this and know that no matter what, she had two wonderful children who loved their mother to the moon and back.

"Will you help me carry it out to the car?" I asked, dropping the paintbrush into the water.

"Yes, but it will cost you," Warrick said, stepping up and cupping my face.

I smirked, knowing what was coming next. "How many kisses?"

"I'd say about ten," he answered. "It's a steep price, but I'll let you put a down payment of two kisses now since we're in a hurry."

"My hero," I teased, popping up on my tiptoes to pay the man his fee.

"No, nope, you two can't be doing that," Gareth ordered. "If you do, then you'll start taking off her clothes, and we all know what that leads to, so wrap it up."

Warrick muttered under his breath something about Gareth being a buzzkill. Sneaking in one more quick kiss, Warrick grabbed one side of the painting while Gareth took the other. I followed them out of my studio into the showroom where Vili and I were creating our new business. After much thought and many conversations with lawyers, Vili decided he would no longer offer his designs to Silveda. Instead, he was going to create all new designs and start his own jewelry line. We hadn't come up with a business name yet, but that will come with time.

Since Randall trashed most of the downstairs, we needed to remodel it. We divided the workspace for Vili and me to share along with creating the upstairs to be his showroom floor. I didn't need the whole upper level as an office, so we made a small room on the main floor showroom instead. Not only was I thrilled to watch Vili create something amazing, but it made me feel much safer in the studio.

My brain understood Randall was in jail and would be there for the next thirty-five years. Yet when I was left alone in the big building, I couldn't help but feel like someone was going to jump out of the shadows at me. My therapist felt this would pass with time but not to be too hard on myself. What happened to me was a traumatic event, and I needed to accept that reality. The upside was nightmares no longer were a problem, but I still didn't want to keep my phone on me all the time. Thankfully, I had a monitor I could wear so my guys knew where I was at all times. Plus Waffles, my faithful shadow, would never let something happen to me.

When we arrived at my parents' house, I knew we were far later than I expected. "Didn't Mom say the party would start at three?" I asked.

"Rosie, it's almost four," Lysse pointed out.

I cringed a little, knowing I lost all track of time when I was painting.

"Don't worry about it. I called Jolene and told her what you were up to, and she understood," Lysse assured me.

If anyone understood my bad habits, it was my mother. She's witnessed firsthand this particular trait many times. Once parked, I decided to leave it in the vehicle and give it to Deanna later. Right now, it was better for us to just get to the damn party.

Yun-Sun helped me out of the car and wrapped my arm around his as we walked down the path to the patio. It was such a beautiful day with the sun shining and the last blooms of the season, as fall headed our way. Mother spotted us first and rushed over to envelop me in a hug.

"Oh, there's my girl," Mother cheered. "Better late than never, as they say."

"Sorry, Mom, I can't believe I lost that much time," I apologized.

Mom tapped my nose with her finger and gave me a wink. "Think nothing of it, darling. It's not the first time, nor will it be the last. You are who you are, and that's exactly who I love."

Moving on from me, Mother hugged the guys and gushed over Vili, making the poor man blush.

"Thank you, Jolene. I am honored to be part of your family," he said as Mother squished his face between her hands.

"Come, come, the others will want to greet you all," Mother urged, herding us further into the backyard.

There was a flurry of hugs from Crew, Eli, Daddy Rawr, and Lysse's parents.

"Oh, I just knew you two were meant for each other. I've always felt like you were a daughter to me." Lysse's mother sobbed as she dabbed at her eyes. "I just can't believe this moment has finally come for you both."

Wrapping my arms around her for another hug, I squeezed her tightly. "Thank you for raising such an amazing son."

That set her off, and Mr. Ford had to pry the clinging woman from me, giving an apologetic look. Then a trio of serious-looking men I hadn't met before stepped up and bowed instead of offering a handshake or a hug. Yun-Sun stepped up next to me and returned their bow, yet no one spoke a word. They parted, and a stunning Asian woman stepped forward, offering a sweet smile as she also bowed.

"It is a delight to finally meet you, Bailey-Rose. I am So-Ri, Yun-Sun's mother," she greeted. "We were honored to be invited by your mother to this party to celebrate the bonding of your pack." So-Ri looked to one of her Alphas, who handed over a white envelope with a beautifully written word on it in another language. "It is tradition in my culture to offer a gift and a blessing to the new pack. Please take this as a sign of the prosperity and happiness we wish for your family."

Unable to be anything but authentically me, I stepped forward, took the envelope, and hugged my mother-in-law. "Thank you so much for taking the time to come, and I hope we will see more of each other."

So-Ri stiffened initially but relaxed at my words and returned my hug. "My son is lucky to find an Omega with such a pure soul and sweet spirit. Many happy blessings upon you, Bailey-Rose."

With that, we parted and moved on to mingle, meeting a few other family friends. Dr. Arbour and his pack came, which meant the world to me. We exchanged stories of the adventures we'd been on, and I showed him the tattoo I'd gotten at the temple.

"See, these are the experiences I look forward to having," Dr. Arbour said, hugging me to his side. "Learn from an old man, kiddo. Don't believe the lie the world tells you about having all the time in the world. You'll blink, and the next thing you know, you're old like me."

"Stop, you're spry as a fox," Phil, Dr. Arbour's Omega, said, playfully smacking his arm. "Although I have to say, it's been wonderful to have you home more."

It was clear to see the love between them, and I hoped things would be the same way for my guys and me. With all that we've been through, I don't see it being a problem. We've defied all the odds from the start, so I don't see why we can't finish that way.

I was sad that Warrick's family didn't make it to the party. Instead, they sent a gift with a letter of apology. It was just simply too short notice for them to fit it into their busy schedules.

"Shh, don't be upset, Care Bear," Warrick murmured as he cuddled me close. "This is who my family is and has always been. If they showed up, I would have probably passed out because of how shocked I was. Trust me, they would have absolutely brought down the energy level here... they don't know how to have a good time. Besides, the only family I need is you and the guys."

Mollified by this answer, he coaxed me into a better mood by grabbing the painting for Deanna. I took a clean napkin and blindfolded her until the guys got it set up on one of my spare easels.

"Are you ready?" I asked, trying not to bounce in excitement.

"Sweetie, I am more excited than a bag of jumping beans," Deanna shared, her accent a little thicker from the wine she'd been enjoying with Lysse's mother.

Pulling the knot free, the cloth fell from Deanna's eyes to reveal the masterpiece. We'd managed to make a brief stop at the hill before the rain started again on our way back to the house. It had given me the real setting to base this moment on, but I took a few liberties and put the Bailey-Rose spin on it.

Gareth stood at the top of the hill watching them as Deanna and Callie lay at the bottom watching the dandelion seeds float through the air. Only I had the little white puffs shifting into butterflies, adding even more emotion to the moment. One blue butterfly sat on Deanna's nose to represent Callie's spirit still being with her even now.

"Sweet baby Jesus, I feel faint," Deanna gasped.

Gareth rushed forward to catch his mother, and Lysse hurried over with a chair. Deanna sank onto the chair, and tears streamed down her cheeks. Reaching out, she took my hand and held it tightly like she was worried I would disappear.

"You, my dear girl, have a gift," Deanna said once she'd composed herself. She pulled me to stand in front of her, holding my hands and locking her gaze to mine. "Promise me you will never stop painting. The world needs to see the world through your eyes, Bailey-Rose, and the only way that can happen is if you show it to us. Words cannot express my gratitude for seeing this memory brought to life. I will treasure it always and no matter what, it will be hung in a place where everyone can see it."

Deanna and I clung to each other for a moment before she shooed me away. "Don't let a weepy old woman steal the show. Today is about celebrating you and your Alphas, so go, enjoy yourself."

I kissed Deanna on the cheek before heading over to the drinks table. As I poured myself a glass of raspberry lemonade, I spotted my mother and Eli talking off to the side. The stunned expression on his face had me concerned. Heading over, I noticed Eli was looking at something, and when I got closer, I realized it was a photograph.

"Eli, what's wrong?" I questioned, resting a hand on his forearm. "You look like you've seen a ghost."

Without saying a word, he handed me the photo of four smiling men. Three were older, attractive, and gave off Alpha energy the way they cuddled around the man in the middle. The fourth was slender, had a youthful-looking face, and wore thigh-high socks, short shorts, and a baggy sweater that fell off one shoulder. While not all Omegas were easy to pick out, this man screamed Omega to the max. He also struck me as someone I wanted to meet, and his unique sense of fashion reminded me a little of Zelly.

"I don't understand. Should I know who these people are?" I asked, looking between Eli and my mother.

Eli rubbed his brow, something he typically did when he was upset or overwhelmed. "According to our mother... these men are my pack."

"What?" I squeaked. "I don't understand?"

"Join the club," Eli muttered.

"Look, you can say that I'm a meddler all you like, but I knew it was wrong of the Scent Matchers to keep you from joining the program. What does it matter if your father had the genetic mutation, you don't. So, I used my skills and influence a few years back to find out if you have a pack. There was no news until a year ago when these men found their scent-bonded Omega, Fawn. The pack developed around the Omega, and these men didn't know each other before then," Mother explained. "This is *your* pack, the people you belong with. Stop hiding in your office now that you can't hide behind your sister. It's time for you to get a life, my son."

"Mother," Eli snapped, cutting her off. "How the hell do you expect me to make that happen? This pack has been living life together for a year. They're bonded, for fuck's sake."

"Watch your tone," Mother shot back. "I understand this is shocking, and you don't take surprises well, but get over it. Trust me, Eli, none of that matters because you were always meant to be part of this pack. You witnessed firsthand how powerful the connection is between an Alpha and their scent-bonded Omega. It will be no different for you when you meet Fawn."

I could fully appreciate the anger that comes with a surprise like this, especially when you've believed all your life it would never happen. Yet I couldn't help but feel joy for my brother who deserved this and so much more.

"Eli, Mother is right. Just meet them. Give them the chance to know they've been missing a piece of the puzzle this whole time. There is nothing more I could wish for in life than to see you as happy as I am. All we're asking is don't slam the door on the idea just because it's scary. What's the worst that could happen?" I challenged, offering him back the photograph.

Letting out a heavy sigh, Eli took the image and studied it. "All right, you guys win like always, but I can't tackle this issue until I've found a new assistant. Too many things are falling through the cracks. I can't risk failing at my job and a new relationship."

"Taken care of," Mother said, waving off Eli's concerns. "Your new assistant is starting next week. This way, you have time to adjust to the idea of having a pack so when she starts, you'll be able to switch focus.

"I'm sorry, Mother, are you saying you hired an executive assistant for me?" Eli demanded, his brows furrowed.

Mother shrugged. "Why not? I own the company. Why can't I hire staff when there's a need? Oh, and you can't fire her. She's relocating her entire life to Windermere on the company's dime. Her contract with us is for two years minimum."

My jaw dropped. "Mother?"

"Oh, don't you start. Now that I've got my youngest bonded and out of the house, it's time I get my boys settled with families of their own," Mother reasoned. "Speaking of which, darling, shouldn't you be getting back to your party? These guests are here for you."

Giving us both cheek kisses, Mother headed off back to

the party, but I wanted to make sure Eli was going to be okay.

"Little B," he whispered, lifting his gaze from the photograph. "I have a pack."

Grinning, I threw my arms around him. "It's going to be amazing, big bro. Trust me, I know a thing or two about dreams coming true."

The End

Don't want to leave this world of sickly sweet omegaverse? Then keep a look out for Eli's happily ever after coming in 2024.

About the Author

Elizabeth is originally from Illinois but is now living in sunny Phoenix, Arizona. Though she is newer to publishing, Elizabeth has been writing for nine years. She started in YA Fiction but recently found herself loving the Reverse Harem genre. Like her favorite books, Elizabeth loves to write about strong women of all varieties. Not all strength is flashy or apparent at first glance—some lie just under the surface.

Don't Miss Out!

Be the first to know what is coming next by following Elizabeth's social media! You never know when or what will be coming next!

Website: ElizabethKnightBooks.com
Facebook: Elizabeth Knight's Unicorn Queens
Instagram: elizabethknightauthor
Newsletter: sign up here

Also by Elizabeth Knight

<u>Hidden Empire Series – Complete series</u>

Book 1 - Two Tricks

Book 2 - Three Tricks

Book 3 - Four Tricks

Book 4 - More Tricks

Book 5 - Our Tricks

<u>Hidden Empire Novel</u>

(Suggested to read after Four Tricks)

Harper's Renegades